Julie,
Fall in
with this story!

DOYENNE.

ANNE MALCOM

Anne
Malcom
xxx

For all the women with big dreams and fractured hearts.

1

I've always been fascinated with my own death.

Not suicidal. It's important to make that distinction.

But inappropriately interested in my demise.

Since I'd gotten to what most people would consider the peak in my professional life, I'd stare off into the distance from the forty-eighth floor, idly wondering about what would happen if I found a way to break the glass and hurl myself into the air.

I felt myself falling.

Imagined, in detail, the impact of the ground. The way my bones would shatter, my organs burst. My skull would explode, and the brains that had gotten me to that spot on the forty-eighth floor of my ivory tower would be nothing more than gray matter.

I didn't take the subway. People like me had drivers. But I had daydreams about wandering down into the bowels of New York and hurling myself in front of an oncoming train.

I was desperate to experience my death over and over again. Safely within the confines of my own mind, of course.

But then again, safety was a farce. My own mind was more dangerous than a fall from forty-eight stories.

Not tonight, though.

No, tonight, the streets of New York that I strolled in thousand-dollar heels were more dangerous than even my poisonous mind.

I'd spent my adulthood working my well-toned ass off trying to break through every stereotype that worked as a wall to progress.

I smashed my way through glass ceilings, kicked through walls, all the while not damaging my six-inch heels.

I clawed my way up a ladder that only catered to middle-aged men, forced my way into the 'old boys club' and did everything to break the mold patriarchy had created for my sex. And I didn't even chip a nail.

It was a daily struggle, even now, the CEO of a multibillion-dollar empire, I was fighting for legitimacy. I'd become comfortable with it, worked it to my advantage in most situations. By no stretch of the imagination did I *like* the misogynistic, sexist, elitist environment—but I accepted that it was something I would most likely have to fight against for the rest of my life.

I just didn't think my life would be so short.

Nor did I think my life would be ended ironically in a manner that reinforced every patriarchal ideology I'd been fighting against. That I'd built my life on.

"On your knees, bitch."

Yeah. The helpless woman in the dark alley rendered incapacitated in a laughably short amount of time, despite her weekly krav maga classes. The trope that I'd battled against so violently would be the one that killed me. Despite my utter abhorrence for fairy tales, I wouldn't mind a white knight and his furry steed to be riding in right about now.

Even his chubby brother on a donkey would be welcomed.

Cold steel bit into my neck and a blossom of pain exploded in my collarbone.

"You fuckin' deaf?" the voice snarled, rank breath close enough to taste. "I said, *on your fucking knees.*"

The intention behind such a command had my stomach roiling. I was about to be *raped*, potentially killed afterward. Rape and murder happened to *other* people. It was tragic, heartbreaking, *despicable*, and something you witnessed from a distance.

Not something you *experienced*.

But rape and murder didn't know the bounds of class or wealth. Or the ignorant confidence I'd been feeling on the subject prior to now. I'd been convinced life had dealt me my share of tragedy, of ugly violence, that I was done. But tragedy and violence were not finite.

The knife pressed in harder, hard enough to draw blood that dribbled down my collarbone and trickled onto my white suit jacket.

I just got this dry-cleaned, I thought, my inner voice sounding cold, detached, exactly like my outer one.

It didn't take much work to convince the world that I was cold and unfeeling. It took a heck of a lot more to convince myself. But I did it. My life, up until right now, had depended on it.

I jutted my chin up, despite the pain, despite the terror almost paralyzing me. Despite the overwhelming urge to do *anything* to save my life.

Would it be a life worth saving if I sacrificed everything I'd made myself into, everything I'd escaped? If I sacrificed the one thing I might not be able to get back—my sanity? I'd worked too hard to maintain that, and losing it would be worse than death for me.

"No," I replied, my voice clear, strong. Unshakeable. Exactly as it had been when I addressed my first shareholder meeting, where I'd never been more scared in my life.

Current moment excluded, obviously.

I had learned to embrace that fear, change it, use it for motivation, make it bend to my will, use it as the fuel in which to power my life.

The trail of blood flowed faster as the knife pressed deeper, pain a lancing sensation through my upper neck. He leaned in, eyes the only thing visible from his mask. They were empty, cold, devoid of anything. Empty like a dried up old pool in an abandoned motel.

"You think you've got a choice?"

It chilled me. His utter confidence in the control he held over this situation. As if he had me in a locked room, not an alley only slightly off the bustling streets of Manhattan. Though, at midnight on a Tuesday, they weren't exactly bustling.

It may have been the city that never slept, but it wasn't averse to a cat nap. The flickering of car headlights gave me hope and despair every time they illuminated the dark corner he'd yanked me into, and then plunging me back into the transparent darkness that he'd used to his advantage to drag me into. Was it minutes ago? Or seconds? Surely Ralph would note my absence by now. I had told him when I was leaving my cosmetics offices, discouraging him from meeting me directly outside my security building, it was only a two-minute walk after all. I owned this block, some of the most expensive real estate in the world. What was the worst that could happen?

I wondered if this was what everyone felt, what everyone did —clung to a flimsy hope that surely this couldn't happen to *them*. This was a nightmare. The real world would bustle in and save the day.

But maybe, this *was* the real world. Cruel, empty, and unsympathetic. And ultimately, fatal.

Death didn't come with a crescendo, a warning, or at a time when you were ready. No, death came when you were hurrying the two blocks from a meeting that ran long and were snatched by the collar of your custom-made jacket.

I tried to mimic that same coldness in my eyes as I regarded him, my blood pulsing. "I have control over whether I willingly kneel in front of the man holding a knife to my neck, like a *coward,"* I spat the word with a hot fury that cut through the previous chill in my voice.

Something flickered in his eyes. Rage. Even that was welcomed. A human emotion beneath the inhuman film over his eyes gave me something to grasp onto. He was no longer just a monster, but a human. But maybe that was worse, seeing the monster inside a human, rather than the human inside the monster. Then it was gone, the human, the monster, the slice of time that had opened up in between my rape and murder for such philosophical contemplation.

A blinding pain erupted in my legs and I crumpled down onto the concrete, my knees jarring as I made contact with the unyielding stone.

He bent down, his figure blurred as my body tried to reconcile the physical pain and mental terror. "Control is something a bitch like you thinks she has, with your fucking companies and your titles that you got from opening your legs," he hissed, the knife pressing deeper now.

It was surprising, the pain. I'd heard and read about victims going numb in the face of such things, but I lived my life making sure I was numb, so it made sense that my death would be nothing but pain.

"*I'm* the one who holds the blade inches from your carotid artery." He moved it, dragging the tip along my skin.

More pain.

"*I'm* the one with the control. Power," he whispered the last word, the truth of the statement as cutting as the knife itself. "You have *nothing*. You are nothing. This is where you should be. Where you belong." He yanked the back of my head back, using my hair as a handhold so my entire neck was exposed and the sharp edge of the knife poised to slit my throat.

Like all the times I'd seen myself hurtling from my office to the street, I felt him rip through my skin, through the flesh, to the bone. I visualized the blood gushing down the front of my jacket, spilling onto the concrete, my body collapsing and finally bleeding out.

I saw it all in the handful of seconds he kept the knife pressed there, a promise of death.

Tears edged out of my eyes as I gritted my teeth to stop from crying out. It was something I was itching to do, scream for help, shriek like a banshee for any form of assistance. All my life I'd refused help, now I yearned for it. But the steel at my throat hindered that.

I blinked at him through my tears, holding up a shaking arm and yanking off my watch. "Take it," I hissed, my voice garbled from the unnatural angle of my neck. "I don't have cash on me, but this is worth more than you deserve and will hopefully stop you from compensating for your lack of masculinity by robbing women in the near future."

Such a comment was probably not wise, considering the man could end my life in an instant. And I was smart. Very. Every decision I made in life was calculated and measured. Made to propel me toward the life I wanted and away from the life I'd been born with. This little outburst? Quite possibly the dumbest thing I'd ever done.

The knife slipped from my neck for a split second as he swatted the fifty-thousand dollar watch onto the pavement where it tumbled into the shadows. I watched it bounce off the concrete, the little twang of metal against stone the loudest sound in the world, drowning out everything but my pounding heartbeat.

That was it, the slipping of that knife as he was distracted by the clang of a watch against concrete. Quite possibly the only moment I'd have to save myself. And I missed it.

The knife was back at my neck before I could grab the moment, perhaps the last one I'd have before he did...whatever he was going to do. I was frozen, paralyzed with fear. I'd always thought I was strong, that in a life or death situation I'd jump into action and be the heroine. Or at least not sit like a rabbit in the headlights trying to control my bladder and terror.

Yet here I was, shaking, bleeding, and almost about to wet myself.

It's a confronting moment when you used to consider yourself the heroine of your own life, when in reality, all it took was a man with a knife and opportunity to turn you into the victim.

And maybe you'd always been the victim. Maybe it was the cruelest thing of all to die with that stark and unadorned truth flickering in your eyes.

It didn't matter how hard I worked, how many companies I owned, the corner office, the world breaking stats. That I was on top of the world. It didn't mean I couldn't tumble down. It just meant I had a heck of a lot farther to fall.

His breath was hot on my face. "Now that you're not struggling I'll be able to do this the right way. Make it look perfect," he murmured, his voice seductive, as if he was a lover muttering sweet nothings in my ear.

Not that I knew anything about sweet nothings. The men I took to bed knew that they were there for a purpose, not affection.

A single tear escaped my eye as the knife pressed deeper still and I prepared myself for oblivion. I squeezed my eyes shut, not wanting the last thing I saw to be those empty eyes.

In preparation for my death, the knife exerted pressure on my neck, I expected pain, a lot of it. But there wasn't any. At least not mine.

There was a grunt and the thump of a body hitting another and the knife left my neck, cold air kissing me with its emptiness. My eyes snapped open and in a blur of motion, the man in the mask hit the concrete viciously and a large man on top of him threw a gun I hadn't realized my attacker possessed, it scuttled to the ground almost at my feet.

I watched, transfixed, hypnotized as the large form wrested

the knife from my would-be murderer and without hesitation, brought it across his neck. The wet, gurgling sound echoed through the open alleyway, drowning the city sounds. Death replaced whatever hustle Manhattan offered.

I didn't look away. I couldn't. Instead I watched the blood gush from the gaping wound in his neck as his body twitched and he continued to make that wet, death sound.

Then, silence.

The man got to his feet, staring down at the body for less than a moment. Then his attention turned to me, still on the ground, bleeding, almost wetting myself, my heart thundering with such intensity it rattled my ribcage. I didn't move, didn't speak as his electric blue eyes glowed in the dim streetlight, fixed on me. He moved toward me, his steps even, confident.

I didn't move. Scream. Or grab the gun inches from my shaking hands.

That would have been the smart thing to do.

Tonight I wasn't smart.

I wasn't the self-made woman with billion-dollar companies she built from the ground up. The CEO who graced covers of finance magazines and didn't blink at sharks in suits who made it their mission to destroy, belittle, and demean her.

Tonight I was a stranger wearing the familiar body but inhabiting an unrecognizable mind.

A cowardly one.

I watched the man who had just taken a life, after saving my own, approach me.

In that couple of seconds it took for him to get to me, I drank him in. Yes, *drank* him in, because he was a tall drink of water. A mountain of it. He took up my whole vision, his form swallowing the still and blood-stained corpse he'd created. He was wearing a weathered tan leather jacket with only a white tee underneath, hugging what I guessed was a lot of muscle. Jeans encased his huge thighs and combat boots stopped in front of me. The boots were worn, like the jacket. Old, but not bad quality.

I could appreciate good shoes.

"Nice boots," I said, my voice dreamlike. "Though, they look like they've seen a season too many. You should invest in a new pair."

Silence.

I guessed it was a peculiar thing to say after he'd just killed someone in front of me. He didn't bend down, ask if I was okay, call 911—none of that. His gaze just flickered over me. My own was still fixated on his boots, there were splatters of red blood on them. Those small splotches hypnotized me, reflecting the death they represented. I knew his gaze was on me, though. It was physical, the shiver that went over my body as those icy eyes traveled the length of it. The boots left my vision, going over to the side of the alley. I didn't move my eyes to watch the journey of the boots. Which meant my gaze focused on the body. The blood spilling in a pool around it.

My stomach roiled.

That was a dead person.

That could have been me. Twitching. Bleeding. Then just a corpse splayed on the concrete of a dirty alleyway.

Nothing but a stain and empty flesh.

The boots returned just as my body started vibrating with the force of my shaking.

He knelt down this time, and I was relieved when his face took up my vision. Not relieved enough to stop shaking. But I wasn't too far gone to appreciate his face. When confronted by the angular, sharp, utterly masculine and lethal features of a man like that, you appreciated it, even if it was seconds after he murdered someone. It was a kind of beauty that made you stop and look. Perhaps marvel. Definitely fear it.

His jaw was covered in stubble that was almost a beard and cloaked half of his tanned face in shadow. The nose had been broken, its crookedness perfecting the features of what would have been too classically handsome otherwise. His hair was long, wayward and brushing the shoulders of his leather jacket.

His eyes were blank. But not empty.

There was something wild about him, about those eyes, like a wolf's when venturing too close to humans. The animal in him was wild and untamed, yet it seemed to mean me no harm.

They focused on me with unwavering intensity as my hand was lifted, cool steel kissing the prickled skin on my wrist.

"You saved me," I whispered, my words floating into the empty air.

He didn't respond, though I didn't expect it. After all, you can't talk to wolves, can you?

Instead, his eyes flickered with something mixing with the wildness, but I couldn't put my finger on it because sharp pressure erupted in my wrist and then there was nothing.

No wild eyes.

No weathered boots.

No blood.

No wolf.

Just nothing.

"Char, what are you doing here?"

I glanced at Vaughn, who'd launched up from his chair and was regarding me with his perfectly manicured brow arched.

"Well, that's the CEO's office." I pointed to the door which had 'Charlotte Crofton' engraved in sloping script. "And I'm *Charlotte*, the CEO, so I guess I'm in the right place," I said dryly, not stopping my journey to my door.

He was quicker than me, even in heels. His patent leather Louboutins met mine, stopping me from entering my office. Now it was my turn to arch my just as perfectly manicured brow in challenge.

"You need to go home," he instructed, folding his arms.

I eyed him evenly. "You need to remember that I'm the one who signs your paychecks so ordering me around is a role reversal I do not appreciate," I said.

My tone was foreign, at least with Vaughn. I had a reputation for being a hard ass to work for, some might even call me a bitch, because assertive women were always labeled as bitches, but I wasn't that way with Vaughn. At least not at six a.m. when he was the first one in the deserted office, like always.

Vaughn was the closest thing I had to a best friend, and I paid him for that duty. He'd been with me since I started my first company—Crofton Cosmetics, as makeup was his first love. Evidenced by the flawlessly contoured and highlighted face with a cat eye sharp enough to cut steel.

We enjoyed a warm relationship. Warm, for me, at least.

I didn't do slumber parties with ice cream and heart to hearts. My heart, if you listened to most of my employees, was made of ice. Or coal, depending on who you talked to. It didn't bother me. If I wanted to be at the top, enjoy the power and control afforded mostly to men in this industry, complete agency over my own life, I didn't have time to consider other people's feelings. That was not in the job description. I didn't even consider my own. Nor did I stop long enough to inspect whatever feelings that were buried deep beneath the shield I'd created to help me survive in this world.

The shield that was broken, battered, and all but destroyed last night with the knowledge that years of accruing power and agency could be snuffed out in a moment.

That was something that I didn't need to think about. Now. Or ever. Thinking or crying over it wouldn't change anything. The past was where ghosts lived. The present was for the living.

And the dying.

I'd come close enough to the latter to be determined to stay the former. This meant continuing my day as usual, as if I hadn't almost died. And my day, in fact, my *life*, was work. This building. This company. This empire.

Living, for me, was getting into the office at dawn, like always and not leaving until well after the sun had disappeared.

I focused on Vaughn, who was assessing me.

He didn't even blink his thick lashes at my tone. "You were almost *killed* last night."

His eyes went to the scarf covering the bandages at my neck.

I didn't flinch, nor did my expression change. I'd hoped that I could avoid anyone commenting on that particular accessory or the reason for it. Because I was poetic, it was a blood red vintage Hermes paired with a sharply tailored black Yves Saint Laurent pantsuit.

My shoes were blood red too. Black and red. The two colors plaguing my memories and the precise one hour of sleep I'd been able to snatch after I'd spent two hours at the hospital and another hour getting interviewed by the police.

Though that wasn't rightly true. Another color cut through them all. Ice blue, like a glacier sparkling in the sunlight, alive and yearning to break free from the earth that constrained it.

Lock it down, I instructed myself.

My attention moved back to lined eyes that were not wild but irritated. And concerned.

"Ralph called you," I surmised.

He nodded.

"He was under strict instructions not to do so. In fact, that's in breach of his confidentiality agreement," I said tightly.

Ralph was my driver, had been for the last six years. And those six years had been eventful, to say the least. The media loved a woman working her way up from nothing and becoming a success in a man's world, apparently. After I moved from a well-established cosmetics brand I'd built from the ground up and moved to tech and security software companies, I'd become somewhat of a sensation in the media. Being a woman and a CEO of a makeup company was somewhat accepted. Lipstick and mascara were the 'woman's domain'—not my words, but a male writer for the *Financial Times*— but a security software company with international and government contracts?

No.

A woman couldn't be trusted with that. With all our *emotions*. Not with national security at stake. Could we make the country vulnerable to attack just because a suit with boobs had a bad bout of PMS—that one wasn't the *Financial Times* but from one of my direct competitors. Another male.

Regardless of gender, he was wrong. I'd put every single cent of profit I'd gained from my cosmetics company into investing in a high risk, high return startup. That moment could have broken me. I would have been bankrupt and damn near destitute had my venture failed. But it didn't fail. Our security firm was the top in the business and leading the way in the IT sector. I was ice cold and more ruthless than most of the people leading the attacks I was defending against. That was child's play. As were the men who tried to doubt me. The worst attacks didn't come from anywhere outside, it was when I looked inward the trouble began.

Ralph was loyal to a fault, he'd been with me since I made enough to afford a driver and turned into a driver/bodyguard when it became apparent I needed that too. I had some death threats, a couple of borderline violent confrontations, nothing serious, but something that Ralph had made sure he took care of. That, in turn, made me change his job description and up his salary.

And also add some points to the non-disclosure.

I didn't precisely think I'd need such a frivolous piece of paper. He was unlikely to sell any details of my life to the tabloids, no matter how much they offered. This was because I paid him well and because he was loyal.

Or so I thought.

Vaughn rolled his eyes. "Seriously? You're talking about confidentiality agreements when you were almost fucking *murdered?*" His voice ended on a slight screech.

"Vaughn—"

He held up his manicured hand. The long nails were curved into sharp points, hot pink and rhinestones today. "Don't 'Vaughn' me," he snapped. "I want to know why *Ralph* had to call me and then threaten bodily harm if I came down to the hospital, which if I didn't like my face so much, I would have." He paused. "I even drove halfway there—you're worth risking plastic surgery for. Plus, I've been thinking of getting a new nose anyway." He scrunched up the aforementioned nose. "What the question should be, is why Ralph had to call me, *why didn't you?*"

I frowned. "Why would I call you?"

He tilted his head to the ceiling. "Are you insane?"

The question, though more hysterical than literal, speared through the broken edges of my shield. I sharpened my gaze. "Not that I'm aware of. Though asking such a question to your employer could be considered so."

Vaughn ignored this. "You were mugged. At *knifepoint.* Then taken to a *hospital.* You should have called me."

I folded my arms. "Why? What would calling you have done? Apart from interrupted your sleep and made you whine about how tired you were for the rest of the day? You being there wouldn't have changed anything. I was fine by myself," I lied.

I was a borderline mess the night before, if I was being honest. Years of keeping my emotions locked up tight was the only thing that kept me together as I rode to the hospital in an ambulance, which I argued was completely unnecessary, which Ralph had sternly disagreed against, showing a side of him I hadn't seen before.

Though I hadn't seen anything like how my fifty-year-old driver was when I awoke, surrounded by him and paramedics.

From what I could glean, someone called 911 and he had gotten there only a hair before the paramedics.

I had been found slumped unconscious against a concrete wall. Alone. If you didn't count the dead body beside me.

"Calling me would have meant you weren't alone and that you had some support, no matter how much you think you don't need it. No woman is a fucking island," Vaughn snapped. His face cleared. He took a breath. "Now I'm going to get us Venti Caramel Lattes with an extra punch of butterscotch and cream on top and you're going to go into your office and wait right there." He opened the door and pointed to the white suede sofa facing the floor to ceiling window, which had a view of the rising sun against the Manhattan skyline.

My mouth opened to argue.

"Nope," Vaughn cut me off before I began. His eyes narrowed. "Even if you've the means to buy one, you're not an island, Char," he said more softly. "Now relax on that fucking sofa while I go and get our lattes that may or may not cause diabetes."

And on that, he turned on his eight-hundred-dollar heel and left.

I watched him snatch his purse from his desk, then I went to the sofa and sat down.

But I didn't relax. I replayed.

The wolf eyes. The boots. The shaggy hair. The leather jacket. The stubble. On repeat.

I was getting scared I imagined him. Maybe Vaughn was right, maybe I was going insane. The thought chilled me, right to the bone.

Insanity.

It ran in the family and you couldn't run from genetics.

No, he was real.

Despite there being no trace of him once Ralph found me.

"Can you describe the man, Ms. Crofton?" the officer asked, scribbling in his notepad as I recounted what happened. How I'd been inches

from death and then I just...wasn't. I'd just told him that the man had saved me and killed my attacker in self-defense. Though, I guessed that wasn't technically true. He didn't need to defend himself, he had him on the ground, his considerable size and obvious penchant for violence making him the threat in the situation. But he'd killed him anyway. In cold blood.

That should have bothered me. It would have bothered a normal person. But I didn't feel normal.

"No," I said firmly, maintaining eye contact with the officer while I lied. "It all happened so fast, then I must have passed out. All I know is that he saved my life. And I wish I could have thanked him."

I don't know why I did it, lied so blatantly to the officer who had been nothing but professional and kind, despite recognizing me. He'd done everything he could to maintain my anonymity. I could have given him exquisite detail of the man, heck, I could have drawn his likeness right down to a wayward strand of hair slithering across his eyebrow.

But I didn't. Because I had an inkling that a wild man like that had a past. One that would not mean good things if the police questioned him over a murder. Wolves couldn't be caged. Not ones that wild. The thought of it made me flinch. As if I knew him as something more than a hero or a murderer, or both, if such a thing was possible.

The officer bought my lie, nodding and glancing up from his notebook. "That's understandable, Ms. Crofton. This was a very traumatic incident. It sounds as if you are lucky to be alive."

I nodded. "Yes. Lucky."

I blinked away the past and focused on the skyline, the city waking up. It was usually the best part of my day. Sipping coffee in my quiet office, having a moment of peace before my fourteen-hour workday began.

This time it wasn't.

The quiet felt wrong, sinister. The emptiness of the office was heavy, tangible with my utter aloneness.

"Coffee!" Vaughn declared, strutting into my office with two giant to-go cups and paper bags.

I took the caffeine gratefully, sucking it down. It would be the first of at least five, but I'd switch to black after this. Like a certain billionaire in a certain book that sat hidden behind the first editions in my library, I liked control in every aspect of my life. Especially my diet.

It wasn't about being thin and measuring up to society's ideal version of a woman, it was about the control. I could control how much I ate, how many miles I ran, how my body was slender and athletic. How my chocolate brown hair was always shiny and cut precisely into a short bob that framed my petite face, making it look a smidge older because, even in my thirties, my features were girlish, innocent. I didn't need to look innocent, to invite some wannabe hero to take care of me. I could take care of myself.

Or so I thought.

But then Wolf Eyes did the saving. And he wasn't a wannabe hero, the more I thought on it—which was a lot—the more I understood his gait, his tight jaw, his wild eyes. He was a reluctant hero.

Maybe even the villain.

Vaughn sat down beside me, jostling me out of my thoughts. "I got us free muffins because the barista totally has the hots for me. I've got to use my wiles to get us free things, you know, 'cause we'd starve otherwise," he deadpanned, looking around my all white corner office that cost as much to decorate as a deposit on a home.

The corner of my mouth tipped up as I took another sip.

"I saw it," he said with triumph. "The crack in the ice queen. I did it."

I shook my head but stayed silent.

Vaughn, of course, didn't. "Now, spill," he demanded.

I swallowed. "I was under the impression Ralph already filled you in," I replied, my tone glacial.

He shook his head, not blinking at what would have most employees staring at the carpet and escaping as quickly as possible. "Ralph gave me the clipped basics while trying not to have a panic attack. He was loath to leave you for even the couple of minutes it took to threaten my face if I came down to the hospital."

I quirked my brow in disbelief. Ralph? Panic? No. The man was unflappable. In all the years he'd worked for me, he'd never once broken the façade of the tough, weathered ex-marine.

Though, I saw the shadow of something behind his eyes at the hospital. He'd refused to leave my side the entire time. Silent, sentinel and hard-jawed. He dropped me home after I refused his offer to stay with him and his wife for the night. Or the few hours of the morning that remained.

Vaughn nodded. "Panic. This close." He held his thumb and forefinger together, millimeters apart. "I swear it on my limited-edition Gucci backpack. Now...details." He reached to squeeze my hand. "Talking about it might stop your head from exploding and also might chase the demons away...the worst of them at least." Something flickered behind his made-up eyes.

We both knew about each other's sordid pasts. Me, because I did background checks on all of my employees—*extensive* back-ground checks. I knew about the demons behind his eyes. I was responsible for punishing those that put them there, though I'd never tell him that. Vaughn knew about mine because of two bottles of Pinot on the one day of the year that had my shields as weakened as they could be. He'd listened, squeezed my hand and given me support that night instead of pity. We'd never spoken of it since.

Maybe it was that glimmer of a kindred soul that made me do it. Or the gentle squeeze against my hand. Or just the presence of someone who cared about me.

So I did. Spill. All of it. Even the Wolf Eyes. Vaughn had signed a non-disclosure agreement too. It was unnecessary, I trusted him as much as I could anyone, but that didn't mean I was stupid. Nor would I take risks, even with the closest of my staff.

Betrayal only comes from those who were once loyal, after all.

"And then, he touched my hand and then there was nothing," I finished, glancing down to my wrist where I was fiddling with my watch. The one he'd retrieved and fastened back on my wrist before I blacked out. There were scratches on the diamond face, marring the beauty with evidence of the ugliness that I'd known all too well the world was capable of.

I didn't think I was much for fainting, but last night taught me a lot about myself.

I didn't notice the silence until I swam out of my own thoughts and glanced at Vaughn's granite face. He literally looked like he was carved in a statue. His inky black hair artfully messed in a way that looked effortless but I knew it took him forty minutes. His makeup that was always flawless and worn with confidence, his custom-tailored suit, which, instead of a bow tie or tie had a diamond broach fastened to the top button. His jaw was masculine and angular but always covered in makeup, he'd had his facial hair lasered off years ago. He was beautiful and handsome at the same time.

He shook himself out of it. "Holy fuck," he muttered.

I nodded, sipping my coffee.

"And you didn't tell the cops about him, Wolf Eyes?"

I shook my head. "And it goes without saying it does not leave this room."

He waved his hands dismissively. "I may have big lips thanks to Dr. Evans, but I do not have a big mouth. At least not when it comes to you," he said. "But seriously, Wolf saved you, killed a guy, fastened on a fifty thousand dollar watch instead of stealing it, which most likely says a lot considering he sounds homeless then he knocks you unconscious? Girl, I knew you were all work and no play, but when shit goes down with you, *it goes down*."

I frowned at him. "He isn't homeless. He didn't knock me out. I fainted."

Vaughn shook his head. "Maybe not homeless, but millionaires don't hang out in alleyways in the middle of the night wearing beat-up boots and stabbing people." He looked down to the wrist I was fiddling with, gently taking it in his hands and turning it over so my watch slipped slightly. He touched a slight discoloration, the size of a thumbprint with his pointed, bright pink nail. "He knocked you out."

I snatched my hand from his grasp to inspect my wrist. "You can't knock someone out by touching their wrist, Vaughn. I must have knocked it at some point during the...incident. I bruise easily." Evidenced by the purple and black rings on my neck and collarbone.

Vaughn looked from my wrist to my face. "You can. If you have the right training and knowledge of how to rapidly lower blood pressure to cause unconsciousness. Wolf is most likely ex-army or something worse."

I gaped at him, usually I kept my emotions and mask locked down tight. "How do you even know that?"

He smirked at me. "I have a life outside of here, you know."

How, I had no idea. He was here as much as I was and helped run my companies. You would think he wouldn't have time for weekly manicures, let alone a life. But he did. I heard about the parties, the boyfriends, the dates, the art gallery openings. I was invited to them all—minus the dates. Invites, I, of course, declined. I went to necessary company events, and when I did, I took one of the men in my book. Men who owned good suits knew their way around a bedroom and knew what I wanted from them.

Nothing but a plus one and an orgasm.

No sleepovers.

I knew what I wanted and how I wanted to live my life and I wasn't ashamed of how I went about it. I would never be the woman who dated and gabbed with her girlfriends over cocktails about the latest asshole that screwed her over. Mostly because I didn't have girlfriends. I had Vaughn and Molly—my twin sister who I didn't see enough. I had an empire I built from the ground up that I was determined to continue building. I didn't have time for things like dating and friendships. I had *goals*.

The problem with goals was that once you achieved them, you were satisfied for a minute before the next one came along. Which meant, of course, you were never satisfied, always hungry, never...complete.

I bit my lip while I chewed over Vaughn's words, staring at the purplish tint on the inside of my wrist.

Though I wanted to scoff at Vaughn's words and tell him he'd been watching too many spy movies, it made sense. Was vaguely logical. I worked on sense and logic. Made billions on it. And Wolf Eyes was not someone to be caged in a corner by people asking questions, especially if they were in uniform. I didn't know how I knew that from the handful of seconds I'd been in his presence, but I was certain of it. He utilized the same skills that had him quickly and efficiently kill a man to quickly and efficiently knock me out. And he did it in such a way that I didn't even *know* it happened. No pain from a punch in the face or concussion from being slammed onto the ground. No, he knocked me out like a *gentleman*.

"Why do you think he did it?" I nodded to my wrist.

"Well, it could be because he just killed a guy and was a spy who couldn't be recognized by anyone. Could be that he was on a mission that didn't need complications. Could be that he didn't want to get arrested for murder. Could be he's just an asshole." Vaughn shrugged. "We'll never know."

That wasn't good enough. The attack was on repeat in my mind, tearing the edges of a consciousness I'd long since tamed. Wolf Eyes appeared every time I closed my eyes, even for the milliseconds it took to blink. It wouldn't let up, this harassment. I knew it with a cold certainty that took me through most of my life. And it would be a problem. I dealt with problems. Not uncertainty.

Which was why I had to know. I'd find him. And I'd find out why.

Maybe I wouldn't like what I found. Maybe it would cost me a lot more than I bargained for. In fact, a chilly premonition told me it would.

But that didn't mean I didn't want to find him.

I was a woman who got what she wanted.

2

HIM

He paced the warehouse, the sound of his boots echoing through the open space as he did so.

He glanced down at the faded, tan leather. One of the toes was peeling at the top layer, like skin after being sliced with a serrated knife. All comparisons these days were to do with pain. Suffering. Torture. Death.

But for once, bloodstained memories didn't linger in the forefront of his mind. They retreated back to that shadowed corner that he reserved for them. And for once, it didn't take concentrated and supreme effort to put them there.

No, it was his god damned *shoes* and that memory that pushed them back.

"Nice boots."

Her voice filtered through the air as if she were right there with him. Husky and even, shaking only slightly. The eyes, emerald, almost glowing. With terror. Shock. But something else. Strength. They saw too much, those eyes. Penetrated too deep.

They saw too much in him, but they'd seen too much of the

world. People who'd witnessed the horror and depravity of humanity had a difference about them, a hardness that only someone of the same kind could recognize.

He saw that in her.

His own people he supposed—the hardened, damaged—if he could *have* people. But he couldn't. Even amongst the scarred and fucked up outcasts, he was too broken. So he distanced himself from even the most depraved and damaged. And when he did encounter those people, he made a concerted effort to avoid them, didn't even pretend to care about their suffering.

That was the way of this hunk of fucking rock in this fucked up stretch of time people called a life. Suffering was the constant. Not love or happiness or any of that bullshit.

That's the way it was and there were people that could deal and people that could not. He didn't trouble himself with either kind of people, but most especially not the latter.

Sympathy was for the Devil.

But he had it for her. Inexplicably, he felt a prickling in his gut at the thought of whatever put that hardness in those emerald eyes and what the events of that night would do to solidify those gemstones.

He shook his head as if such a brutal motion could shake her from his mind.

It couldn't.

He worried about this. His lack of power over the one thing he had left to control.

His mind.

Then again, he never really had control of it anyway. Wasn't that the illusion that shattered the moment the warm blood spilled over his hands and he watched the life drain out of that violent lowlife?

He was a killer.

He was little more than an animal, prowling around the streets of the city, scratching at the caged bars of his mind.

The roar came back when he spilled that blood. The animal reared up to take control and he relished it.

But then he met those emerald eyes and it went quiet.

The roar.

The animal.

Everything.

The world—his world—that had been so isolated had a visitor.

Only for a split second. Because once he saw past those warrior eyes and to the expensive skirt suit that encased a womanly figure that made his cock pulse even now, he knew. She was not a world away from him.

He'd picked up the watch, glittering with diamonds and wealth and reminders of what separated them.

She was in another universe.

So when he fastened it onto her smooth, milky white skin that smelled of vanilla and taunted him with possibility, he made sure to close off that universe. Go back to his.

That didn't mean he didn't imprint that gaze onto his soul. That he didn't stay cloaked in the shadows while a man in an expensive but not flashy black suit—former Marine by the looks of him—came rushing to her side. He was older. But the way he'd not even blinked at the blood, unearthed his piece with a cold calculated glare that told him he wouldn't hesitate to use it told him that he was good. Still sharp. Because he'd peered into those shadows like he'd seen him.

But then his attention focused back on the woman, clad in white and wealth, slumped in the dirty alley, whisky hair cloaking the face that had yet to leave his mind.

The woman he'd followed to the hospital.

Then home.

Then he'd watched from the shadows below the glittering tower above him until the sun came up and the shadows were gone and so was he.

CHARLOTTE

The entire rest of the day after I'd kicked Vaughn out after my coffee was a day of meetings, my mind was only half there.

Which was bad, considering we were on the cusp of one of the biggest mergers my company had ever seen. One that would build my empire to dizzying heights and not only put me at the top of the security tech industry, but the industry in general.

My ivory tower was surpassing the clouds, further isolating me from that world I so despised.

Me, a self-made woman, who started with cosmetics and worked her way up to a billion-dollar empire would finally climb over the Armani clad assholes who, at every turn, had tried to belittle, sabotage and sexualize me.

So why didn't it feel better?

Sure, I was shaken from the incident last night, who wouldn't be? But it was something else. Something at the back of my mind that had my instincts telling me to run a mile from the merger with RuberCorp. They were the biggest company in the IT sector, holding the patents on at least ten groundbreaking technologies, frontrunners in the artificial intelligence game and had data banks big enough to sustain our new security technology.

But something wasn't right.

I'd been feeling it since before last night and waved it off as lack of sleep and overworking myself. I'd promised myself a vacation, which I'd treat Molly to after this was over.

I trusted my instincts. They were what got me to invest every single cent of my money earned from a modest and growing cosmetics company to an IT startup which had revolutionary ideas about smartphones and security.

The return on my investment happened within the year.

We expanded and had multibillion-dollar contracts internationally within two.

My cosmetics company had all but become a household name and I'd ventured into two more brand expansions.

My instincts hadn't let me down yet.

Until now.

Staring at the contracts, I was fighting against the urge to put them in the shredder. Until Vaughn interrupted me, insisting I go home and he come too, and we order Chinese food and watch Julia Roberts movies.

I glanced up from my computer. "Boundaries. Ever heard of them?" I asked curtly.

He put his thumb and forefinger to his chin, pretending to look at the ceiling in thought. "Nope. They sound utterly dull, though."

"I don't like Chinese food or Julia Roberts movies, and I have contracts to go over," I informed him, though he already knew this since he'd put the contracts on my desk in the first place.

His gasp permeated the room and I was actually alarmed for a second, thinking another armed attacker had somehow made it through two lots of security and a swipe card elevator.

Only for a second.

"Who doesn't like Chinese food and *Julia Roberts?*" he asked. "She's America's sweetheart. I can get right with the whole no smiling thing and the fact you may actually melt if you get caught in the rain without an umbrella, but not liking Julia?" He shook his head. "I'm going to have to rethink working for a cyborg with no soul."

The corner of my mouth quirked. "This cyborg with no soul is the only reason you're kept in limited edition Gucci handbags, I think you'll find a way to get right with it," I remarked dryly.

I paid Vaughn a lot. But that was because he did a lot. He wasn't an assistant who did my calendar, got coffees and dry-cleaning. He was in charge of the day to day of Charlotte Cosmetics, as well as overseeing all tech developments. He had a degree from MIT, which meant he could run any of our companies but his passion was cosmetics and his unique look meant that he would not run his own security company—the world was a shitty place.

I was a firm believer in getting what I paid for. I may have been known as a bitch around the office, but I always made sure that I paid people what they were owed.

Plus fifty percent.

I did that even when I was existing on Ramen noodles and my CFO was dining at the best steakhouses in New York.

"For Gucci, I will let it slide," Vaughn decided, leaning against my door.

He paused for less than a second, in which I didn't even entertain the thought that he'd given up. And, like always, I was right.

"How about Greek?"

"Vaughn, I need to get these done"—I nodded to the contracts I was scribbling on—"then I'll go for a run, then I'm sleeping. I don't need to be babysat."

"It's not babysitting, it's looking out for my friend who was attacked last night," he said quietly.

Somehow, by miracle of all miracles, the incident stayed out of the press. Mostly because my lawyers paid a lot of people a lot of money to keep their mouths shut. No one at the office had caught on since my scarves had stayed on all day.

They didn't need to know.

No one needed to know.

Weakness was not something that needed to be broadcast.

I straightened my spine and gave Vaughn a level gaze. "I'm fine." It was so close to being the truth because I'd tricked even myself into believing the lie.

He sighed. "It's okay, you know," he murmured. "Not to be. Okay. *Anyone* would be shaken. On the edge of a mental breakdown. It's normal."

"I'm not anyone, Vaughn," I replied tersely. "I'm the CEO of three companies and have two stacks of cybersecurity contracts for an entire nation in my hands right now. Theoretically hundreds of millions of lives. I've got my shit together. I've got to have my shit together. Otherwise"—I nodded downward—"these people would be in a lot of trouble." I paused, my mind venturing a little too close to the rattling locked door at the corners of my head. "And there's no such thing as normal. It's a construct made to make us strive for something that will turn us insane."

Vaughn's gaze was shrewd, even beneath his lashes. "You're not like her. Having feelings isn't being like her, you know. Losing control for a split second after you *almost died* isn't the same as what she did. You know that." His voice was soft, but the words were sharp enough and the memories that followed were little more than fatal.

"I know," I snapped. "Though I think you have well and truly overstepped whatever boundaries we have left. I'd appreciate you not doing so again."

Vaughn flinched at my harsh tone and that would have affected me had I not been in my shell that protected me from such feelings of guilt, remorse, vulnerability.

I read somewhere that an incredibly large percentage of successful people were high functioning psychopaths, and not for the first time, I wondered which percentage I belonged to.

I had the genetics for it.

He nodded once. "Yes, Ms. Crofton." His eyes met mine. "I'll be here. Day or night. Just a phone call away."

He turned to leave.

"Vaughn," I called to his well-tailored suit-clad back. "You tell Molly any of this, I *will* fire you," I promised.

His eyes flickered before he nodded.

Then he was gone.

And I was alone.

Not truly alone. No one ever was, not when ghosts of the past were always there. Those constant companions we all tried our best to ignore.

Even with those ghosts, the utter loneliness was stifling.

Despite the fact I knew that Ralph was sitting in the lobby, waiting for me. He'd wait all night, even though I told him I'd be working late and could call a car service. Even though he had a wife waiting for him. Cold beers. Some sort of football game.

Some sort of life, presumably.

Yet he remained.

I didn't let myself puzzle on such a gesture. Instead, I pushed any thoughts or feelings connected with it aside and focused on my contracts and tried to breathe around the stifling feeling of loneliness and blink away the wolf eyes staring at me from the shadows of the room.

"You didn't need to walk me up," I said to Ralph as we rode up to my apartment. The floors ticked past as the P button stayed illuminated in the starkly bright elevator.

His gaze was flat, yet the grayish eyes surrounded by shallow wrinkles and weathered skin twinkled with something. "Yes, I did, Ms. Crofton."

I pursed my lips. "It was a one-time thing and could have happened to anyone. This is New York, after all."

He eyed me. "You're not anyone, Ms. Crofton."

I could have argued. I was good at that, my job relied on me to be able to talk my way out of anything, much like a defense lawyer. But better.

Always better.

I stayed silent instead.

The emptiness in the air was usual for me and Ralph, since I hated small talk and he knew me well enough not to try to engage.

So he waited.

And for once, I was the one to proverbially blink first, the silence much too loud for my liking.

"You'll apologize to Jilly for me, for making you miss dinner," I said as the doors opened to the foyer of my penthouse, the glittering lights of the city illuminating the room.

He laughed, deep and throaty that somehow cut a cord within in me. Completely different than the deeper and rougher one from my childhood, yet it reminded me of my father.

The sound breathed life into one of the silent ghosts trailing behind me. Until I shut my shields.

"She wouldn't likely accept that apology, Ms. Crofton," he replied. "She'd be angry if I made it to dinner and heard I'd left you working to find your own way home."

I set my white Prada bag on my vintage side table, regarding my tired face in the ornate Victorian mirror before settling my attention on Ralph, who was staring at me while holding the elevator door open. "I'm a thirty-two-year-old woman, Ralph. I've found my own way for decades. I would have been able to handle myself."

He nodded once. "Yes. You would," he agreed.

There was a loaded pause before he stepped back into the elevator.

"Goodnight, Ms. Crofton. Try and get some sleep tonight. I'll see you at six."

"Six, Ralph," I agreed, as if it wasn't the same time he'd been picking me up for six years. "And pass those apologies to Jilly," I added as the doors closed.

I caught a glimpse of his weathered smile before the doors took him back down to earth and I remained in my penthouse.

Alone once more.

How I used to like it.

Until exactly twenty hours ago.

But that was impossible, an interaction—albeit a life and death interaction—lasting less than five minutes could not change fifteen years of habits.

I learned a lot of things in fifteen years, one of the most important being that almost nothing was impossible.

The stifling feeling followed me as I wandered around my open plan living room, decorated by the best designer in the city, tasteful, elegant, expensive and not a touch of personality in it. Apart from a scattering of framed pictures Molly had given me for Christmas every year since I could remember.

Thinking of my erratic, beautiful and completely opposite twin had me yearning for her.

I'd lied to her, for the first time in...forever when she'd called earlier today.

We might not be identical, her naturally blonde hair was dyed to a shade of midnight, cut into choppy layers that brushed her shoulders with dipped tips of purple which seemed to reflect off her iridescent skin. She was the same height as me, yet she was much thinner, with no muscle as she flat out refused exercise. It was offensive to her mantra of 'do no harm.'

"Who are you harming when you exercise?" I'd asked her after the ridiculous statement was uttered.

"Myself, of course," she deadpanned.

That was not where our differences stopped. In fact, the only similarities we had were our eyes and the fact we'd shared the same womb.

She was a vegan and I loved a tenderloin. Her entire left arm was covered from shoulder to wrist with an ornate and colorful sleeve tattoo. She shopped at thrift stores, and I doubt she owned anything black. Everything about her was bright, warm, exciting.

Me? I dressed in the uniform of the elite, not a single patch of ink decorated my body, I'd never dream to put a color in my brunette head, and I'd go insane without the structure I lived for.

My home mirrored my life, angular, cold and not a single speck of dust out of place.

Her loft apartment in Chelsea was always littered with paint, to-go boxes and more often than not, various people strewn about the surfaces after some sort of party.

I owned the apartment, gifted it to her and I paid for what she'd let me, which wasn't much. Though her paintings were starting to sell so she might be able to pay it herself in the near future.

Not that she would.

I was three minutes older. Therefore I'd take care of her.

Always.

My sister. My best friend. If soulmates existed, then she was mine.

And even with her, the one I shared a womb with, there was a distance I couldn't find it in me to cross.

An entire universe.

If there was any more evidence I was emotionally handicapped, it was that. I couldn't even let down my guard with the one person who loved me unconditionally. The person I'd literally come into this world with.

So, instead of reaching for the phone that was always near my person, I walked to the fridge.

Inside was a rather destitute situation that conflicted the wealth of the apartment, of the white marble kitchen and of the huge industrial refrigerator. It was empty apart from wine, a couple of condiments, a sad looking lettuce and a packet of string cheese.

Not even mine.

Molly's.

It was the rubbery vegan kind that had more chemicals than toilet cleaner, yet she ate disturbing amounts of it.

I liked to shop for myself, yet Antonia, my housekeeper, begged me to let her do it the last time she saw the state of my fridge. And the five hundred times before that.

The large Italian woman with five sons and thirteen grandchildren nearly had a heart attack seeing no food gracing the shelves.

She already knew she couldn't bring around her home cooking because I didn't eat carbs.

Another thing she almost had a stroke at.

Yet I didn't let her shop for me.

It was the one thing I had that gave me peace. Even though I waded through the crowds of the East Village as I did it, it was the part of my week where I had quiet. Quiet amongst the crowd.

I hadn't had my quiet in a while, what with this merger eating up my time for peace. And for anything. Apart from muggings and attempted murders. I was able to squeeze those in.

I shuddered away the feeling of foreboding that came with that rogue thought.

It was a one-off. This is New York. It was bound to happen.

Why didn't I believe that? Why did the prickling still remain at the back of my neck like premonition? Why couldn't those wolf eyes be banished along with that prickle?

It needed to be. I worried that Molly would sense something was up.

I was not into spiritual things, ghosts, magic, psychics. I believed in science and reason. But there was one exception. Me and Molly. Ever since we were born, we were two parts of a whole. Our father used to say that as soon as the other cried the next would join in. As if we could feel each other's hunger.

Or pain.

When Molly was five, she fell from the steps in our old apartment and broke her wrist, Dad said that I cried out in pain.

We had been at the park four blocks away.

Mom was watching her.

Or at least meant to be.

My father had rushed home because he knew of that connection and didn't second guess it.

Neither did I.

Though in times like this that I wanted my sister naïve and happy, I resented it.

A text dinged as soon as I reached into the fridge to get the wine bottle.

Molly: I'm sending someone to kidnap you and take you to a small deserted island with no cell signal. Don't be disturbed.

Molly: I'll also be buying you some form of pet. You need a companion. I'm thinking German Sheperd or Poodle. A cat will just eat off your face when you drop dead from exhaustion.

Molly: And don't worry, he's also attractive. The man I'm sending to kidnap you, not the German Sheperd. Though I'm sure he's attractive too. He's here to treat your work addiction and give you another one entirely. Again, man not dog.

I smiled, shaking my head as I reached into a frosted glass cupboard for a wine glass.

The pop of the bottle echoed through the quiet apartment.

Molly had a lot of energy. And even more ideas. Hence the fact she could never just send one short text. It was always at least three and usually more than five. Each of them was like shaking up a snow globe, her thoughts whipping through the screen like little snowflakes. But it was *her.* I loved that about her. That she didn't need rigid control over herself to stay sane. Or at least her version of sane.

I used structure and order to stave off the bitter and cruel insanity that lurked in the dark corners of my mind. She fought fire with fire. Warm, kind and beautiful insanity to counteract the thing that lurked in our DNA.

Then again, she didn't have the memories that I did. Thankfully I could shield her from that.

I couldn't see her. Not yet. We were twins. We were something more. Our connection was deep and that meant the moment she laid eyes on me, she'd see. And I'd see the reflection of myself in her eyes. I wasn't ready for that.

Me: Can you give me a raincheck? Kidnapping doesn't fit into my schedule today. How about a week from Friday?

The responding text was immediate. I imagined Molly in some loud, dirty and crowded bar in the Meat Packing District, glued to her phone while doing a shot of something. In the city that never slept, neither did Molly.

Molly: Fine. I'll just get him to kidnap me instead. We're having brunch on Saturday. No excuses or I'll burn your office to the ground.
Love you
xxx

I rolled my eyes and treated myself to a small smile before it disappeared.

Me: Being arrested for arson is something you can tick off your bucket list. You'll look great in orange.
X

I set the phone down, not turning it off, it was never off.

I let the sweet wine kiss my lips and roll down my throat, stinging my teeth slightly as I did so. It was rather amusing, if one thought of it, that the glass I was sipping from was ten times more expensive than the bottle itself.

I glanced down at the crudely designed pink label. The bottle teenage girls got their hands on, sharing sips from, giggling as the rancid sweetness of the bubbles sent their toes numb and gave them confidence to talk to the captain of the football team. That was, of course, before their renewed confidence and lowered inhibitions had them losing their virginity to the captain of the football team in an awkward, painful and so not the romance books experience.

The really unlucky ones got a souvenir nine months later thanks to that pink bottle and a broken condom.

My experience was pretty much that exact story, thankfully sans the screaming and filthy child.

I could afford the stuff that was made by monks, aged for years, could be used as the down payment on a house. I certainly drank it whenever I was out—I had to keep up appearances after all. A billionairess didn't drink wine for...*simple* people.

What would Page Six say?

But when the weight of my own world started to pinch at that spot at the back of my neck even New York's best masseuse couldn't reach, I reached for the cheap and nasty pink wine.

Because, to me, that pink wine didn't taste like too much sugar and teenage pregnancy. No. It tasted like the happiest day of my life. One that just happened to be followed by the very worst in my existence, seventeen years earlier.

I woke to Cyndi Lauper screaming in my ear that girls just wanted to have fun.

"Wakey wakey, my princess number one," Mom's husky voice floated over the music.

I snapped my eyes open to see my mother holding two tall stemmed wine glasses in one hand and a crown in the other.

She pushed it onto my mussed curls as soon as I pushed up, rubbing sleep from my eyes. She had a feather boa around her neck and was still wearing her dusky pink silk nightgown that hugged her slender body and lace trim where it ended at her ankles.

It was Dad's birthday present to her.

She loved it.

So much so, sometimes she didn't take it off for days.

On good days.

I took the glass of pink bubbly liquid, taking in Mom's smile and eyes that were full of sparks and beauty.

Today was a good day then.

"Mom, it's a school day," I reminded her back as she twirled around, snatching another glass off my bedside table and moving to the doorway just in time for Molly to come prancing in, her choppy hair mussed from sleep, topped with a crown of her own. She was already dancing to the music and grinning from ear to ear as she took her glass off Mom, taking a huge gulp of the pink liquid without hesitation.

Molly never hesitated. Never. She jumped in with both feet. Which was what everyone loved about her. She was willing to try anything. That's why she was not only the captain of the cheerleading squad but also the chess club. She tore through stereotypes as if she didn't even know they were there.

Me? I cradled the glass with more than hesitation. I didn't jump. I dipped my toe in, testing the water before making an informed decision. That's why I was president of the study body. And editor of the school paper. Things required order, control.

Mom whirled once more, then stopped.

"School?" she repeated, screwing her nose up. "We don't have school on holidays!"

I sat up, careful not to spill the liquid that filled the glass to the rim. "It's not a holiday."

Mom continued to sway to the music, her bright green eyes glowing as they met mine. "It is my beautiful daughter's sixteenth birthday. Of course it's a holiday, it's only the best day on the planet. When the sun shone a little dimmer because you stole some of its light."

She whirled, feathers shedding off the cheap boa and floating silently to the ground.

"School," she scoffed. "No. We are having a girl's day. And girl's days must have these things. Crowns, because we are royalty." She pointed at the plastic crown on her own head. "Pink wine, because you are always happy with pink wine." She sipped her glass.

"And my beautiful girls." She snatched Molly's hand, then mine, sloshing some liquid on it and barely noticing it. "The two most precious treasures I could ever hold in my two hands."

And so the day was spent with wine, and laughter, and dressing up. And happiness.

It was a hollow kind of happiness.

I didn't know that until the day after. Then I looked back at saw into my memories. That slosh of wine on my hand, the way Mom's eyes shined just that little bit too bright to be merely happy. The way madness flirted with her gaze. I was too busy at the time to see that.

Molly still visited her. Every Wednesday. She said she seemed better on Wednesdays.

I wouldn't know. I hadn't gone in fifteen years. Not since the first time.

I didn't go to visit my father's grave either.

I didn't see the point in staring at cold stone meant to represent a soul long gone from this world. Standing on the grass atop his bones. He wasn't there, in some desolate graveyard where life had no place even shadowing the headstones.

It was the same with Mom. She wasn't in this world anymore. Not really. Her gravestone was just a little different than Dad's. Not cold, unyielding stone. Flesh built to look like the woman who'd let me wear fairy wings to believe I could make magic. Who told me the world was mine, hers and Molly's and that nothing bad ever truly happened. Who let us drink pink wine for breakfast on our sixteenth birthday. Her light had left this world and I had no intention of ever staring at the reminder of that. At the empty eyes devoid of sparkle, instead the glassy stare of nothingness welcoming me to the party. Or the funeral.

Why would I?

It wouldn't change anything.

My father would still be dead. She would still have said goodbye to the person that she was. My mother was dead.

The best thing I could do for either of them was to remember that I wasn't. And maybe try to forget that they were.

3

"I don't think you understand the gravity of refusing this merger," Abe, my CFO told me across the boardroom table.

Outside of this room, he was also my uncle. The man that took my sister and me into his expensive and emotionally cold brownstone for two years before we both escaped into adulthood, into two very different versions of it.

He wasn't exactly the warm and kind uncle who kept candy in his pockets and doled out cheesy jokes, but he was there for us when we needed him and gave us whatever his limited emotional capacity enabled. And he'd supported me growing my company, even when my success surpassed his own, he came on as my CFO without hesitation. He was integral to the company. Because he saw things a different way and didn't mind disagreeing with me when he saw fit.

Sometimes he was right. Others, he was wrong. Like this time.

He may have been my uncle outside the boardroom, but I rarely saw him anywhere else and I treated him exactly like I would all of my other employees.

I rose my brows at him and glanced around the room at the scattering of people wearing expensive suits and a variety of stifling perfume. The men wore more than the women. Because they didn't know the delicate touch was all that was needed.

Luckily, the women sitting at the table outnumbered the men. Because I'd made it my mission to source as many of the best women in the field into my employ. I scouted colleges for extraordinary young women, paid for the rest of their tuitions and gave them internships right out of school. I gave them chances that even now, their gender wouldn't normally afford them. But they still had to work hard to get seats at the table. I wanted the best.

"I assure you, I do have all of the information and understand what is at stake," I replied, my voice even and flat.

His caterpillar-like brows narrowed. "If you understood what was at stake, then you wouldn't be using your controlling shares to stop a merger with one of the world's top security firms. I understand that you might not understand the logistics of the company, being young and..." he paused, eyes trailing over my slim fitting white sheath dress, lingering far too long on my breasts. Not in a sexual way, he wasn't *that* kind of uncle either. Everything he did was to make a point. "Inexperienced," he finished instead of stating 'a woman.' Verbally at least. "I've been in the business for years. I *know* these men. I also know mistakes."

I took an even breath, schooling my expression so none of my frustration showed. Emotion had no place in the boardroom.

My life was the boardroom, everything was careful, measured, emotionless.

"And you think it would be a mistake not to get into bed with a company who is headed by a man with no less than three rape convictions that were conveniently dropped when the women disappeared, and whose offshoot security firm was involved in a massacre in Eastern Sudan where a village was looted and all women and children brutalized?" I asked, my tone flat.

People moved uncomfortably around me. Stephanie, my in-house counsel, bit her lip to hide a grin.

Abe's eyes flared slightly at my speech. He hadn't expected me to know this. All this information was buried deep. I knew how to find skeletons in the closet, because I invented the best hiding places.

"I do my homework before signing over my life's work and information about millions of clients to a 'top security firm,'" I informed him. "The money they're offering isn't worth the price I'd have to pay."

The flesh on his neck above his expensive shirt bulged and turned a crimson color as he struggled to compose himself. My uncle stood to make a lot of money from this deal too, I had no doubt he not only knew about this but actively tried to hide it from me. Not to sabotage me, but because he thought he knew what was best. Men always thought they knew what was best for women.

"I understand that such incidents are...upsetting," he said through gritted teeth. "But we need to take emotion out of business decisions. I understand that will be harder for you." He paused long, purposefully. "It's just...nature. But, with all due respect, you should reconsider. It might take a little more hard work than you're used to, but getting your hands dirty is sometimes necessary in this business," he finished, his tone superior and patronizing. "A conscience is all well and good in theory, but in this business, it's about as useless as tits on a bull. And your shareholders would not respond well to your conscience, costing them a fuck of a lot of money."

His threat was clear. Though I held majority shares, he could cause some serious trouble for me if he misrepresented the situation to the shareholders. Or even if he represented it exactly as it was. Because he was right, this business didn't bother with morals when money was concerned. They didn't care about bloodstains on a contract, heck they'd sign in blood if it meant more zeros at the end of their already bloated bank accounts.

I stared at Abe over my papers, gaze focusing across the room with cold indifference, like his was nothing more than an annoying fly.

My pause was long, purposeful and much longer than his. Long enough to make the stuffed suits shift uncomfortably in their chairs. The women smirked knowingly. I stayed stock still, not moving my gaze.

"I would *advise* you not to belittle me, nor make any assumptions about my work ethic based on the fact I wear heels," I addressed Abe mildly. "Because, that, my dear uncle, would be a grave mistake." I leaned back in my chair slightly and crossed my legs, so the red soles of my shoes flashed to the table.

"You see, the fact I wear these shoes makes me so much more dangerous than you could ever be because I do everything you do, except I do it *better*. And I do it wearing shoes that you couldn't even walk a centimeter in, let alone a mile. There is nothing more dangerous than a woman who does everything a man can do, and all the while gritting her teeth in the pain that her six-inch heels cost her." I didn't move my gaze. "Nothing. You'd do well to remember that before you make any more threats, veiled or otherwise." I stood, straightening my skirt and not addressing the variety of stares and slack jaws. I handed my iPad to a grinning Vaughn while I kept my face blank and tone empty. "I apologize, but I have other meetings to attend to. I assume we're done here?"

Without waiting for an answer, I turned on my thousand-dollar heel that sent spikes of pain up my calf and walked out of the room like I was in my comfiest slippers.

That was the trick. Even when the pain was so deep you thought it might cripple and scar you for life, you never let on. You outwardly acted like there was nothing that could hurt you. Because if you acted otherwise, then *everything* could.

I didn't know why it surprised me, considering the fact that I'd been almost killed the week before. But maybe that's why the man in the apartment did surprise me. I somehow thought I was safe. That I escaped with only scars of just how deep death's grip had sunk into me.

But no one escaped death. And it seemed death had its eye fixed squarely on me.

I was surprised, because I was glancing down at the three-page email Abe had sent me after the meeting. I was dealing with lawyers who were advising the best course of action in exiting the merger at the last minute.

None of it was an excuse to not notice the presence of a stranger in my apartment. But living in one of the most expensive and well-protected buildings in Manhattan gave me a misplaced sense of security. Ivory towers, no matter how tall, were never as safe as they seemed. In fact, tonight, my ivory tower was about as safe as a dirty and dark alley.

I didn't scream when he came at me. It wouldn't have been prudent, anyway. I had the entire top floor. No one would hear me. I could've run, I supposed, but in the time it took for me to register his presence and assess my options, he was already dead.

Because there wasn't just one man in my apartment.

There were two.

The second was standing beside the body he'd just created, his knife dripping with blood, crimson droplets landing on his scuffed boots.

I blinked down at the body slowly leaking blood along my marble floor. Freshly polished, too. I made a note to call my housekeeper.

I stepped to the left to avoid my shoes bearing evidence to its journey. Whatever cool detachment had been keeping me level started to shake as reality set in. I couldn't lose it. Even when I'd just witnessed another man murdered. In my apartment no less.

It was not the dead man's wide and empty stare I should've been focused on.

My gaze moved up to a stare that was anything but empty.

Eyes that had been regarding me since the body of my would-be murderer hit the floor.

Wolf eyes.

I focused on them. Tasted the texture of the gaze that was both wild and caged at the same time.

I licked my lips.

The wolf eyes followed this movement.

"That's number two," I observed, finding the key I'd been struggling with to shut the door to my mind. The one where your right and left combine. Where it was a free for all between logic and pure human instinct. I had to struggle to keep the left on top, instinct, feelings could be the end of everything. I was no longer under the illusion that I was safe. Even with the man who'd tried to kill me dead. Danger still permeated the air.

Wolf eyes flickered, betraying confusion while staying silent.

"Number two on the list of people that you've killed," I clarified.

He laughed then. It shocked me at first, the way it bounced off the bitter air and tasted sweet. The chord of it was throaty and masculine, underlying a rough growl.

"Number two," he repeated, his voice that same rough growl. Deep, thick, like he was unused to using his tongue to form words. Like he was testing them out, rolling them around in his mouth.

I nodded.

He stepped forward and I wished my body didn't betray me by involuntarily moving back half an inch. Retreat was a sign of weakness. He noticed this and his eyes hardened, but he didn't stop his approach.

Then he was there. Close enough that the fabric of his leather jacket brushed against the silk of my blouse. Close enough so the weight behind the intensity focused on me was suffocating.

"Two perhaps a number for another list, but not that one," he rasped, searching my face.

I searched his back, hoping for answers to the enigma that was this man. The answer behind his words was death. The promise that he'd dealt it. Yet somehow I couldn't bring myself to care.

"What's the other list?" I asked.

For some reason, perhaps insanity, I wasn't threatened. Or scared. For my physical safety anyway.

His eyes flickered over me, cool and hot at the same time, his gaze caressed me with his hands fisted firmly at his sides. He didn't speak so I guessed this was his non-verbal reply. He didn't need to speak.

The other list was about me.

It was comforting at least that this obsession wasn't all in my own head. Sharing an obsession with a man who'd murdered two human beings without hesitation shouldn't have been comforting.

But it was.

The eyes that have served as wallpaper in my brain were now here, unblinking, cold, ruthless.

Now I was staring at them, up close in all their wild beauty, tasting the scent of his presence, I didn't want it to become a memory.

So I did something impulsive.

Or said something impulsive.

"Do you happen to have a job?"

Wolf eyes flickered and his face tilted with confusion. He still didn't speak. What he did do, was step back.

"It seems to me that there is someone rather intent on causing me harm and you've been in the vicinity to stop that from happening...twice." I frowned at him, and at myself for not choosing to question him on how he came to be in the vicinity twice. The alley was explainable. My apartment, not so much. But I didn't query about that. I kept speaking.

"I'm taking an educated gamble that if it was you that wanted me dead, you could have just sat back and watched the show the first time around. Or the second." I glanced around the room that smelled familiar—blood and death was a scent that was an unwelcome but permanent fixture in my brain—I chased away the memories that came with it. "And, if you really wanted to, kill me, that is, I'm sure you could. Now. Third time's a charm."

I waited. The silent invitation filling the air while his eyes, never leaving me charged it with something else.

Something else that wasn't murder.

Yet it was carnal all the same.

I blinked it away. The desire. I reasoned it was connected to adrenaline and the near-death experience. My body was clutching onto something that wasn't pure terror. I had a hauntingly beautiful man right in front of me. It made sense.

"So. You're not here to murder me," I deduced when he didn't use the knife he was still clutching to slit my throat. "I don't believe in coincidences, we'll have to address how you happened to be *inside my apartment* to prevent my death at a later juncture. For now, let's start with a simple question. Are you gainfully employed?"

He stared at me another beat, perhaps gaging my sanity. He didn't speak.

I crossed my arms, partly for the gesture but mostly to hide the way my nipples decided to harden at an inopportune moment. "I'll take that as a no. As it happens, I have a position available that you'd be perfect for." I glanced to the body and swallowed the bile that came with it. I kept my mask on my face. It was always on. Even when I was alone. Especially when I was alone. The most important person I needed to hide from was the reflection in the mirror.

"You've already aced the interview," I continued. "So I'd like to formally offer you the position. It's a generous salary and comes with full benefits."

"Position?" he repeated on a low grumble.

I nodded, his voice hitting me physically. "As head of my security."

Again, that ripple flickered across his gaze. "I killed a man in front of you, inside your apartment, a place I should not have been, and you're not asking me why I was here, you're offering me a job?"

"Correct," I replied. "Though I will have follow up questions on how you got in here. For now, I'm alive and I have you to thank."

"I'm not a bodyguard," he clipped.

I glanced down to the body once more. "I beg to differ."

He scowled at me. "I'm not the man for the job."

"You seem quite suited."

He gripped his knife, his eyes emptying of whatever had been there before. Humanity, perhaps.

Real fear came creeping back in, caressing my spine with its claws.

"You don't even know me," he said, registering my fear but not doing anything to quell it, if anything, he schooled his features to increase it.

I nodded after swallowing roughly. "No, I do not. And you do not know me. Yet twice you have risked a lot—killed—to stop me from becoming nothing more than a stain on that floor." I nodded to the marble. "I doubt anyone I meet and do an expensive background check on will be able to boast the same."

He stared at me, *into me*, it seemed. But then that fire in his eyes wouldn't be burning if he saw into me. If he glimpsed the rotten core.

"I don't need a job."

I raised a brow at him, staring pointedly at his boots. I didn't know why they had become the signifier that the man needed a job, but they somehow were. Because everything about this man, from his sculpted muscles to his entire *energy* told me he would not be the kind of man to walk around in scuffed and almost ruined leather boots if he could help it.

"I freelance," he all but growled at my silent assumption.

"What does that mean?"

His eyes narrowed. "Means I freelance."

I tilted my head. "Does that mean you're a hitman?"

His mouth twitched. "No."

I nodded. "Okay. Well, whatever it is you do isn't affording you enough resources to buy you new footwear, so how about you do a week trial?"

He stared at me. "You offerin' me a job protectin' you despite the fact not one second ago you thought I was a hitman."

I didn't waver my own stare, hadn't in the years I'd been in business, but in a decade, I'd never had to try harder to keep my face impartial. "You disputed that."

His eyes were glaciers. "I could have lied."

I raised my brow. "I don't think you did."

He stepped forward again, the fabric of our shirts, our worlds, brushing once more. I didn't feel the fear this time, because he did it deliberately to prove a point. You didn't get to where I did without recognizing when men decided to use their size to intimidate.

Terror was what any normal person would feel having a brute of a man—a killer—do such a thing as step forward with wild eyes and clenched fists.

I wasn't normal.

"A hitman would've lied," he murmured, his voice a blade.

I swallowed. "Yeah," I agreed. "And I would have been able to tell."

He eyed me. "I'm a good liar."

I eyed him right back. "I'm better, baby," I rasped. "I may not be able to hit like a man." I glanced down to the fists. "But I can lie like one, fuck like one and recognize sincerity, or lack thereof. You're not a hitman. Yet you've killed people." My gaze flickered over him, the way he held himself. "You're most likely a Marine, or at least a high-ranking officer in the army, in a branch that the government would never admit existed."

He stepped back suddenly and glanced from the body to me. "You know that, how?"

I shrugged. "I'm observant." My eyes went to his bicep. "Semper Fi."

His eyes went there too, for a split second looking at his own skin as if it were foreign, as if someone had etched the ink onto it without him knowing.

Or maybe it was the face of someone looking at their solid, corporeal skin, when they realized they were not invisible as they pretended to be.

As they needed to be.

Or maybe I was just reading far too much into it.

Because I was reading far too much into him.

His gaze quickly met mine once more, eyes shuttered, blank. Animal once more.

"Doesn't matter who I was," he growled. "That's a different life. I'm a different man now." He paused. "I'm *not* a man now. And I'm not someone to be protectin' anything."

And then, with one more loaded moment, with one more second of a pause in my heartbeat, he turned on his boot and walked out of my apartment.

He left bloody footprints in his wake.

"This is the second time you've been attacked, and a dead body was left by a mysterious stranger, Ms. Crofton," the same detective from last week said, looking up from his iPad.

We were in his office now.

Or *someone's* office.

I doubted that this man had an office of his own, even if he was a detective. There were no such luxuries as a police officer. Then again, this was New York. Police officers didn't need offices because their office was the streets. It would be a cold day in hell before this violent city banished law enforcement officers behind a desk pushing paper.

But I was high profile.

I had a reputation.

I needed privacy to be interviewed.

Or interrogated.

His tone didn't exactly betray suspicion or accusation, merely curiosity. It was rather obvious I hadn't committed the murder since my white sheath dress didn't even have a speck of blood on it, nor did my smooth and steady hands. I had called in the body mere seconds after a man left bloody footprints and a shaking soul in his wake.

The police arrived mere minutes later.

I was Charlotte Crofton. A member of the elite. The one percent. The people that ran the world and could get away with murder (and they did, routinely, though not usually with their hands dirty) as long as they had enough money and sway to do so.

Of course, *rich* people got convicted of things all the time.

But it was not just about the money.

Money was easy to make.

Easier to lose.

But it was power.

Power was one of the hardest currencies to become wealthy in. But once gained, it bought more than billions of dollars.

And I had it.

Hence me sitting in what I guessed was the chief's office with a glass of sparkling water—that I had no idea where they got— comfortably sitting across from the officer who had found me at a murder scene for the second time in as many weeks.

"Yes, I do agree it's all rather dramatic," I said, my voice calm.

My mind was not focused on the office with a laboring air

conditioner causing my glass to sweat like a criminal in one of the interrogation rooms. Nor the shrewd and probing gaze of the detective, his whisky colored eyes inspecting me. My mind was on a very different pair of eyes. Eyes that did not inspect me. Eyes that dissected me.

Boots that smeared blood on marble as they strode away from me.

"Dramatic and unusual," Detective Maloney, 'but please call me Dominic' said. "Something beyond a random act of violence, like we deduced last time."

He said *last time* with a heaviness, a weight that settled on me with the memory of my terror. My weakness. My power being snatched away from me.

Of course, I didn't betray that outwardly.

I never would.

It was tantamount to suicide in my world—admitting weakness. And that was amongst the men. Me, a woman, one who paid dearly for her position, it was something a lot more than that. Because the thing worse than death for me, was being helpless. Powerless.

"This is a violent world, Detective Maloney," I replied, my voice steel. "A violent city."

He narrowed his brows at me. The gesture itself was not threatening or aggressive, he was a man trying to figure out a puzzle.

"It is," he agreed. "But in this violent world, it is an anomaly to be saved by a stranger *once*. Let alone twice. Factoring in the fact that this stranger killed both attackers with skill and efficiency only possessed by career criminals, or professionals, it is not random." There was no question in his words yet one in his tone.

He waited for me to answer it. He was good, I'd give him that. His stare was harsh yet not overtly accusing, his demeanor brisk but friendly, his words probing and not forceful on the surface yet there was a quality to them that yanked at the human instinct to answer. To comply.

I didn't comply with anything.

I evenly met his stare, not speaking, making sure my mask was firmly in place.

He blinked first.

They always did.

"Are you sure you don't know this man?" he said, a small twinkle of appreciation in his eye. Likely he wasn't used to being bested. And unlike many men, it did not rouse a kind of fury at being bested by a woman, no it was a respect that lay beneath his gaze.

Rare, those men.

"Am I sure I don't know a man that knows how to kill assailants in a handful of seconds, one who hangs around in dark alleys at midnight and doesn't hesitate to not just come to a woman's aide but end a life?" I asked.

More eye twinkle.

A nod.

"Yes, I am sure that I do not have an acquaintance with someone like that," I said dryly. "And I can say with complete honesty, this man, if we can call him that, is a complete and utter stranger to me. And these acts of violence are as baffling to me as they are to you. I assure you."

All of those statements were, in theory, true.

Lying only worked best when you used the truth to deceive.

He regarded me for a long moment. "Do you have any enemies, Ms. Crofton?"

I laughed, long and cold. "Yes, Detective Maloney, I have plenty of enemies," I said, my voice as chilly as my laugh. "A woman does not get to the position I am without them." I paused. "But do I have enemies that would have me attacked not once, but *twice* in a rather messy and inefficient way?" I raised my brow at him, pausing for a handful of seconds.

"No. I'm sure a lot of men I've stepped on along the way, would love to see me dead. But every single one would be too cowardly to actually do something about it. And the ones that weren't, and I'll say this is very few, they'd be efficient. I wouldn't be sitting here talking to you. I'm sure I'd be in a closed casket while at a tasteful, and impressively attended funeral."

The detective who I had been sure was little more than unflappable blinked in shock at my words.

I wanted to smile at the expression.

Of course I didn't. Smiles, like tears, were a form of weakness.

"Now," I said, standing and positioning my Hermes in the crook of my arm. "If there's nothing else, I have a company to run. Well, I have four, but you get the point."

He recovered quickly and stood, rounding the table to lean on the desk in front of me.

He was rather attractive, in a conventional way. Slightly older than me, if the gray in his temples was anything to go by. Then again, I guessed with his job it was an occupational hazard to go gray early. Either that or die before you had the chance.

The rest of his hair was brown, not quite black, but the same whisky color as his eyes. It was short but slightly ruffled, unstyled, and mussed as if he had been running his fingers through it continuously. His jaw was chiseled and free of stubble, nose straight. There were slight bags under his eyes, another unsurprising physical quality. Detectives didn't keep regular hours, since crime didn't.

He was wearing a middle of the line button down shirt, slightly wrinkled, open collar, no tie. It was tucked into worn jeans, an expensive leather belt fastened around them. He was trim, lean but with muscles that told me, he most likely ran daily and did weight training a couple of times a week.

So he was healthy, not paid well for the number of hours he did—evidenced by the tidy but inexpensive clothes—didn't sleep —the eye bags—and was hardened by the world he'd chosen to become his life. But not jaded, if the slight warming in his expression was anything to go by as he crossed his arms and regarded me.

"Someone is obviously looking to hurt you, Ms. Crofton," he said. "And I fear that the third time will not be lucky for you. If you would like me to organize a protection detail—"

"I appreciate the offer, Detective Maloney," I interrupted. "But the New York City police force are stretched thin as it is, with not enough funding to combat constant crime. I, on the other hand, have the resources to hire my own protection detail. I am not going to be glib with my safety, I assure you. Nor will I be dense about the obvious position I'm in. I plan on hiring an effective security team to make sure there is no third time."

A slight lie.

I *was* going to hire a team. But not to protect me. To find *him*.

Because I was good at reading people.

At picking up small details and adding them together to give me information to get what I wanted.

And this last attack was not in a darkened alley when I didn't have time to assess the situation.

There was light.

I had information.

Maybe not enough, but I'd make it enough.

Because I always got what I wanted.

4

"I don't understand, Mr. Thatcher. Your reputation hails you as one of the best private investigators in the country," I said, looking down at the paper on him for effect rather than anything else. I'd memorized it. Knowledge was always power.

"The lack of information tells me otherwise. And I'm paying you a lot of money for you to tell me nothing." I screwed up the paper, focusing on him with my even gaze. "So here's something I can tell you, for free." I tossed the paper in the trash. His eyes followed it, but I kept my gaze on him. I waited for him to resume eye contact.

"I've taken great pains to ensure my word has weight in this city," I continued. "In *all areas* of this city. I'm thinking with your clientele, clientele who listen to me because they respect me, fear me or because I control their companies. If I were to share my disappointment with them, I would hazard a guess into saying you'd never work in New York City again." I paused as his face reddened. "Perhaps you might afford a ramshackle office in New Jersey with a laboring fan for the summer and nothing but a space heater for the winter, getting measly paychecks from overweight and jealous husbands or pinched faced paranoid housewives." I leaned forward, placing my palms flat on my desk. "Worlds away from your current offices in Manhattan, with an impressive client list and a paycheck that ensures your wife doesn't have to work a day in her life and she can shop at Hermes and get massages every week. And so that you can finance your mistress in her apartment in Soho."

The man's cheeks had reddened from the moment I started speaking, now his eyes bulged to comical proportions, somehow widening his relatively thin and not completely unattractive face.

But his expression and lack of control over his emotions was what made him unattractive.

It was weakness.

I'd been able to strip him of that smarmy false strength he'd sauntered in here with moments before in mere seconds.

"How the fuck do you know that?" he hissed, using anger to blanket his fear at my words and the very real promise behind them. He wasn't an overly stupid man, therefore he knew that I had the power to do everything I said and more. I'd done it before. I didn't do empty threats. Nothing about me was empty, except perhaps my soul.

I tilted my head. "Do you think I look dense enough not to have my investigator investigated?" I leaned back in my chair. "I had to be assured that you are the best, and I do not judge you for your infidelity. I couldn't care less. I do judge you for your lack of skill that you are charging me thousands of dollars for."

"It's impossible!" he yelled. Men did that too, yelled when they were failing in front of a woman. As if the tenor of their voices might cover up the exposed nerve that was inferiority in front of the fairer and in their minds, weaker sex.

"Nothing is impossible, Mr. Thatcher," I said, my voice still even. Men had yelled at me many times before, and nothing made them madder than when I didn't yell back, or blanch in the face of their fury. "And you assured me of much the same when I hired you a week ago."

His cockiness had all but filled up my office. He had assured me it would be covered. That Wolf Eyes would be found on the little amount of information I'd been able to provide.

Yet here he was, a week later, with nothing.

"Do you know how hard it is to find a man with no name, no places of employment, no residence listed?" he asked, voice not quite a yell but a low rumble.

"Yes, I am well aware, which is why I hired a professional rather than do it myself." My eyes flickered over him and his expensive suit, making sure my face was structured in a way that it showed I found him lacking. "Or, more aptly, I *thought* I hired a professional." I waved my hand. "I'll no longer be needing your services. Vaughn will validate your parking on the way out, and that's the only form of reimbursement for services rendered you'll be getting from me."

I held up my hand to silence him as he pushed from his chair, presumably to pace and yell. "And before you try to argue on the point of your paycheck, I'll remind you of the retainer I already paid that is well above the amount needed to pay for your time and resources since neither seems to have been utilized. If you leave my office without a word, I'll consider not mentioning this unfortunate experience to my acquaintances and perhaps you'll still be able to keep your wife in Hermes scarves in a year." I raised my brow. "Your choice."

He opened his mouth. Right before the words flew out, the threats, the insults, the excuses, his brain caught up exceptionally fast. Because he knew I had him, proverbially, by the balls.

And not in the way he liked.

The pure hatred and fury in his eyes told me he was liking nothing about this experience, and every instinct he had was urging him to salvage his tattered masculinity.

But he was likely also very attached to his balls.

So he clenched his fists at his sides and stayed silent.

Of course he did.

Before he could storm from the room like an unruly teenager, the door flew open and the entire energy of the room changed.

No, the room became a pulsating ball of energy.

"I have no idea how he got in the building and I honestly value my life enough not to try and physically stop him from getting in here," Vaughn said calmly as he trailed in behind the person who had opened my doors. He held up his phone. "Security?" he asked, a twinkle in his eye.

Vaughn would've called them already in any other situation. And contrary to what he just said, no one would've been striding unannounced into my office unless they first trampled over his dead body.

This wasn't any other situation.

Vaughn knew this. Because I had explained, in great detail the man that had saved my life. Including the eyes.

The wolf eyes staring at me, locked on me, yanking me up from my chair without my permission.

He was calm. Expressionless. Marble in a man.

He had walked purposefully and confidently into the room, like he owned it, like he owned everyone inside it, despite his worn leather jacket, faded jeans and worn boots.

No one had ever walked into my office in jeans.

Ever.

And the men who strode in wearing ten thousand-dollar suits did not create as much ownership as the man who was standing in the middle of my office, boots splayed out, arms folded, regarding me like he had every right to be here.

Like he had every right to do *anything* he wanted.

My skin pulsated hot and cold with his stare, with his presence in my ivory world, yanking it from reality.

It was only when his gaze flickered to the red-faced man beside him did I regain some sense of composure.

Vaughn was grinning at this point.

"No, Vaughn, I'll not be requiring security," I said, my voice not shaking though every inch of my insides were. "Mr. Thatcher will need to be escorted out, though," I continued, yanking my gaze from the wild animal in front of me.

"Who is this guy?" Mr. Thatcher demanded, not appreciating the fact that the man beside him dominated the room.

I raised my brow, thankful for the opportunity to be distracted and play the part I knew how to play so well. "It seems you can't even do your job when it's literally staring you in the face," I commented dryly. "I'm rethinking my generous retainer. I'll expect the balance back in my account by end of day tomorrow. Otherwise, I'd be looking at real estate in New Jersey."

I paused, dared him to speak. The silence hung on for a long while. I didn't blink. The man I was speaking to blinked profusely, red-faced, hands clenched at his sides, expression structured into a hateful grimace.

I didn't change my expression. "That's all."

I gave Vaughn a pointed look.

"Mr. Thatcher, I'd advise you listen to Ms. Crofton's generous offer," he said, voice holding a bite that was dampened by his obvious amusement. And he'd obviously been listening to the entire conversation through the intercom, as he did regularly.

I reached down and pointedly turned it off.

He only grinned wider.

Mr. Thatcher stayed rooted in his spot, out of shock or malice I wasn't sure. Maybe a mixture of both.

"My time is money, Mr. Thatcher," I said. "If you keep wasting it, I'll add my bill to the amount you're refunding me. And I'm not cheap."

His eyes flickered with more rage, but not enough to have him be stupid enough to say anything.

He turned on his heel and stomped out, just like I predicted.

"Please go and add him to the blacklist," I instructed an awaiting Vaughn. "Make sure he never works in this city again."

He grinned. "I thought you told him you weren't going to do that?'

"I've changed my mind. Women tend to do that. Emotionally unstable and all that," I said, my voice cold.

Vaughn nodded once, still grinning. "Can I get you anything Mister..." he trailed off, waiting for Wolf Eyes to follow with a name, a title to somehow encompass everything in front of me.

In front of me as in, *in my office.*

Not in my dreams.

Not in my nightmares where he'd resided for the past fortnight.

But here, without explanation.

He didn't speak.

Didn't even offer up the small sliver that worked as a social nicety.

"Water?" Vaughn probed. "Coffee? Herbal tea? Whisky? The blood of your enemies?"

I gave Vaughn a look.

He nodded once and left the room, not before winking at me as he closed the door.

Wolf Eyes didn't speak.

Neither did I.

My knees wobbled as they struggled to hold my weight and I forced myself not to brace my body on my desk. That would be betraying my weakness, showing him that he had power over me.

As would speaking first.

I let the silence take over the room. Regulate my breaths. His stare flayed my very skin, making me want to crawl into myself to escape it.

"I won't wear a suit," he all but growled.

Him speaking first should've given me the power I needed.

But he still grasped everything in his hands, in his stare.

I tilted my head, regarding the weathered leather jacket and the plain white tee underneath. Nothing special. Yet somehow they did more than a five thousand dollar suit did for GQ models. They molded to his muscles and size like they were made for him.

"Why?" I asked. My tone was curious, nothing else. The sharp bite I usually reserved for people who refused me was absent here.

Even if I wanted to, I didn't think I could call it up.

He regarded me, the wolf in his eyes glowing, glimmering with the wild air. "Because they're cages," he said after a beat. "Suit and a tie. Chains to a world, a life, that I'll never belong to. That I don't *want* to belong to."

I stared at those eyes, imagined a wild animal at the zoo, all spark gone from a creature torn from everything they once were. I nodded once. "You don't belong in a cage," I replied. "Wild things don't belong in a cage," I all but whispered. The words and the soft tone of them surprised me. Never did I speak without calculating my words, measuring them.

His jaw hardened and his gaze flickered as he stepped forward, with surety that had been absent from his earlier demeanor.

Yet the eyes still danced with something not entirely human.

"You think I'm wild?" he rasped, his voice cutting through the air, and dampening my panties, along with his proximity. He was still a few feet from me, still keeping his distance, yet my heart sped up as goosebumps erupted on my arms from the taste of him. Or the *possibility* of the taste of him.

I didn't move my eyes from his gaze. Nor did I answer. He seemed to be plucking everything from me, every idiosyncrasy I clung to. Every consistent fact about myself. All my power.

"You're right," he said, taking my silence as confirmation. "I am. Too wild for you. Your world."

"We live in the same world," I whispered.

A ghost of a smile kissed his lips. But it wasn't pleasing, nor happy. No, it was filled with bitterness and pain. "No, Boots. We don't."

The words were final. Resolute.

"Perhaps you could...commute," I said once I found my tongue.

"From your world to mine. I'd pay you handsomely for the journey, of course." I slipped back into my tone I reserved for business and instead of the comfortable cashmere sweater it usually felt like, it was wrong, unpleasant. Itchy.

I didn't want to be like that with him.

That false and sanitized version of myself.

His eyes darkened. "I don't need that. Don't give a fuck about money."

The harshness of his words and of his gaze was doing things to me. Shaking me up, making me clench my thighs together against the need for him. Against the desire so chaotic, it almost repulsed me. Because it was nigh on uncontrollable.

I worked to control my expression. My words. I tightened my features and sharpened my gaze. "Everyone gives a fuck about money," I said. "Even the people that say they don't, *especially* the people that say they don't."

Nothing about his expression moved, he wasn't betraying an ounce of feeling, that I was doing anything resembling what he was doing to me. "I'm not people. And what I need, can't be bought with money. Can't be bought with anything."

"And what is it that you need?" the words came out as little more than a whisper. As somewhat of a plea, betraying my desire to know more of him, to find his loose threads and unravel them until he was in pieces in front of me, until I could dissect him like he was doing to me.

But he didn't speak. He just stared at me, challenging me to probe more. Doing that would be showing more than I already had. Betraying that victimhood he had roused within me.

"You're not curious about other aspects of the job?" I asked, deducing his silence, his presence meant that he was taking me up on the offer to protect my life.

To ruin it.

He shook his head once.

"Don't want to know why two people have tried to kill me in the same amount of weeks?" I continued.

"Tried," he said. "And failed. That's all I need to know. And the fact that everyone after the fact will fail too. My job isn't specifics. That's what police are for. To protect and serve. Gonna protect you. Won't fuckin' serve you, though."

I clenched my thighs together. "Contrary to what many of the people in my employ might say, I am not a tyrant," I said, welcoming my old tone with relief. "I simply require people to do their jobs."

"Since my job is keepin' you alive, I'll be fuckin' doin' my job, Boots."

I sucked in a harsh breath.

"We'll have to do something about that," I said, forcing myself to sit slowly back into my chair. As if I weren't doing it because I didn't trust my feet underneath me.

He didn't move, though I nodded at the seat in front of him. "About what, Boots?"

I met his gaze and weathered it. "That," I said through pursed lips. "My employees refer to me as Ms. Crofton."

To my face at least. I knew there were plenty of other names they said behind my back. No one had been brave enough to address me in any other way. Until Wolf Eyes.

"I haven't remarked on this...nickname before primarily because each of our previous interactions have been under...somewhat strained circumstances."

Something moved in his eyes. "You're callin' two men trying to kill you and me killing those men 'strained circumstances'?"

I pursed my lips. "I am. Do you have another description that serves better?" I made sure I had the appropriate bite to my voice as to respond to the slight teasing in his own.

I must've imagined that, of course I made it my business to read people. Small facial tics. Inflections. Stance. All giveaways to a current state of mind and a permanent state of character.

But I was getting *nothing* from him.

And there was somehow everything in that nothing.

He didn't respond to my sharp words, not even a shake of his head. It was meant to unnerve me.

It worked.

I didn't let it show.

"My point was, from this moment on, you are in my employ and the way in which you address me will reflect that." I paused and waited for a response. I got none. I itched to stare him down, not blink first, but I knew he would stand there all day. And as much as I was quite content to stare at him for the remaining nine hours of my workday, I couldn't afford to do that.

My time was precious.

Priceless.

Therefore it was accounted for every moment of the day, down to the minute.

"Are we clear?" I asked, for the first time in my life, proverbially blinking first.

His expression didn't move. "Crystal clear, Boots."

And before I could say anything else, primarily reprimand him, he turned on his heel and walked out.

HIM

Fuck, she was beautiful.

Hard, but beautiful.

He didn't find women beautiful until her. They were all too soft, too weak, to unbroken for him to notice. If he noticed them, then he'd have to come to terms with how absolutely broken he was. How beyond redemption. He didn't invite introspection, for survival purposes. Therefore he didn't invite women into his life.

She wasn't beyond redemption. But she was broken. And beautiful.

A fucking enigma.

Her skin was ivory, everything that had happened to her in the past two weeks should've shredded it, but instead it bounced right off that façade that she'd almost perfected.

Almost.

He saw through it.

Only because he saw through everyone. He was trained to do it. He was trained to figure out a human being's exact weakness and use it to tear them apart.

He'd relished that. Figuring out how people ticked so he could destroy them. At first, it was okay because those people were the enemy. Those people were monsters creating pain and havoc and threatening his country. He was doing his job tearing them apart.

But then he liked it too much. Then he began to look just like the monsters he was so sure he was protecting his country from.

Then shit got bad.

Bad enough that when he came back here, to the place he'd given his soul to protect, he didn't fit. Anywhere. Certainly not back into his old life.

No way was he whole enough to create an entire new one.

He couldn't do the only thing he was good at—killing. The only thing left inside his hollowed-out shell so he had no purpose, apart from prowling around the city, if only to quiet the monsters rattling against the bars of his mind, desperate to get out.

It led him to her.

And he let the monsters out before he knew what he was doing.

Twice.

He had promised himself that he wouldn't follow her.

That he would forget her.

If only to protect her from destruction.

But he had broken every single promise he made himself so what was another one?

So he followed her.

Every single day.

She fascinated him. She was unlike anything he'd ever witnessed, and he'd witnessed a lot—most of it horrible. She wasn't horrible, she was fucking magnificent. He did his research, because that was what he did, he collected information just like he collected black marks against his soul.

She had created a billion-dollar empire from nothing in just shy of a decade.

He couldn't find shit on her life before, most likely it was the reason for that hardness behind her eyes. The reason why she'd survived in a world that ate up people and spat them out, and then they were trodden on by stronger, more ruthless and soulless people on the way to the top.

The top.

Exactly where she was positioned.

About to merge with one shady motherfucker. He knew about this man because in his previous life, this man was fucking notorious. But he helped Uncle Sam with the things that they couldn't officially sign their name to, so he was on their side.

It was war, after all, they were fighting monsters. And they needed monsters of their own. Of course they never told the general public that. No. Publicity needed loyal and moral soldiers.

Morals didn't win wars.

Monsters did.

He knew what kind of fucker this guy was.

It made his skin crawl thinking of her getting wrapped up in that. She could handle it, no doubt. Because she'd handled everything up to this point, but he didn't *want* her to.

And he was sure that this was the reason for two separate skilled assassins trying to take her out.

They would've succeeded, had he not been there, stalking her because his fucked-up brain couldn't let her go.

That haunted him. The vision of her empty eyes staring up at him the first night in the alley. So that's what had him doing the stupidest fucking thing in the world and going up to her ivory towers and taking the fucking job that would have her close to him every fucking day.

Closer to destruction.

He was playing with fire.

But everything about him had been ice cold for as long as he could remember, so he was relishing the heat.

"Jacob?" the voice on the other end of the phone uttered in disbelief. "Bro, we thought you fuckin' *died*. You dropped off the face of the fucking earth."

His hands tightened around the phone with the familiarity of the voice. The concern. He hadn't talked to someone who knew him in what felt like a lifetime.

"Need some info," he bit out, not responding to the greeting. Technically he was alive, his organs were all working. But your heart could beat and you could still be dead inside.

Luckily, he'd called the right person, Nate was not one to ask for details when no one offered them. He was a cold mother fucker and he only let a certain amount of people in. And once you'd committed sins with someone, you were connected for life.

Nate had committed almost as many as he had.

"Tell me what you need."

Jacob told him.

He might've told Charlotte he wasn't going to investigate shit, but he lied.

Because he didn't have a conscience to ail him.

Plus the sooner he eradicated the threat from her life, the sooner he could leave it.

5

CHARLOTTE

I hadn't expected him to come back, despite the fact he'd given his word and he seemed like a man of his word.

After yesterday; his exit seemed so cold, so final, I thought maybe he saw the world that I was asking him to be in—the cage I was asking him to be in—and he ran.

I should've known better.

He was not one to run.

So he was at the curb outside my building at six sharp. I stopped full on as Ralph opened the door to my car, and the man whose eyes watched my nightmares appeared in front of us.

Instantly, Ralph was on alert, his hand going inside his suit, and eyes to the man who had melted out of the early morning shadows.

"It's okay, Ralph," I said, recovering quicker than I expected, holding my hand up but my eyes staying on icy eyes. "Um, this is my new employee..." I trailed off.

I realized I hadn't gotten his name.

How in the hell had I gotten this far, gotten in this deep with a man and not even *knowing his name?* I'd employed him yesterday. I knew everything about a person before I employed them, including the person they lost their virginity to and the teacher in college they'd bribed into giving them an A.

But I knew nothing.

Not where he lived.

Not where he was from.

How old he was.

If he even had a college degree.

Not his fucking *name.*

"Jacob," he said, the voice smooth over the rough morning air.

His eyes flickered to Ralph, who was eyeing him with a wariness that told me he knew what this man was.

A threat.

The man himself was a threat.

Jacob.

That was his name.

It didn't suit the man in front of me.

It was too bland. Too *normal.*

There was nothing bland, nothing normal about him.

Jacob was who he used to be, I suddenly thought. Just like Lottie was who I used to be. We're given one name to carry us through our lives, as if we were only going to be one person. As if life didn't kill the person we were before with every new tragedy. Every new sunrise. A name could only survive so much. But we were stuck with it, no matter the fact that sometimes the world turned us into something that could never resemble the person we had been before.

So we were stuck with the name of the dead. The ghost.

But he wasn't a ghost.

He was corporeal. His scent imprinted to my very bones as he strode forward, moving slightly in front of me, his eyes on Ralph's hand, which is still inside his jacket—most likely clutching the

Glock that he always wore in a shoulder holster—not extending his hand or softening his features.

"You hired more security, Ms. Crofton?" Ralph asked, not taking his eyes from Jacob.

There was something behind his words. Perhaps hurt. Because me hiring someone else to do the job he'd done for years was an insult to this loyal and fiercely protective man. It was telling him I didn't trust him to do his job.

Which wasn't true. I trusted him as much as I could any person. He was exceptional at his job—he wouldn't have remained in the position if he wasn't. But he was advancing in years, and he was not tasked with providing serious security, nor did I want to subject him to dangers that would take him from his wife or grandchildren.

He'd fought enough in his life

He'd paid his dues.

I would not be the one to try to charge him more.

I wasn't going to say this. Charlotte Crofton didn't think like that. Nor did she hesitate on the feelings of her employees when she was making decisions.

"Yes, with everything going on, I thought it would be somewhat sensible to expand the security you already provide," I said smoothly, as close as I would come to the truth.

Most people wouldn't even get an explanation.

Something flickered in Ralph's eyes as he inspected Jacob. As if he could see what he was.

I suspected he could.

Which was why it took him another three seconds to take his hand from his jacket, the gun inside it and straighten his spine.

"Ah, very well, Ms. Crofton," he said. "I am going to have to agree, anything that will reduce the chance of harm coming to you, I will approve of."

I pursed my lips, the warmth in his tone hit me somewhere that it shouldn't. The true concern like that of a father.

Pain speared the area where my heart used to be.

"I didn't do so for your approval," I said, moving forward toward the car. "I did it because I cannot have any more attempts made on my life when I've got a business to run." My voice was sharp and the edges of it cut me more than it did anyone else.

I paused halfway inside the door, making a point not to look at Ralph because I couldn't face the disappointment or hurt that might lay on his face.

Instead, I focused on pensive wolf eyes.

Jacob.

"You will sit in the front with Ralph, of course. He can get you up to speed with my schedule. The two of you can coordinate."

I didn't pause for his response, I just slid into the cool leather interior, flinching when the door shut beside me.

I closed the partition between the driver's seat and the back of the town car. I never usually did so. Ralph and I didn't speak in the mornings. He knew my stance on small talk. But we did enjoy companionable silence. I'd catch his twinkling eyes in the mirror whenever I looked up from my phone and it was nice.

But no way could I face those eyes now. Especially since I likely stole the twinkle.

I heard the driver's door slam shut.

I expected the front passenger's to do so too, my eyes glued to my phone.

Instead, city noises rushed in as the door across from me opened and shut and the air turned from air-conditioned and leathery to stifling and full of him.

My gaze hit him as the car took off from the curb.

"I told you to sit in the front," I bit out.

"And my job is to protect you," he replied, looking forward. "Not to sit in the front seat."

"Your job is to do as I say," I said, voice ice.

"You're used to that. I'd hazard a guess you could get most people to bend to your will." His eyes cut to mine. "I don't bend, 'cause I'm already broken. And I ain't here to submit to your will, Boots."

I gritted my teeth. "We talked about that name."

He didn't reply. He just stared forward.

He was ignoring me. No one ignored me. Ever. And if they did, they'd be fired before they could blink.

I blinked rapidly three times, staring at his profile, his powerful body sitting across from mine. Jeans worn, boots worn, soul worn. Heat erupted in my body and I had an almost uncontrollable urge to jump across the distance between us.

I was unfamiliar with the feeling. With passion. I was passionate about my job, of course. But with a cold sort of determination. Not with this fire. I didn't know what to do with it.

Him.

I should fire him.

There were plenty of deadly men around the world who I could pay for protection from the people trying to kill me. Men that didn't serve as a danger to my previously stable mind while they protected me.

Instead, I looked back down at my phone, focusing on the emails I was responding to with a fierce concentration I didn't need.

I ignored him.

Or tried to.

I had thrown myself into work as soon as I'd arrived at the office. Which wasn't unusual. What was unusual was the man who accompanied me into the elevator.

"You don't need to come inside the building," I said as the floor numbers went up. "I'm assuming my workplace is safe and not containing people who want to kill me." I paused, thinking of my employees. "Or at least it's not full of people with enough gumption to actually try."

Something in his jaw ticked. "Did you just say gumption?"

Heat flamed in my cheeks, the closest thing to a blush I had ever had. My Midwestern roots had been drummed out of me with sheer will and hours of practice to get rid of my accent. I'd been so sure I'd buried all parts of myself that was connected to that past.

A decade and I hadn't so much as let my accent peek out. Minutes with this man and he'd yanked out a piece of me that I was sure was decayed and rotting.

I gritted my teeth, straightened my back.

"You're not needed in the offices," I said curtly by way of response. I looked straight forward, at the numbers, not moving fast enough. I'd always loved being on the top floor, a literal symbol of where I was sitting.

I hadn't wished to be a little lower. Ever.

Until now.

Just so I could escape this elevator.

Him.

"You assumed."

I blinked. I wasn't going to question him. He needed to elaborate, I wasn't going to tolerate the clipped grunts that served as his version of conversation.

The numbers climbed.

The air thickened.

"You assumed that your workplace was safe," he continued. "And when it comes to your safety, I'm not assuming shit. So I'll be up there. I'll assess. And then *I'll* decide where I'm needed."

I sucked in a breath. "That's not how it works. You don't decide. I sign your checks."

"You want to keep signing my checks, you accept the fact when it comes to me, you don't decide shit."

The doors opened.

He strode out.

I was left staring at his back.

And it was a good back. Wide. Strong.

With a backbone to rival my own.

No one spoke to me like that.

Walked away from me.

Another firing offense.

"Are you gonna stand in the elevator all day?"

Vaughn's manicured hands held the door open. He was regarding me with a raised brow and sparkling eyes.

"What are you doing here?"

"I wanted to get the full effect of the new hottie, our wolf," he said, handing me a coffee as I walked out of the elevator."

"He's not *our* anything," I said sharply as he fell into step with me.

"You're right," he agreed, sipping on his coffee. "He's yours."

The words hit me physically, but I didn't slow my stride. "He's a lot of things, but he's definitely not mine."

I didn't look at Vaughn because I wasn't sure I could keep my expression cold if I did so. Instead, I walked into my office and slammed the door behind me.

I knew it was him the second my door opened and closed. And not just because Vaughn didn't let anyone into my office without an appointment.

And because his energy hit me bodily.

I wasn't a believer in that.

Energies.

A change to the air because of the people entering it.

I was a believer in what made sense.

But sense was the first casualty of his presence.

"You wanted to see me." His voice was whisky. Aged. Dry. Perfect.

I didn't look at him straight away. I took all the effort I could, and I finished the email I was sending to my uncle about calling off merger. It was important, considering I was losing the company billions in what the merger would earn us, and the board would have a lot to say over it. On paper, this deal was everything I'd worked myself toward. But in business, it was more than paper. Especially in my business. Especially when there were bloody fingerprints all over the proverbial paper.

The importance of the email wasn't why I kept typing after he spoke. It was because he'd snatched the power I had in two inter-actions this morning. If I wanted to get honest, it was from the first night in that alley. I couldn't have that. I wouldn't have that. Power was my defining quality. It was what kept me together. I wasn't going to let him tear me apart.

"Yes, I've got something I need you to sign," I said, glancing up with a careful coldness. It was the fact I had to construct that chill was what concerned me. With everyone else apart from Molly and sometimes Vaughn, it was my default. Even to my reflection.

But with him, I had to force it. Pretend.

His eyes were intent on me, as I knew they had been since the second he entered the room. He held his body tight, coiled, ready to spring as if we were in the middle of a battlefield instead of my corner office in the most coveted building in Manhattan.

I pushed the paper across the desk. "I'm going to need you to sign this."

He didn't look at the paper, didn't snatch it from the table. His eyes stayed on mine, as if he knew what his stare did to me. How it unraveled me, tugging on loose threads I'd been so sure I'd snipped off over the years.

"What is it?" he asked after the silence had yanked at those threads violently enough for me to dig my nails into my palms to keep my composure.

I should've told him to read it himself to find out. It's what I would've done with anyone else. No, I wouldn't have even had anyone else sitting here, handing them their contract myself. I never did that.

That's what HR was for.

Though I approved every single contract for my employees.

They were much the same, stricter as the title got more important. As they were given more power and more responsibility.

But this was nothing like any of the others.

Because this man wasn't like any of the others.

He wasn't even a man.

Hence why I spoke. Because I was also terrified of what would happen when he read the contract. I couldn't remember the last time I felt fear. Apart from that night in the alley.

Before then, I couldn't call it up.

No, that was wrong. I could. The day after my sixteenth birthday was the last time I'd been really afraid. Since then, nothing.

You couldn't be scared when your worst fear had already been realized before you had even graduated high school.

But I was scared now.

Of what would happen if he actually did read the contract I'd altered myself.

I'd taken a risk thinking he wouldn't read it. I was so sure I'd collected enough information about him to conclude he wouldn't read it. But there were no certainties with this man. I couldn't figure him out like I did everyone else. So there was a chance he could read what I'd put in.

One of the biggest risks I'd ever taken since I invested everything I had in the company that put me in this office. If he read it, the fall would be so much more brutal than the forty-eight story drop.

"It's a standard employment agreement," I lied, my voice terse, even, professional.

His stare was not.

I dug my fingers in deeper.

"I think you'll find the salary more than agreeable," I continued. "Full insurance, benefits, of course. We offer an accommodation supplement, in addition to an option to live in one of the apartments in the building one of my companies owns."

That last part was also a lie. We were generous, but I didn't give anyone an apartment. Not even Vaughn, though he was paid enough to own his Pre-War on the Upper East side.

No one got a free apartment.

But *he* did.

I'd seen to it myself. High ceilings, converted loft, because I sensed he needed the space.

I sensed he needed somewhere to live.

Normally my employees didn't matter to me as long as they did their jobs. New York was a tough city. It chewed you up and spit you out. That was the way of life. I wasn't here to protect anyone. I didn't want people who needed protecting working for me. That meant they were weak.

"There is also a confidentiality clause that prevents you from sharing anything that you experience during your employment here or once the contract is terminated," I continued. "And I can do so within thirty day's notice, as you will be able to do as well. Depending on the length of time, you'll get paid out. It's standard practice with everyone in the company, though slightly altered due to the...nature of our relationship."

Something flickered in his eyes. "The nature of our relationship," he repeated.

I nodded, sure I must've been breaking the skin of my palms at this point, though I felt no pain. In my palms at least. "Our working relationship, of course. As my protection detail, you'll be working closely with me, hearing and seeing more than anyone else."

His gaze darkened and the air thickened with an energy that

spread warmth into my core. I struggled not to pant at the darkly erotic glint to his gaze. "Oh, I'll be seeing more than anyone else," he repeated, the words soaking my panties. "And you'll be sure I won't be uttering a word."

He reached forward for the pen I'd set beside the contract.

"What are you doing?" I demanded, my voice breaking out of its usual shackles. My soul breaking out of its usual shackles.

He paused the pen, glancing up at me. "I'm signing the contract."

"Don't you want to read it? Get a lawyer to look it over? It's standard practice."

Though it was, any lawyer with a community college degree would see that this was as far from a standard employment contract as one could get.

Jacob would see that in an instant.

He saw everything.

"What's goin' on here isn't standard practice," he all but growled. "And I don't need a piece of paper to tell me that." He scribbled on it, the pen moving violently across the page.

He straightened, gave me one more look and walked out the door.

My hand was shaking when I pulled the paper toward me.

6

"I don't know why I let you make me come here to this hideous place," Molly whined, glaring at her plate.

"This has two Michelin Stars," I chided, sounding far too much how I imagined a chastising mother would sound. Not that I had experience. Our mother never chastised us. No, she would either pamper us when her world was soft and fluffy and devoid of responsibility. Or she'd completely ignore us as that world solidified, became too heavy for her to stand up with it on her shoulders. So she'd stay in bed. We'd tiptoe around her until she got out and made us chocolate cake for breakfast.

My father had been the disciplinarian, though he rarely did that since he doted on us and we didn't break the rules.

Molly rolled her eyes, stabbing at a piece of tofu that was wrapped in seaweed. "A *Michelin Star*," she mimicked. "Wow. Cool. Amazing. That makes it all okay to charge hundreds of dollars for four bites of food when I could have literally bought one hundred pizzas from my favorite joint in Brooklyn for this much."

I sipped my wine. Then glared. Not just because the full-bodied red that cost enough to feed a family of four for a month wasn't the sickly-sweet blend I was used to.

But because Molly was almost yelling she was drawing stares at the most intimate, impossible to get into and hideously expensive restaurant in New York. It was known that the more expensive the food, the softer one should speak while eating it.

Of course, Molly didn't adhere to this.

I loved her for it.

Hence her seeing through the glare that I'd structured out of habit more than anything else.

She grinned at me. "You know you want cheese and carbs instead of this fancy shit. Admit it."

I pursed my lips. "I will not."

Her grin widened. "Come on. Admit it."

I folded my arms. "You don't even *eat* cheese," I countered.

She lost her grin. "I do."

"A mixture of chemicals designed to be disguised as cheese doesn't count."

She scowled down at her food and then back up at me. "It does when no animals were harmed in the making of it."

I rolled my eyes. "Yeah, no animals, just the entire environment that suffers from the fumes coming from whatever factories they were produced in. That's *so* much better."

She continued to grin, her smile lighting up her entire face. Lighting up this entire dark and trendily lit room. It was something very simple, that smile. I envied it. That simple happiness that my sister had that made her so much more beautiful. That made me so much harsher because it was absent from my own, not so identical face. She had seen enough sorrow to turn her into...well, me. Yet she could smile a simple smile and feel that simple happiness from fresh paint or from a nice glass of wine. A stupid TV show or a good book.

People try and tie up the key to happiness in some complicated formula of mindfulness, or religion, or love, or any number of concepts. Yet what most people missed, that gave them a sentence of unhappiness until they figured it out, was how simple it was.

It was the mastery over simplicity that was the trick.

Then the smile left. "You gonna tell me yet?"

The abrupt change in her face and tone had me pausing my beef tartare halfway to my mouth. I made myself slowly chew and swallow before attempting to mask myself in front of the one person who saw through everything.

"Tell you what? That it was not appropriate to wear a 'Meat is Murder' crop top to an establishment that has a dress code?"

Thankfully, the waiters here knew exactly who I was, and barely fluttered an eyelash at my sister's ensemble. Well, it only had to do with me in part. Mostly it was the fact my sister radiated a light that made even the snobbiest of waiters grin at her. She could get anyone eating out of the palm of her hand with her simple happiness.

"Ah, but I'm with you, oh great and powerful one. Codes and rules do not apply to the elite. Or, as it happens, the deplete, which I am." She winked. "And no, you brought me here because you knew I'd be distracted by the snobby waiters, the stupid décor, the irritating food, and the entire *principle* of a place like this." She waved her fork around. "You were hoping that the stupid lighting in here would mask what you are trying to hide from me." She leaned forward on her elbows, despite the fact that elbows on a table were the height of bad manners. "When will you learn, Char Bear, that you can *never* hide from me? I'm the other half of you, remember?"

Her voice was soft, landing in that spot that I reserved for my sister. That tiny little area I hadn't hardened completely.

"I'm not hiding anything," I lied.

She raised her brow.

I feared she might push it.

I feared what would come of it if she did. Because I would never blink in front of some of the most powerful men in the world. Not when they tried to bring me down, not when they threatened my company, my reputation, and more recently, my life. But in front of my erratic, flaky and free-spirited sister's kind gaze, I would crumble. I'd let out the events of the past two weeks and that would be it.

My weakness would be inescapable and all-consuming.

I'd be painting the air with the truth of it all. That fear that had burrowed into me since that night. Those eyes that haunted my dreams, my uninterrupted longing for that strange, violent and wild man.

Molly leaned back, picking up her utensils and shoving a bite of food into her mouth. "Fine," she said, swallowing. "Tell me now, tell me later. It'll come out. You can't hide from me forever."

I exhaled in relief.

But the truth of her words haunted me.

The man with the wolf eyes haunted me.

Until he was more than a ghost.

Until he came back.

Because wolves never left their prey.

"Where are you going?"

The voice was relatively flat and calm, considering it belonged to the man who had just ripped an earbud out of my ear, snatched my wrist and all but yanked me around to face him.

His grip wasn't violent, exactly.

Well, it *was*.

But it wasn't purposeful violence.

It was just...him.

My wrist protested at the firmness of his grip, but my soul cried out for more. Who was I kidding? The throbbing area between my legs cried out for more.

To lose control.

Or more accurately, let him hold onto it with the same ferocity as he was gripping my wrist.

My small pause at feasting on him in the dawn light was as close as I would come to ever relinquishing control. That sliver of a moment in the murky morning air.

I yanked my wrist back, he let it go without a struggle, folding his arms across his chest, the veins of his arms pulsating and defining his muscles as he did so.

"Isn't it obvious?" I said, gesturing down to my body with a slightly shaking hand. "I'm going for a run." Muted sounds from my headphones floated into the air. I pressed pause on my phone more for something to do than anything else. "What are you doing outside my building at dawn?"

He didn't speak for a beat, as if he knew that it would torture me. His eyes went slowly up and down my body, taking in my tight black leggings and long-sleeved compression top. His expression didn't change as he did so, it stayed granite. But somehow my body responded to that cold gaze with an inferno. Like it would if he was devouring my naked body with his eyes.

"You got a gym inside that building, I assume?" he jerked his head to where I'd just come out of.

I folded my arms. "Yes, you assume right. But I prefer to run outside."

"You're not running outside today."

I quirked my brow. "Excuse me?"

"Did I stutter?"

I narrowed my eyes. Could someone really be this broody before the sun had even come up? Then again, I was as sharp as I'd ever be, and I hadn't even had coffee yet. It was for survival purposes more than anything. "We still haven't addressed what you're doing lurking outside my building over an hour before you need to be here," I said, voice sharp.

"My job," he said by answer.

I waited for more. No way was I breaking first. Not this time.

The silence lasted until the birds that could only be heard in a small sliver of time between five a. m. and sunrise started chirping. A truck rattled past on the street and New York replaced nature. The city was a living, breathing thing, highest up on the food chain, swallowing anything and everything beneath it.

Including human beings.

"Know that you're already up and ready at six in the morning," he continued, voice tight. "And know that you didn't work out last night since you went to that dinner." The dinner he accompanied me to, sitting at the bar to avoid questions from business associates. Obviously he didn't come to the one I had with Molly. She didn't need to know about him. Nor did anyone else. It wouldn't do well for it to get out that I was needing to employ security. I was the face of my companies. If I was in trouble, if I couldn't keep myself safe, people would think I was weak. That my companies were.

And in the current situation I was in, that wouldn't do.

"So you came here to lurk outside my building? To try to tell me what to do?" I asked sharply. "That's not in your job description. But it will be in the letter I write as a reason for the termination of your employment."

He didn't even blanch and I used my most scathing tone. "Not dressed for running."

My eyes flickered down to his jeans and boots.

He still hadn't gotten new ones. Hadn't gotten new anything. I'd given him an advance on his first paycheck, considering he had technically started protecting my safety two weeks' prior.

It was generous.

My realtor had told me that no one had taken possession of the apartment I'd reserved for him. He hadn't spent a dime on new clothing, nor had he moved into the five-million-dollar apartment that was now his for the duration of his employment.

I ached to ask him why this was. But I didn't ask personal questions. It sent the wrong message. It also wasted my time. My time was little more than priceless. But he owned that. Something that money couldn't buy and countless people had tried to purchase, steal and ruin, he owned without trying. With just his empty stare.

"I'm not dressed for running, therefore, I can't come with you and I can't do my job, which is to keep you safe, as outlined in the contract I signed," he said, voice harsh.

My stomach fluttered at the mention of the contract, at the slight inflection in his voice as he mentioned it. Something in it betrayed knowledge of exactly what was in the contract. Which was impossible. I'd been there when he signed it, barely glancing at the page long enough to read the first two paragraphs, let alone something that was hidden on the second page.

He hadn't taken it with him, either. It was in the safe in my office.

Therefore he *couldn't* know the exact details of it.

"You're runnin' inside for today only. Tomorrow I'll have the right shit. I'll go with you."

I inwardly flinched at the thought of doing the one thing in my day that didn't require my mask of indifference and consisted only of the simple task of putting one foot in front of the other, doing that with Jacob beside me.

"I assure you that you are not needed on my runs," I said, my voice not betraying an ounce of unease.

His eyes probed past the flat tone, dissecting everything I was trying to hide. "Don't give a shit what you assure or not. Get inside the building."

I narrowed my eyes. "You don't have the right to tell me what to do."

He stepped forward and every part of me froze. His weathered boots almost touched my black, top of the line running shoes. His scent curled around me like an embrace and like an assault at the same time.

"I have every right," he said, voice a whip. "Now get inside."

Any other person on this planet who ordered me to do such a thing would get a glare, some of my choice verbal barbs, a dressing down which would ensure they would finish the exchange in a puddle at my feet.

Metaphorically, of course.

Any other person on the planet but Jacob.

I held his stare for a long time. Long enough for my inner thighs to shake, for my heart to splinter my ribcage and my breathing to become shallow.

His face didn't change.

His hands were fisted at his sides. The knuckles were turning white. His chest moved up and down evenly.

I swallowed.

Took an inhale, held onto his scent inside me, let it imprint onto my lungs and then I stepped back.

I didn't say a word as I shoved my headphones back into my ears and walked into my building.

He watched me the whole way.

As promised, Jacob was outside my building at five the next morning. I didn't speak to him. He didn't greet me. Our eyes met for exactly five seconds—I counted—before I turned the volume of my music all the way up and began running.

He fell into step with me.

He didn't have headphones.

I was a fast runner. I was also fit, I had to be the best at everything and being at peak physical performance was compulsory. Even though I could likely keep pace with seasoned marathon runners, I didn't think that I was any match for Jacob's long stride and powerful thighs. He didn't let on if he was slowing down for me, nor did I take pains to even glance in his direction, to try and gauge whether he was or not.

We entered Central Park, mist still lingering in this strange moment between night and morning.

The park was as empty as it could get, but there were many like me who woke before the rest of the city. Powerful people who started their days like this. Who ran through the stretch of green embedded into a concrete city, competing with themselves before they spent the day competing with the rest of the world.

I had been worried yesterday that Jacob would consume me in the one part of the day that belonged to me—as much as anything could. I knew that despite my bank balance, I could never really own the things that mattered. The mornings were as close as I could get, and they were priceless. Jacob might have limited means, but I had a visceral kind of knowing that he'd be able to buy the thing that billions of dollars couldn't purchase.

Control over my thoughts.

With him keeping pace beside me, I realized the mornings prior, without him, after that night in the alley, those mornings had belonged to him. Strangely, with him beside me, I was able to purge him as much as I could from my thoughts even though he was in the immediate vicinity. I wasn't annoyed with his presence, as I would've been by anyone else. That shouldn't have surprised me, since Jacob wasn't anyone else, and he didn't evoke things in me like others did.

It was dangerous. Because I could easily fall into the routine of having him beside me. When his presence, physically at least, was always going to be temporary.

"Hot Rambo is on his way in," Vaughn's voice filtered through the intercom.

Every cell in my body froze. "Stop referring to him like that," I demanded into the intercom.

All I got was dead air.

Vaughn seemed to think he could push the boundaries now that Jacob had all but destroyed them.

My finger hovered over the phone to snap something at him, chastise him, bark in my cold tone, if only to remind myself I was capable of it.

Then the door opened.

I pointedly powered the intercom down as I did every time Jacob was in my office. Which wasn't often. I wasn't sure where he went when I was inside the building—he'd determined it safe from threats after the first morning—all I knew was whenever I exited it, he was there. He had a copy of my schedule, but even as I left for last-minute meetings, he was there.

I didn't ask him where he was because it was a show of weakness. All questions were, I shouldn't have to ask such things, I had the means to find out, and knowledge was power. Without it, I was nothing. So I didn't ask. But I wondered. A lot more than I should.

He closed the door behind him, yanking all the oxygen from the room. I steeled myself for the interaction. Any interaction with Jacob was a battle. It was a war.

I was never one to back down from a fight.

In the past at least.

My whole existence, my position in this world was a war, so fighting was as easy as breathing for me. *Winning* was as easy as breathing.

But with Jacob, I could barely inhale and exhale easily.

I wasn't too proud to admit I knew I was losing with him.

What exactly I didn't know.

No, I did know what I was losing.

Everything.

But I wasn't giving up. Surrendering.

The smart move was to fire him.

"My sister is coming tonight," I said, trying to drown out those thoughts with an icy tone.

Tonight's event was in my schedule so he knew about it. He had also been to a handful of events with me, staying close to my side, acting invisible. But of course, someone like Jacob was never invisible. There were whispers, as I knew there would be. I told all my business associates that he was a security expert I'd employed as a consultant. This explained away his brooding demeanor and attire as being ex-military. It worked. Mainly because it was a mix between lie and truth. Life always required lies, mine much more than most. The key was to make sure no lie wasn't accompanied without a truth.

But tonight I couldn't explain him away. Primarily because of the fact Molly was going to be there. My sister knew when I was lying and she would've seen through the lie about Jacob in an instant. The alternative I'd decided on wasn't much better but had a higher chance of being successful.

Jacob nodded once.

He didn't ask anything about her, follow up questions, social niceties. Jacob didn't do social niceties. Nor did he do questions.

"She's my twin sister and she is nothing like me," I continued, answering something he'd never asked. Giving information as well as asking for it was a sign of weakness. But I couldn't stop myself.

"And that's a good thing," I continued, glancing down at my phone, if only for a distraction. "That's the reason I protect her from as much of this world as I can. She knows nothing about the attempts made on my life. And for as long as the press doesn't know, neither will she." I glanced up at Jacob's iron jaw and intense expression. "Which is why introducing you as my security will serve as problematic. My sister is smart enough to know me employing extra security means something's happened. And she will not rest until she gets the truth. I'll give her no reason to go looking for it." I put my phone down. "I'm assuming there's no way to assure you I don't need your services tonight?"

He gritted his teeth in response.

One came to learn Jacob didn't speak if a brooding silence or steely glare would suffice.

I nodded. "I thought as much. So you'll be acting as my date. To my sister's eyes, at least."

He didn't respond.

"Molly, she's..." I trailed off. How did I explain Molly to anyone? Why did I want to explain Molly to Jacob, of all people? I didn't share my personal life with any of my employees, except Vaughn. I doubted any of my staff even knew I had a twin sister or a family at all. They most likely thought I emerged from the bowels of hell, to do Satan's bidding. I wasn't being creative, it was something I'd heard in the office when they didn't know I was listening.

I guessed if you asked my mother, I might've been the product of some kind of demon since she murdered my father convinced he was possessed by one.

I never shared personal details willingly. Jacob didn't need to know anything more than what I'd already said. But with him, it wasn't about need. Or maybe that was all it was about, which was why I kept speaking, kept offering more of myself that he didn't ask for.

"She's my twin. Biologically at least," I said. "We look alike. We're meant to be identical. But even with biology telling Molly she has to be the same as one other human being on the earth, she doesn't listen." I wanted to smile at the thought of it. My lips might've even turned up. "She's everything that I'm not, in all the best ways. But she's...soft. She believes in the goodness of the world. Though I know better, I take it upon myself to protect her from that, best I can. She's the best person I know. She's the other half of me. The better half. " I stopped speaking abruptly. I realized what I'd done. What I'd shown with those words.

Weakness.

Jacob's eyes bore into me, prodding painfully at all the nerves I'd exposed.

I sucked in a breath and jutted my chin up, glancing to my computer if only for a respite from his gaze. What a coward I was.

"Anyway," I said after a handful of seconds spent composing myself. "I just need you to understand she's not like any of the other people I associate with. She's...a person. I expect you to treat her with respect."

He nodded once, something moved in his eyes, or most likely, I imagined it.

"I'll arrange for Vaughn to set you up for a suit fitting," I said after a long moment. A moment in which I waited for him to surrender even a hint of something beyond his mask, to offer something more than a cold silence.

There was nothing.

"The event is black tie. You can't wear that." I nodded to his jeans. "I understand your reservations about suits, so if you don't want to attend, I'm sure I can arrange other—"

"I'll wear the suit," he cut in, voice brutal.

I nodded, the movement jerky, shocked by the violence that had seeped into the sentence. I recovered quickly. "Then you should be going to the tailor, it's short notice, but no one says no to me. Vaughn will tell you where to go." My dismissal was clear. It bordered on desperate. I needed to breathe. To regroup. It wouldn't do for me to continue to volunteer information like it was free. Like he was entitled to it.

Nothing in life was free and no one was entitled to anything.

Jacob didn't move. He merely continued to stare.

I struggled not to squirm in my seat.

"Is there something else?" I asked, my voice colder than usual, as if to make up for the warmth in my tone before. "I'm busy."

His fists clenched and unclenched at his sides.

"You're not half of anything," he said, voice a blade searing through all the walls I was scrambling to replace.

And then he turned and walked out.

7

I took care in my appearance tonight.

Granted, I always made sure I looked flawless. I was the face of a cosmetics company, for starters. And no matter what was politically correct, women and men would not buy Charlotte Crofton products if Charlotte Crofton herself didn't look flawless.

With the help of Botox, one of the best facialists in the world, and an extensive beauty routine, I was always flawless.

At the start, even then, being in the business of making women beautiful, being in the business of beauty, it wasn't my goal to be in *Vogue*, though my products and face are regularly featured. No. I didn't want that. I wanted to be in *Forbes*. Not because I wanted to be rich—that was a favorable side effect of success—but because I wanted *power*. Not to wield over others, but over myself. When all my childhood was controlled by the whim of an uncontrollable disease, when it was ultimately ruined by that same disease—power was what I wanted. No, craved. Something to control.

Everything to control.

If I created a life in which I enjoyed control and power over everything on the outside, maybe a favorable side effect might be that I controlled that disease that destroyed my mother. Killed my father. Massacred my family and childhood.

Maybe that was just wishful thinking.

Maybe it lurked, like a silent assassin, waiting to pounce and tear at my psyche and laugh in the face of the work, the blood, sweat and no tears I'd shed to create this life.

But that was not something to dwell on.

Dwelling was a practice of the pathetic and lazy. Doing was an instrument of the successful and powerful.

So I did.

And doing was making sure I was put together at every event I went to. Granted, it was all a lie, what I was selling to people, that my flawless exterior was one maintained by the products that I represented, when it was more thanks to injectables and thousands of dollars, but everyone was selling a lie.

This one was the most important events of the year. Not for business. But for Molly and I. It was a charity I founded, anonymously, of course. For mental health research and support for those suffering from conditions that the government didn't pay enough attention to.

It wasn't about what dress I wore, how my hair was styled or what my makeup looked like, in the end. But I needed my mask. I needed to be the Charlotte Crofton of the present so I didn't resurrect the Charlotte of the past.

That was every *other* year.

This year was different.

I told myself I wasn't dressing up for him.

But I was a liar.

My dress was couture, obviously. Designers scrambled to dress me, every time I wore something off the rack and was photographed in it, it sold out instantly. I wasn't a fashion icon, by any means. But career women in New York knew me, they wanted to emulate me. And clothes maketh the woman, apparently.

I'd gone with a lesser-known designer, as I always did to this event. One struggling and just starting out. I'd had research done on the young man. He happened to be from the Midwest. Living on the fourth floor of a studio walkup with three other people.

But he made art. True art.

And he'd outdone himself for me. The dress was blood red. It was long sleeved, high necked, tailored beyond perfection. I'd had many clothes made for me—in fact, almost all of my clothes were —but not once had something glided over me like this did. It covered me neck to ankle, with a small but striking train in the back. There were tiny embellished studs around my sleeves, sharp but almost invisible.

I was covered, but somehow, I felt sexier than ever.

My hair was yanked back into a low and severe pony, Long diamond strand earrings almost touched my shoulders. I'd had a lipstick made to match the shade of the dress perfectly.

It would go on sale tonight. I predicted it would sell out in less than an hour.

The elevator door opened, and Molly was all but shouting at Jacob, who was stony-faced and looking straight ahead. This might've deterred anyone else—especially since Jacob's entire energy was pure danger—but not Molly, she had a grin on her face and didn't shut up. Not much scared her, even the man who terrified me more than anything else.

She was chattering until her eyes landed on me.

Then she shut up.

And gaped.

Rendering Molly speechless was a damn near impossible feat.

Her eyes ran over me.

I did the same to her.

She was wearing a white lace and beaded dress, empire waist and flowing down her body. Her hair was a mess of curls. She'd dyed it again. A soft red that suited her.

"Char Bear," she whispered. "You look..." She trailed off. "You look like a superstar."

I smiled. "That's you, sis." I walked over to kiss her cheek, trying my best not to lock eyes with Jacob, who was standing stock still, arms clasped in front of him.

"Your date is smokin' hot and a total fucking badass," she whispered in my ear loud enough for him to hear.

I smiled tightly and straightened. "I see you met Jacob in the elevator."

"Met him, bowed down to his badassery so he didn't shoot laser beams at me and incinerate me on the spot." She shrugged. "Whichever you prefer."

I shook my head, closing my purse. "You don't have a date? Color me surprised."

She grinned. "Good thing I didn't, whoever I brought would've likely had their manhood shrink up right in front of this one." She jerked her head in Jacob's direction, who still hadn't moved or spoken, he was just staring at me in a way that made it hard for me to think straight.

"Plus, I much prefer to third wheel with the two of you." She winked at me. "Never have your dates been so...interesting." She glanced at Jacob pointedly. "Or silent. The last two I had to share an elevator with bored me with stories of their stock portfolios and summer in the Hamptons." She gagged. "Seriously. Silence is absolutely *refreshing.*"

I shook my head. "What's refreshing is that you're actually on time and we won't be running late, for once. We've got to go now."

Jacob held the elevator door open.

We all got in.

He was somehow positioned behind me. And although my sister was chatting animatedly to the both of us, and I was responding, all of my attention was focused on Jacob's heat at my back. My heart in my throat.

I stopped breathing the second I felt fire on the back of my arm. It was searing through the thin fabric of my dress.

His fingers only brushed my arm for a second, at the most, but I felt the touch the entire ride down and for the rest of the night.

The night was a blur, as most events such as these were.

It started with the flashing of cameras, the yells of photographers as soon as we emerged from the car. Molly and I posed for exactly thirty seconds, as was my rule—this was the only event I even acknowledged the paparazzi—and then Jacob led us inside.

And the role of being Charlotte Crofton began. Not that it ever ended.

Molly weathered two conversations with two of our biggest donors, and then ran off to the bar to likely flirt with the bartender and lecture some oil tycoon about what he was doing to the environment.

I didn't begrudge her for leaving me to do all the schmoozing that was required. I was happy that she didn't do it. I didn't want her part of this world more than she needed to be. The fact she had her wild, chaotic and beautifully happy life was all I needed. This world hammered out all of that, with rules, with image, with the social structure.

I only played the game because I was at the top of it, and that was the only way to stay there.

We got a moment of peace, sitting in a corner that Molly yanked us into, shoving a glass of champagne in my hand.

"I've only seen you take one of these all night," she said, sipping from her own. "That simply isn't enough to handle these people." She gazed around the room in distaste.

I grinned, making sure Molly was the only one to see the expression. It wouldn't do well for New York society to see me betray something as weak as happiness. "These people are *my* people, if you don't remember," I commented dryly, but I took a generous gulp anyway. Not because of the number of people in the room demanding something from me. But the one who still hadn't spoken a word to me all night, apart from burn holes into my beautiful dress. I'd already given the designer's name to eight different fashion 'it' girls. I'd made his career in one night.

"You've changed," she observed with a smile, her eyes saucers for all of the light and happiness in them. "Because of him." She nodded behind me and I didn't need to turn to know who she was gesturing to.

Despite my own sense of happiness that bloomed by seeing my sister like this, I frowned. "That's ridiculous," I snapped. "I barely know him. He's been in my life for a handful weeks. *I've* been in my life for three decades."

It was somewhat of a lie. One I was telling more to myself than Molly.

And of course, Molly saw straight through me.

"Time doesn't mean shit in situations like this," Molly replied, sipping her drink and gazing pointedly and the man behind me.

My brows narrowed. "Would you stop being so obvious?" I hissed.

She grinned wider behind her glass. "Why? He's making no secret of the fact you're the only woman in this room. To him, anyway. And he's definitely making no secret of any murderous intentions he holds toward any men that even glances in the vicinity of your ass." She paused, scanning the room. "Or even in *your* general vicinity."

It took every inch of my considerable willpower not to follow her gaze and lock onto two ice blue eyes. I didn't want to lose sensation in my knees right in the middle of one of the most important charitable events of the year. They were already weak at the weight of his glance on my back.

It was preposterous, but I felt it. Against my bare skin like an icy breeze in January in New York.

"You're being dramatic," I said, sipping my own glass, if only for something to do.

"Of course I am, I'm breathing," she replied. "But not about this." Her eyes turned serious. "This is something more than even I could conjure up. It's like he's been waiting for you all his lives."

She didn't misspeak. Molly vehemently believed in reincarnation and past lives. She'd been burned at the stake for witchcraft in one of them, apparently, which was why she didn't like open fireplaces.

"That's just his way," I dismissed. "He's intense."

"Yeah, he is," she said appreciatively. "But this is something more than that. You don't need a lifetime for someone to change you. You only need a moment." She drained her glass. "Time in the most general of terms is a construct made up by the same patriarchal assholes who wrote that women should have no rights other than to serve her husband. But in this specific instance, it means nothing at all. You change when something shakes your life to the core. Something that does that normally doesn't last long. How many seconds did you see Mom hovering over Dad's body?"

I flinched. Visibly. Ice settled over my entire body like I was standing in the middle of Central Park at midnight in January, naked. It was instantaneous and even more brutal than Jacob's gaze.

It took a few seconds for me to compose myself. A few seconds longer than it normally would have. But I did it.

Outwardly, my features were carved into the same icy façade I was infamous for. Inside, I was screaming.

"You know?" my choked rasp all but destroyed my calm exterior.

"Of course I know," Molly said softly, not moving forward to touch me. She didn't need to, I could feel her warmth and support rolling through our invisible connection. She also sensed that touching me would completely crumble whatever decorum I was clutching onto.

"How long?" I whispered.

"When I started painting," she whispered back.

I swallowed. Thirteen years.

"How?"

"You know how," she said. "I could feel something horribly different about you, like something inside you hadn't just broken as it would have losing a parent in a car crash. Something had been burned to embers. Destroyed. Something very integral. It was damaged in me too. I felt only a fraction of your pain and I could barely stand it." Her eyes shimmered with a pain so visceral it speared through every part of me. "For that year, I tried to believe the lie, but I had to know. So I made it my business to find out."

I clutched the stem of my glass so tightly I was surprised it didn't break. "Why didn't you tell me?"

She smiled through her tears the way only Molly could. "Because, my dear Charlotte, my protector, my other half, my better half, you are so hard on yourself. You've achieved extraordinary things in your short life, and yet you hold yourself up to an impossible standard. You blame yourself for failures outside of your control. Surely you'd blame yourself if you thought you hadn't protected me from the ugly reality of our mother. Of her illness. Of the world. You would do *anything* to keep me out of harm's way." She lifted her hand to lightly brush across my jaw. "The same holds true with me. My methods are somewhat different, that's all."

I rapidly blinked away the strange prickle at the backs of my eyes, searching for something to say to my sister. Searching for a way to regain my composure.

"Excuse me," a smooth masculine voice interjected.

Both Molly and I snapped our heads to look at the handsome, groomed and grinning man standing in front of us.

"I was wondering if I could tempt you for a dance?" he asked Molly.

She beamed back at him like she didn't have a care in the world, as if she weren't just discussing our mother murdering our father, as only Molly could. "I'm always tempted to dance," she replied. She turned to me, leaned in and kissed my cheek. "I love you," she murmured. And then she took the man's manicured hand and let him whisk her off onto the dance floor.

Molly never said no to a dance. Never found a reason not to smile. She didn't run from the rain, didn't stray from pain, she turned it into beauty.

I continued to sip at my champagne watching her, if only so I didn't lock eyes with the man I knew was watching me.

He still hadn't spoken all night, despite being at my side for most of it, still playing his part as my date. I introduced him as a business associate when Molly wasn't within earshot. He glared at the New York elite enough for them to almost run from the exchange, but they fought it because they were leeches trying to suck up influence and power from me. It was rather entertaining.

I knew this wasn't a real date. All of this was for Molly's benefit. And hopefully by the next time, she wouldn't remember to ask about him, the threat would be over, and he would be out of my life.

That was the goal of all of this, right?

Having Jacob disappear from my life was good because that meant people weren't trying to kill me anymore.

Why was I more afraid of him leaving than another attempt on my life?

Maybe the fascination with my demise had consumed me more than I thought. And maybe that's why my fascination with Jacob was so intense. Because he *was* my demise. He was death in a human being.

"What do you think you're doing?" an angry voice hissed.

I looked up at my uncle, who I'd been too lost in my own thoughts to see approach. That wouldn't do. I'd never lapsed into a daydream in a public setting. I was always on, always aware.

It was the only way to survive here.

I focused on my uncle's furious face. "I'm drinking some champagne and having a quiet moment to myself," I replied. "Which I see is over now."

"I got the memo you're killing the deal," he clipped. "I know the meeting we had was...emotionally charged, but I didn't think you'd be so stupid as to kill a deal that would've made the company billions."

I raised my brow. "*May* have. But I don't care about the zeroes when the one man who would be responsible for them is Ethan Kershaw. I make clean money, Abe. Not blood money. Now if you'll excuse me, I've got guests."

I started to walk away, but he snatched my arm.

"All money is blood money, Charlotte," he hissed, eyes wild. "When are you going to learn that?"

I kept my composure, despite the fact this was the first time my uncle had ever gotten physical with me. The first time he'd focused such a menacing look in my direction. It didn't upset me. But it did interest me. He had plenty of money, and sure, he was a man, he wanted more, but it wasn't just that. This reaction signified a stake in the deal that was about more than the zeroes.

"You take your hand off her right now if you want to keep it," a low and deadly voice interrupted my moment of reflection.

I didn't look back at the owner of it.

I *knew* the owner of the voice.

He was also the owner of wolf eyes, my attention, something I was so sure wasn't even for sale.

He paid for it with my life.

With those eyes.

And he would never know that he owned it. I'd buy it back if it took everything I had.

Abe's gaze went to Jacob, his hand automatically letting go of my arm. I wasn't even sure if he knew he was doing it. It was instinct to survive, obeying a voice with that much violence in it.

"Who is this?" he demanded, straightening his blazer as if it would gather the face he'd just lost. My uncle was not known for public outbursts.

Which made this all the more interesting.

Abe hadn't known about the attempts on my life, which surprised me, he was a man who made it his business to know everything. He was good at finding things out, but I was better at hiding things. Which was why he hadn't met Jacob yet, he wouldn't buy the story I'd been telling everyone else.

"This is your reminder to keep discussions about business polite and dignified," I said, draining my glass and putting it on a nearby table. "If you have problems with the way I'm running my business, schedule an appointment with Vaughn."

"I'll do better. I'll let the board know what you're doing," he said, voice cold, but his eyes didn't hide his fear at Jacob's presence.

"I welcome it," I replied to his threat, trying to keep my satisfaction at his response to Jacob hidden. "Then I'll be able to inform them the laundry list of crimes we'd become accessories to should we decide to get into bed with Ethan Kershaw." I paused, refusing to break his stare. "My decision is made. And in case you've forgotten, I'm in charge here. Until that changes, my word is law."

I looked to Jacob, who was still glaring at my uncle. "Shall we go? I'm rather ready to leave."

I didn't wait, I walked away.

I knew Jacob followed me.

"Are you sure we can't drop you somewhere?" I asked, concern not showing in my words, despite the fact I was all but consumed with it. We were standing outside on the street, my car ready and waiting, Jacob standing silent beside me.

Molly grinned. "Nah, I've got friends picking me up." She frowned at her phone. "Or I'm meeting them at a party close." She shrugged. "I'll go for a walk. Hang out with New York for a spell."

"You realize it's a city, not a person, right?" I asked, this time hiding the grin in my words.

She quirked her brow. "New York is all the people I know and love and all the people I dislike all rolled into one. It's no one and everyone at the same time."

I rolled my eyes. "Well, be careful."

She blew me a kiss. "Never! Careful is too dull." She gave Jacob a look. "Keep being awesome, dude. I'll let you know if there have been any nuclear codes stolen that you and your biceps need to retrieve." She winked at him.

It happened so quickly I wasn't quite sure whether I imagined it or not, but the corner of Jacob's mouth twitched.

Molly grinned between the two of us, saying everything and nothing in that grin.

And then she turned and lost herself in the crowd. Or tried to. Molly would never meld into a crowd. She was born to stand out.

I watched her for three seconds, it's all I gave myself, I didn't know who was watching, but it wouldn't do well for anyone to see that Molly was someone who mattered to me.

Jacob saw it.

Because Jacob saw everything.

"Thank you, Ralph," I said as I got out of the car.

He gave me a smile. "Always, Ms. Crofton." His eyes moved to Jacob. "I assume he can accompany you up to the apartment?"

It was safe to say that Ralph and Jacob didn't enjoy a warm relationship. Primarily because Jacob had yet to show that he was capable of any kind of relationship with a human being, warm or otherwise. Also because Ralph was a man trained to distinguish threats and Jacob was a threat. It didn't take an expert to assess that. He was on our side for now, but someone with Ralph's training likely saw the cold killer that was barely hidden. He knew that Jacob was not a man you warmed to if you wanted to stay breathing.

I nodded to him. "I've kept you away from your grandchildren long enough."

He smiled warmly. "You've saved me, more like. There are only so many Disney movies I can pretend to watch before I go insane."

I wanted to smile. For the man with the hard life and the demons behind his eyes going home to a wife, to children to a family. To warmth.

I didn't.

I nodded once. "See you Monday."

"Six," he said.

I turned and walked into the building.

I didn't need to glance toward Jacob to know that he followed me.

It was as constant as my shadow, Jacob's presence. But it wasn't natural. It wasn't easy to ignore. It was impossible.

He still hadn't said a word to me all night. The ride back here was full of silence and me pretending to be engrossed in the emails I was sending. I expected him to ask me about the exchange with my uncle, any other person would. But Jacob wasn't any other person. He never did as I expected. The only thing I could expect from Jacob was stony silence and a gaze to flay at my skin.

The elevator was scarcely big enough for the silence between us. My arm burned from where he'd touched it in this very elevator hours ago. We were alone in the enclosed space, without my sister's warmth and constant chatter. I wanted him to touch me again. I ached to cross the distance between us. For my entire body to be branded with that brutal touch.

I sank my nails into my palms and held my breath.

Never had I had to do physical things like this in order to control myself. Compose myself. Self-control and composure were two things that were as easy as breathing with me. But when Jacob was around, mere inhaling and exhaling evenly was an effort.

It wouldn't do.

I had to fire him.

The doors opened, revealing my stark and empty penthouse. It was a human thing, staring at me, taunting me with the solitude it offered.

I was frozen in my spot for two seconds. That's all it was—I counted. But it was two seconds where I literally didn't have control of myself, all of that was yielded to the man beside me, holding me still with nothing but his mere presence.

I regained control after those two seconds that should never have been anyone's but mine.

I needed to fire him. Right now.

"Goodnight, Jacob," I said, my voice almost a sigh.

I walked out of the elevator and prided myself on the fact I didn't look back at him.

"Boots?"

I instantly turned.

Well, there went all my upper hand.

His face had changed since the last time I looked at it. It hit me physically, the hunger in his gaze. Not human hunger. Brutal, animal hunger. "You look fucking magnificent."

I blinked rapidly, digesting the words. And by the time I opened my mouth to respond, the elevator doors were closing.

8

I knew who was knocking at the door the second the pounding started.

I'd been waiting for it.

"Happy birthday!" Molly screamed the second I opened the door. Then she looked me up and down and scowled. "How are you dressed? It's not even six in the morning. I'm only dressed because I haven't been to *sleep* yet. I was planning on this being the *one* birthday *I* wake *you* up."

I smiled, taking in my sister's slightly too bright eyes, her sequined dress with a chunky knit thrown over the top of it and thigh high lace up boots. Only she could pull this off and look amazing. I did worry about that glint in her eye, knowing it didn't come from cocktails since she barely drank. She was more about saying no to vodka and yes to cocaine. Cocaine was more common than coffee the higher you got to the top, so it wasn't like I wasn't jaded to the drug. I didn't believe in drugs because I was terrified of anything that would take control of my thoughts. There was already a disease lurking in my genes which threatened

108

to do that to me. Almost every CEO needed to take something, it wasn't natural to work the amount we did. The amount I did. Though I didn't need a drug since it was a matter of survival in my eyes.

I worried about Molly, but she had been a party girl since forever, and she somehow found excess in everything but drug use.

"Well, you needed to get here at four-thirty. I've had my workout and two conference calls already," I told her.

"*Four-thirty?*" she repeated. "No one gets up that early. Not even the sun."

I smiled again. "The sun's always up somewhere."

She tilted her head to regard me. "Touché, and strangely sweet for you."

I opened the door fully and let her burst in. "It's not sweet, it's science."

She waved her hand, well, the coffee cup that she was holding. Obviously she had decided to switch stimulants, likely in preparation for seeing her slightly older, more judgmental and less fun sister.

I closed the door and followed her into the apartment. My thighs burned slightly underneath my silk slacks. Jacob and I had gone faster and further than our usual. And our usual was already six miles.

I'd needed more today.

People—my sister included—who believed in the supernatural thought the veil between the living and the dead was thinnest at Halloween.

I didn't believe in the supernatural.

But my birthday worked somewhat like that for memories of death. For ghosts and demons that didn't live in some otherworld, but within me. This day made the veil between my memories and the present almost nonexistent. So I ran hard. Fast. As if I could escape them.

If I couldn't escape them, I could distract myself with the burn in my thighs, the tightness in my chest, the constant thump of Jacob's shoes against the ground.

I used to run with music. I had to. Ear-splitting rock, the lower brow, the better. I didn't need to hear the ground crunching beneath my feet, didn't need to hear my only slightly labored inhales and exhales. I just needed noise.

But since Jacob and I had started running, I'd *needed* the crunch of the ground beneath his feet, his steady inhales and exhales.

I needed *him.*

It was bad. Sick. Dangerous. But I didn't stop.

We hadn't spoken about the extra distance today. He didn't ask. He was Jacob. He just did what he always did, he walked me into my building. Usually he'd go to the gym complex—I'd gotten him a locker and access to full facilities, but since I'd informed him I was going into work late today, he didn't need to be immediately ready. I imagined he was going home. Wherever home was. He still hadn't moved into the apartment. I still had enough self-control not to ask him why, though the question was burning at the back of my throat like some kind of emotional acid reflux. I needed relief. I didn't give in.

Yet

Jacob had been with me for a month, he knew my schedule, likely he'd burned it into his brain by his second day. Ditto with my qualities. He almost certainly knew that me going into the office late was highly out of the ordinary.

Yet he didn't ask questions.

I wondered if it was because of the same reason as me. If he wanted to know, but he knew that asking questions would disrupt the power struggle between us. It would be giving in to me somehow.

Or the more likely explanation was that he didn't care.

The pop of a wine bottle jerked me out of that uncomfortable thought.

I walked into the kitchen and took the glass of pink wine that Molly had poured for us.

She grinned, holding up her glass. "To us, being another year older. You being another year wiser and me being..."

"You," I finished for her.

She smiled wider and clinked her glass to mine.

I tasted the sweet liquid, but it turned bitter with the memories. The last day we'd had with our mother being...whatever was left of herself. The last day we had when our father was alive. Where he'd come home from work with a novel about the most successful women in business for me and a record player for Molly. Where he'd smiled with true happiness, kissed our heads, danced with my mother and lit the candles on our cake.

Molly loved tradition, and somehow extracted the sweet from the bitter, the happy from the terrible in order to continue it. That was the way Molly lived her life in general, I lived mine with the truth, always bitter and terrible.

It made Molly happy to do this, which was why I did it. Why I drank the pink wine at six in the morning, gritted my teeth from the sugar and the memories. It's not like it made me more miserable. I'd have the memories whether I started my birthday with the physical reminder of them or not.

She regarded me over her glass, then she glanced around my kitchen, looking for something. "I didn't expect you to be alone," she said, putting her glass down.

"Why? I'm always alone in the mornings."

She raised her brow. "But that was *before* Jacob. He is not a man that leaves you alone in the mornings."

I knew she saw too much, despite the fact she'd been silent on the topic of Jacob since the charity event.

"You know my rules when it comes to men, Molly. They don't

stay over," I said, taking another sip of the sweet wine and bitter memories if only to escape the taste of Jacob's name in the air.

"I know that's a man that breaks every rule in the book. Even yours," she countered.

"Don't put anything into Jacob and me," I ordered, my voice harsher than intended. "We're temporary."

She pursed her lips. "*Nothing* about that man is temporary."

She was right. The ghost of him was already haunting me and he hadn't even left yet.

Another thing to put on the list of reasons why I should fire him.

Another thing to put on the list of reasons of how he was destroying me, even with the reality of how temporary he was, all I knew was the permanence of what he'd done to me.

What he was still doing to me.

I left Molly at my apartment with the rest of the bottle of the wine, Netflix and a promise she would take a nap before she met her friends for lunch later on in the day.

I doubted she would. If Molly and I had one thing in common, apart from our eyes, it was our lack of sleep. She just snatched her few hours when I was getting up from mine.

All of my employees knew the drill in regards to my birthday —that was to not so much as acknowledge it unless they wanted to be fired.

I had fired three different staff members for doing just that. It promoted too much familiarity, sent the wrong message, and there was probably the small dark part of me that was slightly unhinged at this time of the year.

But if I made the rules, I expected employees to follow them, and if they didn't follow the little ones, it didn't bode well for the larger ones.

Therefore, Ralph gave me his usual greeting as I met him in the car, maybe with more of a twinkle in his eye as he said, "Good Morning, Ms. Crofton."

"Good morning, Ralph," I nodded, with no twinkle in my eye.

Jacob didn't speak, he just slid into the back seat, where he always sat now, despite his knowledge of my discomfort over the fact.

And my discomfort came from the very comfort of his presence. I was only now just able to concentrate on my morning emails and contracts without my brain being clouded by his proximity.

I was thankful he didn't know what today was, though Jacob didn't strike me as a man that would make a big deal over such things.

I managed all the way up to the offices in silence, though that too had become the norm.

Vaughn handed me a coffee. Different than my regular black with an extra shot. I knew this because it was covered in whip cream and syrup. The one allowance I made for him having any kind of statement on this day as it was "a criminal offense to have a birthday without some kind of refined sugar."

He smirked at me, daring me to say something, as his gaze flickered to Jacob. He knew Jacob, and he likely knew that Jacob noticed every minute detail, likely that I had gotten the exact same coffee from Vaughn for the entire time he was working here, and today, for no obvious reason I was getting a different one.

He didn't comment.

Nor did I.

"I've got a meeting with China in fifteen minutes, prep the conference room and make sure that Adams is actually versed on how to exchange pleasantries in Mandarin," I said, taking the coffee. "I will not have another disaster like last time. Oh, and confirm my two o'clock."

Vaughn raised his brow. "Are you sure you want to take that meeting today?"

I raised my own. "I just said to confirm it, so obviously I'm sure," I said, voice sharp.

He nodded once.

I strode into my office.

Jacob didn't follow me. He walked me to my office every morning, to Vaughn's absolute glee, and then he left to parts unknown.

The door opened and closed. I didn't need to look up to know who it was.

I pretended to busy myself with the last of my contracts, steeling myself from his gaze. I wouldn't admit it to anyone, but I did feel delicate today of all days. Not just in general, but with Jacob. As if he had this ability to not only live through and create horror but see my own too.

That didn't make sense.

But it was true to me nonetheless.

I didn't expect him to speak, I knew he was here to escort me to my meeting, as he did with all of my meetings, though he usually waited in the car. But it was impossible to establish a pattern of behavior with Jacob.

"Happy birthday," he murmured, soft voice the same as a yell in my quiet office.

I jerked my head up and blinked in surprise. Not of his knowledge, but his acknowledgment. "I wouldn't consider you to be much of a birthday person." I forced my tone to flatten.

"I'm not," he said. "But this is the anniversary of the day you came into the world. It deserves recognition."

I wasn't just blinking in surprise anymore. I was gaping. Just this morning, I had been torturing myself with the idea that

Jacob's surface indifference toward me ran all the way to the bottom. And then he says something like that.

His words ran all the way to the bottom of me.

To my core.

I sucked in a ragged breath.

"Am I interrupting something?"

My head jerked up and my gaze landed on Vaughn. I didn't scuttle back, nor change my expression. "Not at all."

I could feel Jacob's stare.

I ignored it.

As well as the way every single nerve ending in my body was electrified, crying out for him.

Vaughn grinned. "Your meeting with Ethan Kershaw is in twenty minutes. The car will be ready in five."

I nodded once. "I'll be there."

Vaughn didn't say another word as he walked out and closed the door.

At the moment Kershaw's name was mentioned, Jacob's entire energy changed. He had been holding himself taut, wired, and he was still doing so now. But there was a menace now. Not that there wasn't one before, but it was different. A heat.

This was a chill.

Below zero.

It was unnerving, to say the least.

"You're meeting Ethan Kershaw," he ground out.

I smoothed my pants, inhaling and exhaling before moving toward my desk to gather my things. I made sure my movements were even, practiced, calm. I felt anything but.

"I'm surprised you know of him," I said after a long moment.

His eyes were onyx. "You're not surprised I know him. You know what circles I come from, therefore you know he works in those same ones. It's why you employed me after all, you need a monster to protect you from another monster."

"You're not a monster, Jacob," I replied. My voice was no longer flat.

He gave me a look to melt metal and to flay my skin. "We're not talkin' about what I am. We're talking about who Ethan Kershaw is. *What* he is."

The way he spoke unnerved me. The mere sliver of emotion, of fury into his words, the fact he was speaking them at all scared me. Jacob was not a man to react to just anyone. And someone who Jacob reacted to like this was more than dangerous.

But I knew that already.

"Who I am is Charlotte Crofton, and I have a reputation to uphold. It's only polite to inform him of the breaking of our business relationship in person," I said, slipping my phone into my purse.

Jacob moved in a flash, his hand circling my wrist tightly. "This is not a fuckin' man you're *polite* to. This is not a man *you're* even in the same room as."

I regarded him coolly, pretending I wasn't reacting to his touch. But I was. Every part of me was hot and cold at the same time and my heartbeat increased rapidly. "This is not something you get to comment on."

He didn't break my stare, his grip tightening. "I'm not letting it happen."

I raised my brow, knees shaking. "The fact you're under the impression that you can let me do anything concerns me greatly. This is not your decision."

Pain radiated through my wrist. I didn't show it. "The man is beyond dangerous," he said.

"I'm aware," I replied, my voice ice. "I've done my research. I'm not afraid of him."

"That's the fucking problem," he hissed, emotion seeping into his voice for the first time...ever. "He'll see you're not afraid of him, and then he'll make it his mission to make sure you are when he's done with you."

Something flickered in his gaze.

Something that had me wavering. Which of course was why I yanked my hand from his, positioning my purse on my shoulder.

"He can try. But I don't scare easily. And I didn't get to where I was by hiding in my ivory tower, Jacob."

I turned and walked out the door.

He followed me.

"Ah, the famous Charlotte Crofton," the devil in the suit greeted me, he was still sitting at the head of a long, glass conference table. The New York skyline glittered behind him and his outline was carved stark with the custom black suit, under which he had a crisp black button down, open collar.

It was intended to show off his corded neck, likely to communicate that this man didn't need to wear a conventional suit and tie, that he was both above and below that.

He grinned, showing straight white veneers, that was a jarring contrast to the onyx of his suit. "I've heard so much about you, your pictures don't do you justice." He stood, eyes running over me in a way that made my skin crawl. Not because it was an obvious leer. Because it was the opposite of that. Because his eyes ran down my body like they saw the demons underneath, the weakness.

Everything about the man was smooth, attractive. From his voice to his custom suit, to his hair, to his tanned skin. His jaw was angular, sharp, masculine. He was tall, but not towering over me like the man trailing in behind me, closer to my back than he ever had been. Instantly I sensed he was dangerous, like the man behind me. But in a much different way.

I took his outstretched hand, though my instincts screamed at me not to initiate any kind of contact. "Pictures rarely do anyone justice," I replied, my voice even. I didn't react at the coldness of his hands, the filth that seemed to settle on my skin as he held the contact for a few crucial beats more than was socially acceptable. I didn't try to struggle from the grip, didn't betray an ounce of discomfort, which I knew was his goal.

Energy pulsated from the area behind me from where I imagined Jacob's steely glare on the handshake.

The corner of Ethan's mouth turned up. "Please, sit," he offered.

His gaze flickered to Jacob, but he did not offer him a seat, nor did he remark on his presence or bother to introduce himself. This was a man who never introduced himself.

"Can my assistant get you anything?" he asked, sitting and gesturing to the door. "Fiji? Wine? I have Pastel Paradise, chilled, of course. Celebration is suitable for the day, thirty-three, is it?" His expression didn't change with the offer and neither did mine.

He didn't offer me thousand-dollar bottles of Dom. No, the ten-dollar bottle that no one knew I drank. The exact brand. It was a pointed threat. He had been looking into me. Hard enough to have someone follow me to the supermarket or at the very least go through my trash.

It was meant to unnerve me.

It did not.

The man standing behind me unnerved me with his presence, the one in front of me irritated me.

I smiled. "I appreciate the offer, but it is rather early for me, and I regret that I'm not going to be here long enough to enjoy refreshments. I came as a courtesy more than anything."

He waved off the woman who had place bottled water in front of us, leaning back in his chair. "Ah, yes, you're here to kill the deal that's been three years in the making, that's losing your company at least a billion dollars." He raised his brow. "And that's my lowest estimate."

He didn't take his eyes off me. His tone was mild. Not an ounce of irritation. Only cocky confidence that came with a man who always got what he wanted. Either by persuasion or force. I'd been around men like that before, but not like this. This was more than an upper crust sense of entitlement from men who had everything given to them because of a title, a surname or a bank balance.

No, this was a man that was given things out of fear, and what he wasn't given he took forcefully.

"It isn't the right fit for my company at this time. As a businessman yourself, I'm sure you'll understand." I didn't apologize. I never did. I would if I ever did something worth apologizing for. And I hadn't. Not in business, at least.

He nodded. "Of course, I understand. It's a risk. Keeping your company safe is the first and foremost of your concerns. Since you're the face of your company, keeping yourself safe is another one of those concerns. I'm happy to see you continue to do so." His eyes flickered to Jacob for no more than one second. "Despite your...difficulties."

I didn't react outwardly. My suspicions about my attacks were all but confirmed with the words. With the glint in his eyes. "I don't mind taking risks, Mr. Kershaw," I replied, voice glacial. "With my company or myself. But as you said, I am my brand and my brand is me. I do not consider myself a good person by any sense of the word. But I do have morals. Principles. As does my brand. We're high end. We are worth something. We will not tarnish ourselves or our reputation by getting into bed with someone from the gutter. All you are is a bully with a custom suit." I stood. "You're looking for a victim here, as all bullies always are. Looking for control. But I'm no victim. Nor am I a bully. So instead of fighting with you, instead of speaking in circles as you're so keen to do, I'm going to be brutally honest." I didn't lower my gaze, and he regarded me with that same even look he'd had when I arrived. This was not a man that would succumb to petty rage, which made him all the more dangerous.

"I'm not stooping to your level," I continued. "I know what you had to do with my *difficulties*. I know you've had a lot to do with other people's difficulties." I struggled to keep the contempt from my tone as I remembered the contents of the files I had on him. "That is one of the main reasons you're not going to merge with my company. You resorting to petty acts of violence didn't scare me. It made me confident in my decision. I don't do business with bullies. And I'm not scared of them either."

I turned to walk away.

"Everyone's a victim, at some point, Charlotte," his voice called after me. "Even the most powerful of men. Or women. There's a point where power doesn't save you."

The threat hit my back and paused my step as the energy in the room changed once more.

Jacob moved quickly and I surprised even myself by moving quicker. I was in front of him, between Ethan and him before he could do anything unwise like murder a man with whom I was concluding business with.

"Let us not do anything that would have Detective Maloney speaking to me about yet another dead body in my vicinity," I said calmly. "I'm thinking the third time would not be lucky in this situation."

Jacob's nostrils flared and a vein in his neck jumped. Small things, but it spoke louder than a roar to me, communicating Jacob's fury. His loss of control. It shocked me as much as delighted me, sick satisfaction overruling all fear at Kershaw's words. It was me that made the man unravel, lose control. A part of it was satisfaction in victory, the instinctual part of me that craved winning above all else. A larger part was the knowledge that Jacob was affected by me in the same violent way I was by him. The animal part of me that craved Jacob above all else.

I expected Kershaw to taunt him. To bait him. He may not have greeted Jacob or even acknowledged him, but that didn't mean he didn't inspect him closely, form a very educated guess on who he was. What he was. I knew the threat was as much for

Jacob's benefit as mine. And to gain information about the nature of the relationship between the two of us. Jacob's reaction communicated something dangerous.

There was nothing but silence from behind me and I didn't glance back. Jacob was teetering between violence and resistance. I was the only thing standing in his way.

He took an audible breath, ripping his eyes from the man behind me to focus on me, I didn't relax even though the movement of his eyes signified the movement of his wrath from surface to slightly under. I struggled to keep steady under his gaze when I'd barely shuddered when faced with the man who'd tried to have me killed.

Twice.

And despite me being certain I was anything but a victim, everything had changed that night in the alley.

I was not the victim of the man who tried to kill me.

I am the victim of the man who saved me.

And the gift of my life felt like something of a punishment as he taunted me with his presence.

9

I kept my cool the entire walk to the elevator, Jacob's white-hot fury encasing me as he walked damn near plastered to my side.

I'd just come out of a meeting with a criminal in a business suit, one who not only openly threatened me but all but admitted to the attempts on my life. I despised him for multiple reasons, but his brazenness was impressive. It came from a man who'd done worse things and gotten away with it. He considered himself untouchable, from things like federal or international laws. Likely he was, since I knew he was the government's unofficial attack dog. Information that had come to my desk just this morning.

Any kind of legal action I might try to bring against him would disappear. I would too if I tried conventional means to get rid of a criminal. Conventional means being putting him behind bars.

But eighty percent of the CEOs I dealt with belonged behind bars, none of them would ever get there, of course. Nor would I, I supposed, if I managed to hold onto my power and sway. Not that I'd done anything that would put me in jail. And that didn't matter. If someone wanted to try, really try, they'd find something, invent something.

Framing someone was an amateur move, too risky, too many

variables outside of your control. Which was why Kershaw deduced having me killed was the best idea when I started to look like I might back out of the deal. He'd obviously done his research and knew I wasn't likely to change my mind, knew that I had the deciding vote and if something were to happen to me, the controlling shares of my company would be given to my uncle. Who, just so happened to be very invested in this deal going through.

I thought about it.

He was invested to the point where his trademark self-control frayed, evidenced by the outburst last week. The idea that the man who took my sister and me in after our father's death, put us through school and gave up his own career to help with my company would have a hand in trying to get me killed was likely not something normal people would consider. Normal people considered that such crimes would never be committed by blood.

But in my world, blood meant nothing, power meant everything.

So, walking to the elevator, trying to find my self-control and not have a visceral reaction to Jacob's fury, I considered the highly likely possibility that my uncle had something to do with this.

I called Vaughn.

"I need you to get IT to send all of my uncle's email correspondence to my computer," I said before he could squeeze in the greeting. "And every file he's tried to get rid of." My uncle knew about everything, so likely he knew about this meeting. He was a smart man, he knew me, so if he knew about the attacks on my life—which he only would if he had someone hacking into police records or if he had something to do with it—he'd know my next step and would be attempting to cover his tracks.

There was a small pause and then tapping of keys. "I take it the meeting went well, then?" Vaughn asked dryly.

"I expect the files on my computer by the time I arrive back at the office, and it goes without saying to keep this discreet. Let IT know that if they so much as think about breathing a word of this, they'll be thrown in jail per their non-disclosure," I said.

I didn't wait for the response, I hung up the phone and walked into the elevator that was ready to take us down from hell. Scripture was wrong, the devils and demons didn't reside below our feet in the bowels of hell. They lived above the clouds, in ivory towers, controlling humans like pawns, sipping thousand-dollar wine.

I clasped my shaking hands together as the elevator doors closed on the last person to walk out. I glanced at the numbers. We only had ten floors to go. Ten floors to breathe through the dense air that had become that much thicker with the fact we were alone. I could get through ten floors. Ten seconds. Anyone can handle anything for ten seconds. It had been a mantra I'd adopted since I found my father. I'd count to ten while waiting for the police to arrive. Ten seconds was manageable. Then when I made ten, I'd start over.

The gentle movement of the elevator jolted suddenly and unexpectedly enough for me to totter on my heels.

A firm, bordering on painful grip on my elbow steadied me.

He'd pressed the emergency stop on the elevator.

I didn't even think people did that in real life.

But the man with the wolf eyes, who'd killed two men in front of me and many more in the shadows was not real life.

"You provoked him on purpose, knowing it'd get a reaction from me," he bit out.

I exhaled, making it sound like a sigh of exasperation when it was really a battle for control of my lungs.

I didn't look at him. Not directly. I focused on the area above his dark brows so I didn't have to be assaulted with his gaze. "I don't presume to know what any of your actions are, but I played with all information at my fingertips, and considered your likeliest actions. Even without the show, I suspect my message still would've been well sent."

"The message that you've got a guard dog who answers to you and you only?" he bit out.

The pure fury leeching out of the cold tone had my heartbeats increasing, fear mingled with desire throughout my body.

"I know you think you can do it with everyone, play your games, practice your control, but you can't do it with me. Not fucking ever," he hissed, his breath kissing the top of my head, grip tightening on my elbow.

I tried to move out of his grasp so I could step forward and press on the flashing red button that would restart the motion of me going down and make sure that I would be out of this shrinking space before I started to hyperventilate.

Of course I didn't go anywhere. Jacob didn't want me to move, therefore I didn't.

He yanked on me so my body turned to be almost flush against his.

Almost.

There was a calculated distance between us, so my pointed Choos only just touched his scuffed boots. Less than an inch. But it may as well have been an ocean.

I didn't shrink away from this show of force, I met his eyes, hopefully not betraying my growing panic.

"Let me go," I demanded.

"Not until I make my point, Boots," he murmured. "Not until you understand. And I'll do anything to make my point." He leaned in closer, so his scent and his very presence enveloped me.

My already rapid heartbeat increased at his proximity, the dangerous and erotic promise threaded through his words, through the air.

"Let me go," I repeated, sweat beading on my forehead. My body started to vibrate with the extension of time being stationary inside the shrinking metal box.

My vision blurred.

Panic crawled over my skin at the loss of control and my

response to it. I liked it. Jacob snatching away any and all agency I had over my body and mind. Something that was integral to my identity, my survival. I should've hated it. My panties shouldn't be dampening, my core clenching from the visceral reaction to his violent touch.

He didn't speak. He watched my reaction, and I knew he noted my panic, my discomfort, because he was Jacob and he noticed everything. He saw what he was doing to me, and he didn't stop, just observed me unravel with nothing but his proximity and stare.

"You've made your point," I bit out, struggling to keep my tone even.

"Have I?" he asked, leaning forward so there was only a sliver of air between our mouths.

I could taste him. Mint and menace.

"You try and do shit like that again, you won't need me to protect you from fuckers like Ethan Kershaw. You'll need to protect yourself from me. And even you won't be able to do that."

The threat hung in the air, fear pumped through my blood with more intensity than it had in a room with a glorified mass murderer. My panties were drenched, as if I were turned on with the prospect of my destruction.

I was.

I ached to cross the tiny distance between us, to rip at Jacob's clothes, his skin and unravel him, destroy him in a way he was destroying me.

I actually leaned forward, to commence that destruction, but Jacob flinched back as if I were about to strike him. Something changed in his eyes. Something that wasn't flat menace.

Something that might've resembled panic. Fear?

No, the man could not be afraid of me.

He stepped back, pressed the red button. The elevator moved with a jolt and descended back to earth.

My mind, my heart, stayed up in hell.

Not with Kershaw.

With Jacob.

Because he carried hell around with him.

I wasn't surprised to see the evidence of my uncle's betrayal in the files.

I wasn't hurt either.

Though I was slightly disappointed in him for making them so easy to find. They were banished to a junk folder, not even erased from the hard drive—something that would've taken my IT, the best in the world, slightly longer to find.

There should have been a sense of victory in this, if not some kind of pain at having a family member do such a thing.

There was neither. Just a hollow kind of determination to get him out and make sure I wasn't vulnerable to such things again.

The emails didn't betray any knowledge or involvement with my attacks, but if he had been involved, he was nowhere near stupid enough to leave evidence of such a thing anywhere.

It wasn't beyond the scope. He knew my schedule, and he might've known I was taking the short walk on that night in the alley. He'd been in my apartment a handful of times when I hosted obligatory parties. My doorman—who had been fired for letting in the second man who tried to kill me—knew him and his relationship to me. It actually made perfect sense. But that in itself made me hesitate. Rarely did such deception make perfect sense. It was a straight story—the successful uncle surpassed by the niece he took in, forced to work under her is bitter from the change in power and looking for ways to come back out on top.

It was the plot of too many elementary thrillers.

Life was always stranger than fiction, and never as predictable.

Or maybe there was a sentimental part of me I didn't even know I had who was trying to make excuses as to why it couldn't be him, look for another villain, further removed from me.

But villains were usually the ones with the closest relationships to their targets. I wasn't sure I wasn't a villain myself, in one way or another.

My mind flickered to Jacob, who hadn't spoken to me since the incident in the elevator. He'd left me in the foyer and stalked off somewhere, his promise, his threat imprinted onto every part of me.

No way he was the hero. He was worse than any kind of villain. He was his own monster.

The door opened and closed and I looked up to Vaughn, his face was tight, grave.

"I'm sorry, Char," he said.

Obviously he'd seen the emails.

I should've berated him for looking at them before I did, but I didn't.

"Why?"

He folded his arms. "Because you're sitting in front of evidence that your uncle not only was engaging in corporate espionage at best and was involved in an attempt on your life at worst?"

I snapped my laptop shut, standing. "This is not bad news, Vaughn. It's good. I am cleaning house, at an opportune time since I need to start moving against Kershaw before he tries anything else. Is Abe on his way up?"

Vaughn wasn't shocked at the way I brushed it off, he'd been with me long enough to likely expect my reaction. Or lack of one.

He nodded once. "I called Rambo too, just in case things get—"

"I doubt that my uncle would try and assault me in the middle of the office," I said. "He's not that crass."

Vaughn regarded me. "I'd prefer to have Rambo here, just in case. You've been through enough, Char."

I narrowed my eyes at him, finger on the doorknob. "That statement makes it sounds like there's a quota on how much human beings are given. There isn't. Enough is nothing but the point where weaker people give up."

I opened the door and pretended not to see Jacob, leaning against Vaughn's desk and regarding me with a hard gaze. Hard but cold, all evidence of the elevator exchange gone. From his face at least.

My uncle helped with me wrenching my focus from Jacob, striding into the foyer, cheeks red, eyes narrowed.

"Is there a reason I was pulled out of one of the most important budget meetings this quarter?" he said by greeting.

"You have one hour to pack up your belongings," I replied.

He blinked rapidly. "What?"

I didn't falter my gaze, though Jacob's attention was taunting me with its intensity. I cursed Vaughn for getting him up here. I straightened my shoulders and said, "You heard me."

"You can't fire me," he hissed. "I'm family."

"Yes, you're family," I agreed. "Which is why I'm not having you arrested for corporate espionage."

He stilled. Opened his mouth to likely explain, try to justify, not to lie, because his guilt was painted all over his usually expressionless face.

I held up my hand to silence him. "I was planning on doing this privately, to show you respect. But since respect doesn't mean much to you, I'll save us that conversation. I don't want to have to call security."

Every employee within viewing distance was doing their best to watch without making it obvious.

"You're making a mistake, Charlotte," he said coldly.

"I doubt it," I replied.

He stared at me a beat longer and I was uncomfortable with the chill in his gaze that was something more than the normal emotionless expression I'd come to expect from my uncle.

There was menace in it.

I waited for him to do something more.

Jacob's taut body beside me told me he was doing the same thing.

I hoped for Abe's sake that he didn't do anything more. Jacob wouldn't hesitate to hurt him. And it wasn't the concern of my family member being beaten by Jacob, it was more worry for the man dealing the beating. I knew calling up violence also called up some kinds of demons for Jacob. I wasn't quite sure which, but I didn't want him battling them for Abe.

It seemed like a waste.

But my worry was unwarranted, because Abe gave me one last sneer and turned on his heel and walked away.

I didn't look at Jacob.

"Vaughn, you'll have a list of competent replacement CPOs on my desk by end of day," I said, turning on my own heel and into my office.

I had work to do.

"You don't have to come in," I said to Jacob.

It was the first words I'd spoken to him since the incident in the elevator.

Two days ago.

Even with our limited exchanges, no words—if you didn't count his general intoxicating presence—in two days was somewhat of a record. The memory of our proximity and what he smelled like, what his wild fury felt like encased around my body was all consuming. I couldn't speak around it.

Something had changed.

Definitely.

Not just from his reaction, from him proving that he could control my body without mercy, but from his flinch when he jerked away from me.

The man who embodied fear and death, who'd committed two murders in front of me, who didn't flinch from blood, violence, death, *recoiled from my touch.*

It didn't hurt me, as it would different women, more ruled by singular emotions or self-esteem issues. No, it intrigued me. Made me ache to explore more of it. Dive into his dark and depraved psyche and figure him out. I wanted to tear him apart and inspect his pieces.

He still turned up for a run both mornings. I still abandoned music for his footfalls and even breath.

I still worked, obviously. Nothing short of death would interrupt my schedule. I waited for some kind of retribution from either my uncle or Kershaw.

There was press about the failed merger and my uncle's termination. I'd expected it. Not the sheer volume of it. The office had been all but swarmed with reporters on the first day.

The second day they had disappeared.

Not by choice. There was a story here. A big one. Bigger than most of them would even know. But I had connections that got them shooed. Mostly because I held the notes on some of the owners of their publications.

Press was meant to be the fourth estate, holding power to account, but if power knew the dollar amount of the press's account, then it held the press too.

Every headline was controlled, paid for and orchestrated by those of us at the top. Ideas were some of the most sought after currency in the world.

I hadn't bothered myself with it before. I didn't want to control the public's ideologies. Just my own demons.

I had very few morals left—the higher you got to the top, the more you shed away—but messing with freedom of speech hadn't been a line I'd been willing to cross.

Until now.

Not that I was surprised, I knew that there would be no lines left to cross once I got high enough.

I didn't want some fresh-faced reporter trying to make a name for themselves in a dying medium to sniff the blood that lurked under the ivory façade.

They would.

Eventually.

The smell of blood always found its way to the surface.

Hence me sitting in the car outside Molly's apartment building. I would protect her from this for as long as I could. I wasn't so dense to realize that she wouldn't find out eventually. I just planned on it being after the threat was eradicated. My mind stuttered on that thought. The threat *would* be eradicated. And so would whatever this was between Jacob and me.

"My sister already thinks the wrong thing about us," I continued from the first three words I'd spoken to Jacob in two days. "I don't want her to build on that any more than she already is. Plus, there is only so long she will be fooled by the façade that we are..." I trailed off, my words catching in my throat with Jacob's stare, struggling to put any kind of label on what we were.

I cleared my throat.

"There is no threat inside that building." I nodded to the shabby walk up, quickly being cleaned up by gentrification, to Molly's horror.

"I'll have my phone," I said as if I were ever without it. "If there is trouble, I'll call. For now, wait."

I expected an argument. Not a verbal one. Jacob's version of an argument was a glare and then him disregarding everything I said and following me out of the car.

He didn't do so.

The entire walk up to Molly's apartment, I wondered if he believed in my safety or if the moments in the elevator had something to do with the fact he was still in the car.

I felt naked without his stare.

I should've felt more vulnerable without the monster protecting me. Instead I felt stronger without the man dissecting me.

It took Molly five minutes to answer the door. When she did, she was wearing an oversized men's shirt, a kimono over top, her hair was messy and eye makeup smudged.

"Why are you here so early?" she whined.

My mouth turned up. "It's two in the afternoon."

She leaned against the door frame. "Yes, *early*."

I raised my brow. "Do I need to even ask?"

She yawned. "Oh come on, I was just up all night painting. Canvases. Not the town. For once." She winked and held the door open so I could step inside.

My heels clicked against the wood floors.

"I felt inspired," she said to my back as I stared at the paintings strewn around the place.

They were amazing. All of Molly's were. But this was something else. Violent. Dark.

Unlike anything she'd ever painted before.

Fear clutched my throat as I looked at all the canvases.

I turned to watch her putting coffee into two large mugs. "Are you okay?" I demanded.

She glanced up. "Apart from sleep deprived, fine. Why?" She screwed up her nose. "Oh, because of the paintings. I should've known you'd get all worried about them. You never see the surface, even on first glance."

She padded over and handed me the mug.

"But it's *me* who should be asking that," she said after taking a long sip. "This didn't come from me." She waved the mug at the paintings.

I gaped at her. I knew what she was insinuating. What she meant. I opened my mouth to protest, but then I looked at the paintings again. Something crawled over my spine as I took them in. It was me. All of the prickly, violent thoughts that had been clawing at my mind, they were splashed all over those canvases.

I froze as I spotted one that I hadn't seen on first glance. I don't know why my eyes weren't drawn to it the second I step foot inside the apartment.

Wordlessly, I walked over to stand in front of the canvas that was set apart from the others.

It was a large wolf, depicted in painstaking realism. Which was something in itself. All of Molly's work was abstract. It was chaotic. It didn't bow down to the rules of reality. She created and broke her own rules. She didn't do portraits or landscapes. She was exceptionally good at them, but she never did them.

"I don't want to paint what everyone else sees. I want to paint what I feel when I see what everyone else thinks they see."

But here it was. A wolf. Real in every stroke, apart from the eyes. They were ice blue, so haunting that it could've been Jacob's irises plucked from his head and flattened onto the canvas. There was enough violence in them to make it known that pain created them.

"Molly," I whispered, my voice fractured as I turned to regard her.

She was smiling at me with eyes that were usually full of youth and chaos. But now there was a wisdom to them that only peeked out in these moments.

Our twin moments.

When I forgot all the rules I lived by and realized that my ordered world wasn't as simple and brutal as I pretended it was.

"I think, when we were in Mom's stomach, we were one person," Molly said, by way of answer. "And then, someone, something, maybe even us, realized that we were going to be too much to fit into one mind, so we split into two. It's like the yin and the yang, without us being dark or light, we just *are*. We're okay apart." She looked at me pointedly. "Rather, one of us is more okay than the other."

I glanced around the albeit messy rooms, my own eyes pointedly staring at the clear masterpieces amongst the chaos. "I would disagree on that point."

She grinned. "It's paint on a canvas." She shrugged. "Nothing like thousands of jobs and really serious computer stuff that pretty much holds the fate of thousands of people in the little hard drives or whatever."

I smiled inwardly. *Little* was not the word for our hard drives.

And it wasn't because Molly wasn't wildly proud of me that she didn't know that, it was because it was all far too big for her to comprehend, too invisible. She lived in tangibles. Her paintbrush, the ink on her skin, whoever she was in love with that week.

She squinted at the painting as if seeing it for the first time, as if she weren't the one who painted it.

A moment of dread clutched me with that look, that beautiful confusion so familiar. So reminiscent of the woman who had no beauty left in her stare. None left in her soul. An ugly and cruel disease had rotted her from the insides out.

Schizophrenia was genetic.

It could manifest in women in their early twenties and thirties.

I tasted bile at the thought of Molly being yanked out of herself by her own mind. All of her vibrancy sucked away by drugs that would fight what was wrong inside of her by muting everything that was right.

No matter how visceral my fear was for that to be my fate, if it was a choice between sanity and watching my sister decay like my mother, I'd take the disease.

In a second.

Because it would take more from Molly than it would from me. She had more life in her than I did. Much more to steal. Illness was greedy, darkness was. I knew it'd take from the most vibrant if it was the choice between the two of us.

My eyes ran over the complex brushstrokes of the painting in an effort to shake the demons from my mind. Then I looked back to the wonderful artist that simply *could not* be taken from me like that.

My Molly.

I made a mental note to put another ten million into my research fund for mental illnesses.

I stared at her as if the effort might be able to chase away what lay dormant in our blood. "It's beauty," I choked out, unable to say anything else.

She rolled her eyes with a warm smile, waving her hand. "Whatever. I need to get back to my point, I know I left it somewhere." There was a small pause and I imagined her rustling through the corridors of her mind that likely resembled this very apartment. "Right," she said, eyes lighting with the lightbulb of recovery. "We were meant to be one. Well, in biology's standards. But by whatever else runs the universe, we were meant to be *two*. You were meant to be the strict, regimented and wildly successful, albeit slightly robotic—" she winked—"superstar. And I was meant to be the one who reminded you of your humanity, that it's okay to smile and laugh. You were meant to be the one that protected me from the world. The one outside, and more importantly, the one inside. Three minutes may be long for some people, but not to you. It's the time that defined our relationship, to a point." She smiled wider. "I think even if you were the biologically younger sister, you'd always be the big sister spiritually."

She whirled around the room, the billowing sleeves of her kimono moving with her.

"And I was meant to be like this," she sang. "The strictly unregimented, irresponsible, romantic sister who will always lean a lot to the left. We fit because we don't."

She stopped and regarded me. "We're one person still, because I feel what you're feeling." She nodded to the paintings. "You're not going to tell me, are you?" She didn't need to ask outright, but she knew something was going on. We didn't need words when she had the paintings, when we had our connection.

I shook my head. "Not yet."

She nodded. Didn't argue. Molly knew me well enough to know that whatever she got through our connection was all she was going to get. "It's him, the wolf man, Jacob, isn't it?"

My hand clenched around my mug handle. I couldn't lie to her. I physically couldn't lie to my sister. No matter how much I wanted to. "Yes," I said, little more than a whisper.

She nodded again. "I thought so, only thoughts as dark and painful as that could have been born from love."

I jerked. "I don't love him." The words were sharp and violent. A tone I'd never taken with Molly.

She didn't flinch from it. She didn't argue with me. Just regarded me and faced me with that ridiculous notion. Not that I could fall in love with a man who I barely spoke to, who I'd seen kill two other men. No, that I was *capable* of loving anything. Even the monster that Jacob was. Because I was a different kind of monster. Maybe not as obvious. But a monster nonetheless.

"I didn't come here to speak about my personal life," I said.

"Obviously," she replied, sinking down onto her bright purple sofa sitting in the middle of the room, for no apparent reason. Molly didn't own a TV.

"I came to give you your birthday gift," I said, reaching into my purse to hand her an envelope.

She eyed it. "Is it a car?"

I rolled my eyes.

She took the envelope and opened what was inside. Her eyes flared. "Ten days in an Ashram in India?" she all but yelled. Her mouth stretched into a smile. "I thought you were totally against me going on spiritual journeys."

I folded my arms. "I'm not against you doing anything that makes you happy," I said as response. It wasn't a lie. But my motivations behind such a thing were not purely to make her happy, they were more to keep her safe.

It was an over precaution, one I hadn't spoken to anyone about, but I didn't want to take risks after my meeting with Kershaw. I couldn't rule out anything with a man like him. And having Molly in the middle of nowhere in India with armed guards following her at a distance would set my mind at ease.

Her gaze was sharp and knowing. "There's something you're not telling me."

I hated that she read me so well.

"But I'll wait until you're ready to do so," she continued. "Until after I get back from India." She got up, put her mug down amongst three more on her cluttered coffee table and came over to hug me.

She smelled of paint and strawberries.

I relaxed into the embrace, and despite what she said before, I wasn't the older sister. She was the one that was taking care of me.

"Your present is obviously unwrapped, and your announced house call ruined the surprise," she said, letting me go. "I was going to break into your apartment and get it hung without your knowledge."

"You do realize that breaking in doesn't work in this scenario since you have the key code to my penthouse?" I asked.

She waved my hand. "Don't ruin my fun." She screwed her nose up, concentrating on the painting I knew she had meant for me. "There's still a couple of things I need to unperfect."

"Unperfect?" I repeated.

She nodded. "Yeah, it's too perfect. It needs to be a little..." She trailed off. "Wrong," she decided.

"Yeah, wrong," I whispered under my breath.

Molly left the day after she delivered the painting to my apartment. She had "unperfected" it. I wasn't sure how, it didn't look physically different from the painting I'd seen two days' prior. But it was. Everything about it was.

Wrong.

Beautifully so.

Painfully so.

Now I'd never escape Jacob's eyes, they'd be mounted on the wall in my bedroom, where Molly insisted I hang it.

And despite the damage it would do, I let her because I never said no to Molly.

She had given me one last hug before leaving to go to the airport. "You know I can handle the darker parts of your life, right?"

I schooled my expression, the knowledge of her harboring the truth about our parents in her beautiful brain for over a decade. "I know. I just don't want you to."

She frowned. "But I *want* to. You're not alone, Charlotte. You're not in this ivory tower, cold and without feeling, whatever everyone else says, whatever you tell yourself. There are actually quite a few people around you that love you. That adore you. And not just because they share chromosomes with you."

I stilled.

Her meaning was clear.

I ached to spill everything about Jacob. All of the ugliness, all of my torment, everything that was haunting me.

"You're going to miss your flight," I said instead.

My sister already had enough ghosts haunting her, whether she made it seem like it or not.

She shook her head, smiling. "I'm not going to miss my flight, since even though I've got a commercial itinerary, I'm going to get to the airport and escorted to the private hanger because you know I'd never agree to such a waste of fuel until it was too late."

The corner of my mouth twitched. "Don't tell me you're going to refuse to go now?"

She smiled. "Not this time. But I'll be making a hefty donation to clean air organizations on your behalf."

"I'll call my business manager and get it arranged." Though it was already arranged since I knew Molly would have some kind of stipulation before she got on my jet.

She rolled her eyes and then her expression sobered. "I know something is going on, beyond you and Jacob. And I know that's dangerous, despite what you say. I know there's some kind of real danger. I can..." she trailed off. "I can feel something. So just be careful, okay?" Something dark and unnerving flickering through her light eyes.

I clenched my teeth. "Of course. Only if you promise the same."

She grinned again. "Of course I won't promise to be careful."

She winked and left in pursuit of peace while I resigned myself to stave off chaos.

———

"Are you afraid of flying?"

I jerked up from my laptop.

It was the first words he'd spoken to me since we'd gotten on the jet.

No, it was the first words he'd spoken at all, apart from some clipped responses to Vaughn's questions.

Though Vaughn knew him well enough by now to understand he wasn't going to get anything but the bare minimum of words from Jacob, it seemed to be his hobby to try and get more.

I wondered if he and Molly were in a competition.

Jacob's eyes were on me from his spot across the cabin. I should've gotten used to that near constant gaze, he'd been my security for over a month now. But it was something I'd never get used to. No one should ever get used to a stare like that.

Silence stretched on after his question, one of the first he'd ever asked me.

I dissected what that meant to the power dynamic.

"What makes you think that?" I asked instead of answering with a lie like I would've with anyone else.

Vaughn included.

Vaughn had his headphones on and was typing on his laptop, in a world that was nowhere near this conversation. He was extremely engaged in dissecting the dynamics between Jacob and me, but he was also extremely diligent with his job, and when he focused on something, it was with his full attention. To an almost unhealthy extent, which was why he was my second.

Jacob didn't reply to my question, just tilted his head ever so slightly and gave me a look communicating that I should know that his entire job was noticing things about me, learning things about people, picking out their weaknesses.

"I wouldn't say *afraid*," I said after a long pause. "It just makes me uncomfortable that—"

"You're not in control?" he finished for me.

I pursed my lips, hating that he was right and it made me sound like a total control freak. Which I was. I knew this about myself. But hearing it out loud...

"Not to put too fine a point on it, but yes I suppose that's the crux of it," I replied. "I'm not afraid of crashing. That's ridiculous. I'm well aware of the statistics of people dying in plane crashes, even smaller jets such as this one. I'm more likely to die in a traffic accident, or in my apartment, it seems that assassins are what I have to worry about, not fiery deaths."

"You don't have to worry about that," he clipped, voice cold.

I stared at him, tried to stare into him. "I know."

He didn't make an effort to further the conversation.

He didn't stop staring either.

I could go back to work, pretend I didn't know he was watching, pretend it didn't do anything to me. I'd been doing that for over a month. But I didn't.

"Are you afraid of anything?" I asked, surprising myself with the question.

I didn't expect him to answer. He didn't volunteer personal information. Nor did I, but I wanted to give him all of it, everything personal and ugly about me. I had to actively stop myself from cutting open my emotional flesh and letting it all pour at his feet.

"I used to be," he said, his low rasp taking up all the air in the cabin. "But everything I used to be afraid of died with the person I used to be."

I blinked, glanced to Vaughn, to make sure he was still focusing on his laptop, headphones still blaring. To me, that admission was loud enough to cut through whatever terrible music Vaughn was listening to.

Jacob's ice gaze tugged me back. "Didn't think I'd be afraid of anything again. Gotta have somethin' to lose in order to fear anything."

My heart beat in my throat.

I opened my mouth to say something. Anything.

"Char? We've got Korea on the phone, they want to talk about rolling out our whole brand range in fifty new stores and I need to consult with you on—"

Vaughn's voice cut off abruptly as he noted the air in the cabin after tearing off his headphones.

I tore my gaze from Jacob to my assistant, proverbial life raft.

"It can wait," he said quickly, corner of his mouth turning up.

I tapped on my laptop, calling up the agreement. "Of course it can't," I said, voice ice. "It's what we've been waiting for and I need to go over every inch of the contract before I have a call with them. Organize a conference call after we land and finish the meeting."

"Already done," Vaughn said.

"Good."

I focused all of my attention on the screen in front of me.

Or I pretended to.

I was drunk.

The bottles littered around my suite were evidence of that.

And the fact I was passing those bottles, barefoot, wearing cashmere sweats, no bra and heading to the door.

My face was free of makeup, I'd let my hair air dry after my shower, therefore it was slightly damp and had an unruly wave to it that the best hair stylists in New York usually blew out twice a week.

I was without any of the armor I suited myself with to enter the world. Anything outside of a hotel room or my penthouse required the armor. I couldn't trust New York, all the people in it to walk around with my guard down. Even before the attacks.

It was a testament to how drunk I was that I didn't even hesitate to open the door, close it behind me and walk steadily to another door at the end of the hall.

There were only three rooms on this floor. All suites. Each of which housed the two men who had flown to San Francisco with me. I had put Vaughn in the middle as a buffer, but I knew he would not be inside his room nearing midnight on a Friday. In San Francisco, of all cities. His phone would be on, and he'd be there in an instant for anything work-related, but we were strictly off the clock. Hence me having imbibed so much alcohol after pouring over my laptop for ways I could acquire Kershaw's company.

My gait was steady. I hadn't been drunk often in my life, but whenever I was, the average outsider wasn't likely to notice, since I never outwardly looked anything but maybe a little flushed.

My hand was shaking as I knocked on the third door. It had nothing to do with alcohol and everything to do with the man that opened that door moments later.

He had a gun in his left hand.

The safety was off, even though my vision was slightly blurred, it didn't stop me from noting the subtleties of a deadly weapon.

Which was why I noted something not so subtle about the man who served to be deadlier than a gun.

He was shirtless.

I pretended that I didn't think about what he looked like

without his tight tees and leather jackets. I thought I'd called up somewhat of a pleasing and tempting image in my mind.

It was nothing on reality.

He had the same sculpted muscles I knew he would have, abs that bordered on an eight pack, every muscle that could be carved in a person's body stark and beautiful.

But it was marred by ugly.

By puckered scars covering almost his entire torso, spaced unevenly, textures varying.

Burns. Gunshot wounds. Some kind of tearing of the skin, that didn't look to be from a knife or a bullet.

I cataloged them with absent sterility that was only possible from a drunken mind. The same drunken mind that let my hand lift, move forward and attempt to touch the ruined skin.

Jacob let out a sound that wasn't quite a hiss or quite a growl.

My hand froze, the warning was clear.

I let it dangle there, suspended in the air for a moment. I toyed with the idea of pushing past the pure danger in the noise that he just made, touching him despite every single one of my survival instincts that were roaring at me to retreat. Run.

I never retreated. Or ran.

I did lower my arm.

"Why won't you let me touch you?" my words were soft, the only inkling of my inebriation—lack of flatness to my tone.

Though my inebriation was quickly disappearing, as if spotting the predator that Jacob was was more sobering than coffee, a cold shower or a long sleep.

A hangover was hitting me quick and fast, my head pounding, stomach lurching.

Or maybe it was the reality that I was standing here, unprotected, in bare feet, bare face, bare soul in front of the man without a shirt but still layers of steel protecting him.

He stared at me with the eyes that were wild and caged at the same time. The emptiness unsettling because it was anything but.

Empty, that was.

A chilling thought echoed through my spine. Those eyes would be wild until the grave took him. Haunted forever.

I didn't think he'd answer, just stare at me with those wolf eyes. I was seconds away from backing down, flickering my gaze away and retreating. Me.

The woman who had won stare downs with men who owned weapons companies that could have a hit out on me in the blink of an eye.

Me.

Who had met and fended off numerous Senators and one Prime Minister from sexually assaulting me because they'd thought it their right.

And here was one man without the billions, the titles, and the expensive suits that had me surrendering. Because none of that meant anything. None of that was real power.

"Because I don't have control," he growled, the air thickening with the murmur of his voice.

I blinked, long and slow. His voice was death but it was also sex. "Over what?"

He glanced down at his hands, large, calloused, attached to veiny, sculpted and scarred arms. "Over these," he muttered. Then he glanced back up to me. "I won't touch you with the hands that have ended lives, destroyed them," he spat his words at me, as if he could use them as a physical force to rid him of my presence. To scare me away.

That, coupled with the fresh memories of blood and death and the power humming in the air very nearly did. Scare me away, that was.

But the wolf eyes, the ones that I presumed were also trying to banish me were what chained me to the spot. Tightened me to him in a grip that I was afraid was too tight. That I might never get free of.

He had been waiting for my retreat and since he didn't get it, he stepped forward, his goal to intimidate me with his body, the charge rolling off it. It did intimidate me. But it excited me. To my toes and then back up in between my legs where my panties were soaked.

"I won't touch you, Boots," he murmured. "Not with hands that only offer death and pain. That only *know* death and pain. I don't have control over what happens after I lay them on you. I *have* to have control. Even when I'm ending a man's life, I have it." He paused, the sliver of air separating us feeling like a hair and a chasm at the same time. "Hell, that's when I have the most control. But with you? You offer chaos. And destruction. Yours or mine, I can't figure out. The latter, I'd be happy with if I got to feel your skin. But the former? Not a risk I'll take." Wolf eyes turned from wild to resolute. "Not ever, Boots," he promised. And then just as the chasm began to close, he stepped back and slammed his door.

In my face.

I stared at the door for longer than I would like to admit.

It was only me and his words left in the empty hallway. I could barely breathe around them.

But I did.

Breathe, that was.

I turned and returned to my hotel room.

I opened another bottle of vodka and continued working on a way to bring Kershaw down. If only to distract myself from the fact the man two doors away had already brought me down.

11

The next morning I woke up with a headache.

And a lot more than that.

Memories fractured and out of sequence rushed into my brain as I forced myself up and into my running gear. My stomach lurched once, then settled. I waited for the regret, the shame to rush in with the knowledge of what I'd done last night, what I'd revealed to Jacob.

But none came.

Because I may have revealed a lot. Definitely too much. But he'd revealed a lot too. More of those shreds of himself I was determined to detach from him, collect and own.

I laced my shoes and made my way down to the hotel gym. First, I had to make it through the hallway. The hallway that was drenched in the heaviness from the night before. Walking through it was like trying to wade through the muddy ocean floor.

Especially when I passed his room.

The door stared at me in accusation. Dared me to knock again, and not to pause when my survival instincts warned me not to touch him. It urged me to move past my human self-preservation and surrender to my obsession with my own destruction.

I almost did it.

Almost.

But then I continued moving and took the elevator down to the hotel gym.

I half expected him to be there. It was the usual time for our morning run, and since it was pouring with rain outside, he would deduce that I wasn't hitting the San Francisco streets.

I held my breath as I entered the empty room, five in the morning was too early for even the most exclusive of their business clientele.

The room was empty.

And so was I.

A week went by with the elephant of that night between us. Though of course Jacob acted like it never happened, never mentioned a word, though sometimes I swore I saw him looking at me with something other than his intense but cold indifference.

I could have been imagining it.

I almost certainly was.

The amount of work I'd been pushing myself to do was bordering on insane, even for me. I'd shaved hours off my already short sleeping schedule, falling asleep at my laptop most nights, plagued by broken and frightening dreams.

Not of the traumas I'd been through. Not of blood or of death.

Just him.

The him that was waiting outside my building every morning at five, who ran beside me without a word. Who sat across from me in the car for fifteen to seventeen minutes, depending on traffic. Who escorted me to functions, meetings and anything else that he deemed outside the safe area. His silence should've made him melt into the background, it did anything but.

I became more hyper-aware of him with every passing day. To

the point where my weekends, when he wasn't around, I was sure I felt his eyes following me to the market, up and down the streets of the East Village where I wandered amongst the crowds.

Worry was a constant pinch at the back of my spine. No, not worry. Bone deep terror, that it wasn't Jacob that was unraveling me, nor the man who was trying to kill me, or my uncle's betrayal. No, it was the villain lurking in my brain, in my genes, slowly but surely sinking its talons into the flesh of my psyche until I was its prisoner.

More often than not, those thoughts became most unbearable at three in the morning, when I jerked awake.

I thought of my mother in those lonely hours.

Wondered about her sitting in some tastefully decorated mental institution with great amenities and top-notch staff. Her beautiful surroundings meaning nothing when her mind was rotting from the inside out.

I knew this because that's how I felt in that hour known as the witching hour. My memories a rotting corpse amidst the shiny and expensive things I'd surrounded myself within the ivory tower of mine.

I held onto one thing when I became seriously concerned about my grip on sanity. Well, two things, the eyes staring at me from across the room. The wolf hung directly in front of my bed.

Him.

The reality of him drove me to the edge in the daylight, but the memory of him stopped me from toppling over in the darkness.

Now, those itching feelings were creeping into my days, whether it be from lack of sleep or the start of the disease, I couldn't be sure.

I was on my fifth coffee for the day and it was barely eleven. I was looking at different companies I'd acquired in the past two weeks in order to give myself a chance at taking Kershaw down. No one knew I was doing this. Not even Vaughn. I'd outsourced all legal representation to handle the deals, and I was operating through a shell corporation. All very clandestine and paranoid, but my uncle's actions sat in the forefront of my mind as to just how far people would go to grasp onto the kind of power I was toying with. I was holding onto.

We were at the precipice of something, I knew that. Kershaw had been dormant for too long. And men like him didn't skulk off with their tails between their legs, especially after being bested by a woman. He was planning something. I had to be two steps ahead.

Then there was Jacob. It couldn't continue on like this, despite our time together having an expiration date. The tension was getting so tight between us it was going to snap.

I was going to.

He was chained to my routine, and he was not a man that was designed for such things. I expected to get down for my run one morning and not see him. For him to just melt back into the shadows from where he came.

If I was honest with myself, that was my greatest fear. Not whatever Kershaw was planning. Not the prospect of losing everything I'd worked for. And not even the prospect of losing myself to the disease that claimed my mother and killed my father.

It was Jacob.

Or more accurately, the absence of him.

And on that thought, as if by something Molly would've described as fate and I put down to coincidence, he strode through the door to my office.

The air turned wired with his presence and I was too much of a coward to meet his eyes, cold certainty washing over me that this was it, this was him coming in for whatever sort of goodbye a man like him would offer.

I pretended to look at my screen while Jacob stood in the middle of the room, staring at me, yanking at the loose threads of my soul with nothing but his attention.

I waited. Didn't breathe.

"I wasn't there that night, in the alley, by chance." His voice was a low rasp, gravel and whisky.

I didn't look up. "I know."

There was a loaded pause as I took Jacob by surprise. I steeled myself not to look up so I could witness it. And like with most exercises of control with the man in front of me, I failed.

He was staring at me in something more than the flat and intense gaze that was characteristic, a small change, but important. With people that had such constant control, there were no such things as small changes.

"You know?" he repeated.

I nodded. "Rarely anything in this world happens by chance, regardless of what people like my sister believe. There is no fate, no destiny. Everything in this world is controlled, calculated by people like me. People who pull the strings. It's only once you get high enough that the fall is fatal do you realize such things. So I know you weren't just taking a midnight stroll, kismet for such things do not exist."

"You know why I was there?" he asked. I was collecting his questions, not as victories, as they should've been, but something else.

"No, but I could take an educated guess." I put down my pen. "Though I don't take guesses, educated or otherwise. It seems you're ready to enlighten me."

He clenched his fists. Another small change, another huge signifier of what emotions he was feeling. That he was feeling anything at all.

"I wasn't lying when I told you I wasn't a hitman," he said.

I regarded him. "I know."

His jaw ticked. "But I do shit. Sometimes for money. Sometimes for free." He paused. "Though everything costs something. Feeds something."

I wasn't surprised. I'd accepted as much about him. Maybe

that's why I was so obsessed with him. I was obsessed with death, my own more specifically. He was the embodiment of it. Death itself and my own demise.

"Wrong people got in touch with me, armed with the right information about who I was." He paused again. The jaw tick resumed. "About who I am," he corrected. "Took the information about what they needed. Not so politely declined." His gaze was an anchor on my chest. "Knew it was a woman, and it didn't bother me. I've killed women before. Death doesn't discriminate, so I don't. That's not why I said no. It was who the call was comin' from. People I knew weren't killing for the right reasons, if there ever is a right reason. Knew there was a chance, a high one, you'd be innocent. Still wasn't plannin' on interfering. I walk at night. Lookin' for shit. Or waitin' for shit to find me. My feet found me in that alley. I don't believe in fate or destiny either. Or I didn't. 'Til I slit the throat of the man who was tryin' to kill you."

I blinked at him. Once. Twice. Three times.

I needed to find my composure.

I *had* to.

He had just told me that he got a call about someone planning my assassination, that he wasn't planning on stopping it until he actually did.

If there were ever a reason to call security and get him out of my office and my life, beyond all of the others, this was a huge and glaring one.

I pushed my chair out, got on unsteady feet and rounded my desk. He didn't speak, didn't move his body, apart from his eyes, which followed me.

I stopped in front of him. My breathing was sharp, punishing my lungs. Or was it the air that surrounded him?

I didn't think. I did. My hand was fastened on the back of his neck, yanking him down before I realized I was touching him. And his mouth smashed down on mine and all of my coherent thought disappeared.

The kiss was violent.

There was no other way to describe it.

Every second we'd spent together had led up to this moment. Our mouths clashing in a brutal war for control. I wasn't yielding. Neither was he. It lasted for an eternity and for a mere second until I yanked my head back.

I stared at him. "You're everything that I shouldn't want. Shouldn't crave," I whispered. "You're wild. Chaos. I can't control anything when I'm around you. Not even my breath. I've worked my whole life for it and you're making me want to throw it all away."

He stared at me. "You're everything I don't deserve."

His hand had found its way to my hip, the other was tight on my neck.

"Happiness," he continued, voice rough and his hand began to squeeze.

I reveled in the pain. "I don't think that's what this is," my voice was a low rasp. "That's what we promise." I ran my eyes along him greedily. "We are a lot of things. But I don't think we'll be happy. We'll be better. And worse. And it may destroy us both."

The words hung in the air, an omen, a promise, a death sentence perhaps.

And then there weren't words in the air. There was only the blur of motion as he attached his mouth to mine. My entire body submitted to his control immediately, without question, without fight.

Surrender.

It was always surrender with Jacob.

His hands tore through my carefully styled chignon, tearing at the pins holding the strands together while his mouth's brutal assault of mine tore at the pins inside me, holding me together.

If you'd asked me before this moment whether a mere kiss could tear you apart and not care if you'd ever be put back together or not, I'd call you a romantic idiot and go about my day.

But now, my day wasn't anything but a plea that this would never stop. I worried some little sliver of me that remained logical, whether my day or life might never be the same again after this kiss.

I cried out in surprise, pain, and pleasure as his teeth grazed my lips, sending warm blood into my mouth. His assault quickened with the metallic twang being shared between us, as the wolf craved the blood and went crazy with it.

My hands moved underneath his tee and I raked my nails down his back, tearing through the skin, warm liquid seeped onto my fingers. He let out a grunt at this and the hardness at his belt buckle pressed into me harder.

Maybe I had a wolf in me too.

He let out a low growl in his throat and his hands went to my hips, lifting me, walking us back and placing me—not gently—on my desk. Then, he leaned back, depriving my lips of his.

My pussy clenched the second my eyes met his. There was no control left in them. There was no man. This was all monster.

His hands went to the bottom of my skirt, grabbing the delicate fabric in his rough and scarred hands he ripped. From hem to waist, he tore at the fabric until it was split in half and exposed my garters and stockings.

He let out a low hiss that was not human. That I felt right in between my legs. My legs were spread apart with the same violence the kiss had started with. I didn't expect any tenderness here. I didn't want tenderness. Polite, passionate touches as I'd had in the past.

I wanted wild, fierce, I wanted pain. Agony.

His fingers pressed into my inner thighs with a force that would leave bruises on my pale skin.

My teeth sank into the flesh of my lip until I tasted blood. I didn't even feel the pain, but warmth spread from my lips as some of it escaped.

Jacob's feral gaze traveled up to focus on me. He zeroed in on my mouth, his hand was up, wiping the thin trail of crimson from my mouth with his thumb. He lifted his hand, slowly and purposefully put it into his mouth.

I bit my lip harder, needing more pain to survive this moment. Though I feared I'd need a lot more.

My panties fared the same fate as my skirt once he stopped sucking my blood from his finger. He didn't wait, didn't tease me, or pause. His fingers entered me with brutal beauty.

I let out a strangled moan at the back of my throat as he maintained eye contact the entire time his fingers moved inside me. His other hand came to the back of my neck, leaning forward so our mouths could crash together once more. His teeth grasped my lip, where the skin had opened up. He sucked at it, drawing more blood from me.

An orgasm, brutal and unexpected shattered me as he did this, my entire body breaking apart from his fingers and his mouth on mine.

I was barely over the aftershocks when I started ripping at his clothes, desperate, greedy to have him inside me, for him to fill me up. Or him to empty me completely.

His hands left me so he could yank his tee off, hurling it to the floor and then snatching my neck to pull me into another frenzied and violent kiss.

My entire body shook, and I sank my nails into the corded and scarred skin of his back, eager to draw more blood, I wanted to add my own scars to his roadmap of torment, I wanted to hurt him more than anything else. He let out a low growl as I broke the skin, a growl that made my pussy clench, and my blood sing.

"Fuck me. Now," I commanded, my voice was so husky it was unrecognizable.

Jacob froze. His grip on my hips tightened past the point of pain, right to agony and his eyes bore into me, noting the way I tensed up with discomfort, but he didn't loosen his grip. "You think you're in charge here?" he rasped. "You think this," he pushed his finger inside, my eyes rolled back, "is something else you can control? You think I am?"

My body fought between the conflicting pleasure and pain Jacob was putting through. My mind was frayed, rapidly coming apart in his hands.

"This is gonna be like flyin', Boots," he growled. "You're not in control here, and there's no chance of a safe landing either."

He didn't move.

I didn't breathe. He was right. Despite the fact that with every other sexual partner I'd ever had, I was in charge—some might even call me a Dom—it all fell away, ripped from me like Jacob had torn apart my clothes.

With devastating slowness, he pulled his fingers from me.

He didn't break eye contact, and still, his grip was violent instead of tender, as was his gaze. But the pain was a caress against my rough soul. He unbuttoned his belt and I thought about the situation, the fact he had not locked the door behind him and that anyone could walk in right now.

Not that anyone was able to walk in, they'd have to get past Vaughn, but he could also come in. That knowledge did not urge me to hesitate, to tense and tell Jacob to stop. Nothing would. Not my image as ice cold, Charlotte Crofton being shattered if someone found my bodyguard fucking me on top of my desk.

I wasn't that Charlotte Crofton anymore. Not under Jacob's gaze. Not with his touch. I wasn't anyone or anything.

I moved to grasp his belt, desperate for him.

His grip tightened. "What the fuck did I just say?" he growled. "Hands flat on the desk."

I obeyed his command immediately. The only man I'd ever obeyed in my life. The only person.

His body was taut, pulsating with an energy that mimicked my own.

I watched him, rapt, as he undid his belt with devastating

slowness, one hand still tight on my neck, tight and warning me about doing anything under my own volition.

When he freed himself, I let out a harsh hiss in between my teeth.

He didn't give me time to examine a part of a man I'd never been intent on inspecting...ever. With Jacob, it was different.

With Jacob, everything was different.

With Jacob, I was different.

I wanted not only to examine him, but to worship him. I wanted to sink down to my knees and do what the man with a gun had tried to get me to do in an alleyway two months prior. The man that Jacob killed.

But there was no time for that.

As soon as he was freed from his jeans, Jacob surged inside. Right inside.

The second I was about to cry out from the brutal and beautiful intrusion, his palm covered my mouth, stifling my scream.

Another thing a man had never done before, physically or metaphorically—silence me.

And I *loved* it.

My teeth sank into the flesh of Jacob's palm as he moved inside me, fast, hard, magnificent.

My hands were still flat on the desk, because he hadn't told me to move them, and somehow, I'd became a slave to him, I wouldn't exhale if it weren't under his command.

"Touch me," he grunted. "More blood."

I moved immediately and hungrily, clawing at his back once more.

He let out a guttural noise in his throat as I opened his skin, my orgasm came at the same time his blood trickled onto my fingertips.

Another scream into his palm.

My entire body shook, split apart, shattered in his grip.

He moved his hand and replaced it with his mouth as I milked his own release from him.

His lips stayed on mine, tasting like mint, man and a coppery aftertaste of blood.

A mixture that spelled the end of me.

12

I didn't make bad decisions in my life.

Every move I made was calculated, measured, purposeful.

I'd failed in my life. Because success was impossible without some kind of failure. But all those failures didn't signify mistakes since I had something to gain from each of them. I was made of my failures, not my success.

But *this* was a mistake.

I knew it.

I wasn't gaining anything.

No, I was certain I was losing a lot.

Everything.

He'd already taken enough, there was nothing to control how he got the rest of me.

It was a foregone conclusion.

I wanted more from him. I'd given in, let him inside me, in every way possible, and then he'd disappeared. Not technically, since after we'd dressed—me in a new skirt, luckily I kept spare clothes in a closet in my office—he'd left the office without a word, but with one last brutal kiss. He'd been waiting in the car when I finished for the day and gone straight to a business dinner.

He'd been there on the ride home, the energy in the air humming with the knowledge of each other's bodies, each other's pleasure, and more importantly, pain. The way his gaze had seared into me, I expected him to touch me, to fuck me in the back of the car, with nothing but thin glass separating us from Ralph.

I ached for it.

But he didn't.

His fists stayed clasped atop his knees, gaze cementing me in place the whole ride. I knew what he was doing. He was manipulating me, asserting his power with nothing more than a look and the memory of his brutal touch still fresh on my skin.

I submitted to it. Didn't fight it, though my entire body was desperate for him like I assumed a drug addict might've been for a fix.

I'd been careful to avoid drugs because anything that had the power to alter your mind had the power to control your mind. And that's what Jacob was doing, altering everything about my thought system, so nothing, least of all my thoughts, were under my control.

Drugs could ruin lives.

Not like people could.

Humans were the worst substance on earth.

I'd gotten out of the car on shaky legs, said goodbye to Ralph and walked up to my apartment.

Alone.

He didn't come in the shadows, like I'd lain awake expecting him to do all night. He was controlling me with his absence.

Saturday morning, instead of going grocery shopping, or working like I should've been, I was here. Trying to take my control back or abandon it completely.

For once, I was certain of nothing before acting.

"Are you sure this is the place, miss? my driver asked, looking up at the building and the surrounding street in concern.

The weekend was only time I could do this, since I didn't have Ralph to ask questions and this was the one day Jacob wasn't with me as I informed him I'd be in my apartment.

With additional security. Whom I'd sent home.

I didn't need anyone tracking my movements. Hence me using a new car service. Reputable, of course. Expensive. And discreet.

I glanced around. It was a bad neighborhood, there was no mistaking it. But New York was a bad neighborhood in itself, I'd almost gotten murdered in one of the most expensive parts of the city, so the men loitering on the street staring at the car didn't bother me. Outright danger was always safer than false security. "Yes, I'm sure," I replied. "I expect you can stay here until I call to tell you otherwise."

The driver glance at the same men I did with unease, but he met my eyes. "Of course, ma'am." The tone was professional. He knew who I was. He knew that if his answer was anything else that I'd have him fired and that he wouldn't work in the city again.

I nodded once, opening the door and closing it purposefully. I didn't glance at the men, not when they whistled and shouted. I strode to the building purposefully like I had every right to be there. People tended not to target those who radiated confidence, ownership of the situation—because cowards only tended to attack those whose grip on themselves seemed tenuous. My grip on myself was tenuous, but I was an expert at making it seem otherwise.

The building was meant to have a security door that only opened when residents buzzed up visitors. But at some point, this had been broken. A landlord hadn't come to fix it, since I walked right in without a problem.

The foyer stank like stale Chinese food and a baby screamed from the depths of the building.

There was an elevator to the left, but I chose to take the stairs.

I passed no one in the stairwell. Different smells lingered together. Old takeout, human sweat, general misery. It was a building for the damned and the hopeless. People who had no other choice than to live in the concrete, cold, cramped and old apartment block that was designed to hold hundreds of people's sadness within its walls.

I didn't feel anything about this in general. People made their own decisions, and life was hard. It was a fact. But the thought of Jacob being in here, breathing in this smell every day, letting this hopelessness sink into him...it *unnerved* me.

I was uncomfortable with this feeling. You couldn't survive at the top in this world if the suffering of others affected you.

My hand was steady as I knocked on the door to 25C.

There was no going back now.

There hadn't been any going back since that night in the alley.

The door opened and a shirtless man with a spoon in his mouth and a jar of peanut butter in his hand answered.

One that was most definitely not Jacob.

He was young. Attractive. Had a pleasing body, covered in various scars that weren't as extensive as Jacob's, but still a lot more than a regular human should've collected. His hair was growing out from an Army issue buzz cut. His eyes were too light for what the rest of him communicated.

His gaze traveled up and down my body.

The spoon left his mouth and he grinned in a way that likely made women forget a lot of things, their inhibitions especially.

"I would ask you if you're lost, but you strike me as someone who is exactly where they intend to be at all times," he said by greeting.

His tone was flirty, sexy, playful even, which didn't connect with the scars and the shadows hidden behind his eyes.

"Depending on whether this is the residence of Jacob Lucas, I'll be able to tell you whether I'm exactly where I need to be," I replied, keeping eye contact with him, my voice flat and purposefully unaffected by the teasing in his tone.

Where I needed to be was in my office, researching different companies with data banks we needed, making offers and figuring out how to consolidate each company, figure out how to come out on top. That's where the Charlotte Crofton I'd constructed should've been.

Not here, in front of a shirtless man with playful eyes eating peanut butter out of the jar, with scars that were familiar and a happiness that was alien.

The playfulness in his eyes disappeared and his form stiffened.

"I don't know anyone by that name," he lied.

I quirked my brow. "You're a good liar. But I'm better. I'm his employer. I'm not here for trouble."

His eyes went up and down me pointedly. "Yeah, you are. Just not the kind Jacob's used to," he muttered.

Something in the words jerked me. There was a familiarity with Jacob in his tone. It was strange. I didn't think of Jacob having people who knew him well enough to make such statements. I didn't think of Jacob having anyone. It made me jealous in a way that I couldn't explain. Shouldn't I be happy that there was a man with smiling eyes that knew Jacob? But I wanted him to myself, I didn't want smiles or happiness for Jacob, I wanted something more than that. I wanted him to myself. My greed knew no bounds.

"Are you going to make me make this difficult?" I asked, taking half a second to recover.

His eyebrow went up, as if he could calculate what that small pause meant. "As much as I would *love* to see you make it difficult, I feel like Jacob might kill me," he replied playfully. "Though he's likely gonna kill me for giving out his location. It's just a matter of how violently I'd like to die."

He made me want to smile, this man. He was easy. Despite the scars on his body telling me that life had been hard to him.

He reminded me of Molly.

He was the kind of man I'd like for Molly to have. Someone who made her laugh but had the hardness of the world inside him so he could protect her from it. Granted, I wanted him not to live in squalor eating peanut butter out of the jar shirtless in the middle of a workday, all things that Molly would likely love about the man.

I waited as he pretended to think on his statement. It was rather amusing, and the view wasn't exactly bad, despite the surroundings. I was not a person accustomed to waiting. I knew there was something about me that made people not want to make me wait. They wanted to get me out of their presence as quickly as possible.

Not this man.

"You gonna put in a good word for me when you see him?" he asked. "Plead the case about how it'd be such a hassle to dispose of my body?"

The corner of my mouth twitched. "I'm known to be convincing, so I'll make sure you don't end up in the Hudson."

He regarded me, sharp and soft at the same time. "I think you'll make sure he doesn't either."

His words struck me again, but then he was rattling off an address and I stopped my thoughts in their tracks. I didn't know the area well, but I knew that it wasn't likely to have many residential buildings.

"You gonna write it down?"

I straightened my spine. "I'll remember."

He grinned. "Yeah."

He didn't say anything else. He didn't need to. There was a knowing in that single word that made me uncomfortable.

I nodded. "Well, thank you, Mr...?"

"Everyone calls me Shooter," he said.

"What does the IRS call you?" I asked, my voice curt.

He grinned, big and wild. "They don't call me much, since I'm kind of not in contact with them anymore," he said playfully. "Usually I have to kill the people I tell my first name, but I'll make an exception for you. Donald." He held out his hand.

I raised my brow as I shook it. Donald was the least likely name for a man like this. It was comical enough for me to lose the control over my expression and my mouth moved less than an inch.

Of course this man noted it. He only grinned wider. "See why everyone calls me Shooter?"

I let go of his hand. "Thank you, Donald."

His laugh followed me down the stairs.

"Are you sure you don't want me to wait?" the driver asked, peering into the seemingly abandoned warehouse with obvious unease. "Doesn't sit right, leaving you here alone."

He had seemed to forget about the professional distance that was required of him for these situations. I wasn't sure why. It's not like I'd treated him warmly enough to warrant him caring about my wellbeing other than making sure he got the hefty tip that people like me were known for giving services such as this.

Maybe it was the concern for his tip and not my wellbeing that had him acting out.

"I'm not alone," I said in response. "Thank you for your services and your discretion today," I continued, reaching into my purse and handing him the envelope I'd had in there for this exact situation.

He took it with wide eyes. "You walked into that apartment building with *that* in your purse?" he asked in disbelief. "I would've walked in with you if I'd known."

I almost smiled at the five foot nothing man who was barely over twenty wanting to protect me. Or protect the tip that would likely pay his rent for the next two months.

"Well, now I don't have it and I assure you I'll be okay."

I was out of the car before I could taste the uncertainty in my own voice. I was most certainly not going to be okay. Not if I went in there. The smart, Charlotte Crofton approved thing to do would've been to get back into the town car and right back up to my ivory tower where this place was nothing but a dark spot on the landscape. Where he was nothing but a searing hole in my memory.

Some part of me knew if I did that, I'd never see Jacob again. That I might be less safe from assassination attempts, but my overall physical and mental security would be better off.

I walked into the warehouse anyway.

I strode around the yawning space before me, my heels echoing through the wrought iron walls, the sound catching on the wind breezing through the boarded-up windows. A bitter smell carried in the air, forgotten poverty, hidden demons. Forgotten sorrow, hidden pain.

There wasn't much in the space, an old weights bench that had rudimentary weights on it and little more. In the other corner, a single cot, made immaculately with military corners. A rusty mini fridge was humming beside it. Though this was little more than a ramshackle warehouse in the middle of the Manhattan that was forgotten by the glossy Matthattanites and inherited by those with no new hotspot to migrate to, it was clean. Bare. But clean.

I focused on the ice blue eyes that had been watching me. He hadn't acknowledged me when I entered the abandoned building, though he likely knew I was here the second I stepped my heeled foot onto the floor.

No, he would've known I was here since the car pulled up at the curb. Maybe even before, if Donald had called to warn him.

He didn't speak, didn't even look surprised to find me in his...whatever this was.

Jacob would never live in actual squalor.

He was just squatting in a building.

Despite the fact he had an apartment, paid for and empty on Park Avenue. Despite the fact he was earning enough with me to rent his own property wherever he wished. But he was here.

It didn't make sense.

Then again, Jacob didn't make sense.

He stood statuesque in the middle of the room. It was jarring, that image. Such a beautiful and broken damaged man in an ugly, broken and damaged space.

He didn't fit.

There was nowhere that Jacob fit. Inside me, maybe. In situations where he took human life.

"You live here," I deduced.

He nodded once, never breaking eye contact, not questioning why I was here.

I stared back with effort. "Why?"

He knew the depth of my question.

He glanced up, breaking his eyes from mine. I should've felt relief, instead the loss of his attention was physical.

I followed his gaze. Like any warehouse, the ceilings were high, towering above our heads with rusty and crumbling exposed beams. Old spider webs blanketed the ceiling.

"The décor?" I guessed dryly.

The silence yawned before he answered.

I'd come to expect it. Get used to it, even if it was something that I never tolerated in whatever passed for my everyday life. I didn't wait for people to answer, I demanded it. And most people were either scared of me, wanted something from me, or hated me enough to give me an immediate one.

Not him.

I found myself willing to wait until forever for one. I feared and hoped it would take forever to get them all.

The answers.

"Space," he rasped. His eyes flickered around the empty expanse of the room. "You don't get that anywhere here. Not without a few million and then some. Didn't have that. Couldn't live in the box my pension gave me. Even with supplementary income." He paused. I knew the supplementary income he spoke of. Killing people. I didn't imagine death came cheap, but then again, life was cheaper than a deposit on an apartment building in New York City.

"I was a POW," he continued. "Seven months, three days, eight hours, three minutes and thirty-three seconds." His tone was brisk. No nonsense. I recognized it.

It was empty.

Almost.

Hiding the pain.

It was the same one I used every day of my life.

"They put me in a box just tall enough so I could stand, lie down if I curled into a ball. Next to my own filth. They wanted me like that. An animal." His eyes glowed, the wolf alive, the monster in control.

I got it now. The wolf wasn't just alive, it was what was *keeping* him alive. You couldn't go through *that* without finding a way to cope.

I killed everything human in me to survive what I went through.

He did the same but called up something less than human. Something more.

"It's what they got, an animal," he continued. "I came back. Went home. But my family, friends, they were waiting for the man that left. He was gone. I had a wild animal in his place who didn't know how to be free. Who suffocated in a town that knew, or thought they knew, it all."

I gaped at him, a lone tear rolling down my cheek. I was in too much shock to understand it was the first tear I'd shed since I was sixteen years old. "Why here?" I choked. "New York is one of the busiest and stifling cities on earth."

His gaze was hot and uncomfortable as the ice-cold tear

trailed through my makeup. "Exactly. I could get lost in it. The horde. The concrete. It's not the crowd that makes me feel stifled, Boots. It's the space. It's the wide-open spaces of my hometown."

"But you need space," I said, glancing up at the roof yawning above us.

He stepped forward, then caught himself before he could come too close, his jaw hardening and the fists at his sides clenched. "Yeah. When I'm alone, so I can sleep, I need it. As much as I can get. Because that box apartment was a fuckin' joke. Couldn't close my eyes in there for a second. Not when it took me back there."

I flinched at the roughness of his voice, the way the pain filtered through the air to fill this wide-open space. I thought about that building that was held together with questionable labor practices, sorrow and poverty. No way he could exist there. Survive. Whatever little of him that was left.

I'd wished he'd talked more, throughout the time I'd known him and come to be obsessed with him. I'd craved him to speak more than clipped sentences and hoarse demands when I was at his mercy. No other time had I been more aware of the phrase 'be careful what you wish for.'

I wanted to go to him. Comfort him. Though I'd never been good at that, my hands itched to run through his hair, to give him whatever support I could. But the way he held himself warned me against that. He'd erected a barrier between us, one I didn't have the skills or kind words to climb over.

"Makes sense," I said finally, the words lackluster and hollow. "I'm sorry," I ended up on more than a whisper.

His eyes glowed. "I used to be too. Not one to dwell on the past, or cry over shit. But I did curse those mother fuckers every time I tried to sleep in the ranch my grandfather built from the ground up. When my sister looked to me with real terror in her eyes. When I had to leave and never contact them for a year, because the alternative is too much. Being faced with my own weakness is not enough." He searched my face. "I wish I could kill them thirty times over for that. It's the soundtrack to my night-mares. Their screams. My lullaby. I hated it. Until now. I can't bring myself to hate it that much. Or at all." He stepped forward, not crossing the barrier between us, but bowling through it.

He was in front of me, not touching me, with his hands at least. His next words wrapped around me so tightly I almost couldn't breathe. I didn't want to. Didn't need to.

"Now, I'm thinkin', Boots, that I don't want to bring them back from the grave and kill them again like I have for four hundred and eighty-four days." His hand clutched my jaw. "Wanna fuckin' *thank* them. For that. For turning me into this. If I wasn't this. Then I wouldn't have been brought to you." His entire frame stiff-ened. "That man in that alley might have been successful." He shuddered. "And that in itself, you livin' in your world. That's worth seven months, three days, eight hours, three minutes and thirty-three seconds in a box. Easily. A trade I'd likely make again. Without blinkin', baby."

I didn't blink at his words.

Didn't breathe.

Not without his command at least.

Because this was the last point of battle.

It was the point of surrender.

And I did.

13

He was now in my offices for meetings with employees.

Vaughn was told this was because the possibility of Kershaw having turned another one of my staff. Which wasn't outside the realm of possibility since it seemed it had taken little effort with my uncle, who was *family*, not that that meant anything when it came to business. My staff didn't share my blood and definitely didn't share any warm thoughts toward me. But they were treated well, were paid a lot and had signed non-disclosure agreements that would ruin their lives if they *thought* about doing what my uncle had done, so it was a low risk, but a risk nonetheless.

And that tiny risk was one of the reasons my acquisitions of Kershaw's smaller companies under different shell corporations was kept completely separate from everyone. To cover for this, I made sure we had acquired smaller defense companies with much less impressive data banks than RuberCorp—they would serve our purposes but would not make us the most competitive outfit on the market. In my business history, I'd never settled for second.

If Vaughn was surprised about my seeming lack of frustration about this, he wasn't showing it. Then again, I never seemed frustrated. Even when I was in debt up to my neck, eating one meal a day and still paying fifteen people's salaries. Calm was key in battle and in business.

Which was what I had been trying to act in Jacob's presence, he had entered a handful of seconds before my meeting.

Jacob was a battle.

Despite the fact he'd already won, I continued to cling onto my façade of calm. Until his hands touched my skin. Then everything slipped off me. No, everything was *torn* off me. His touch was pain. Even amidst the pleasure. It was every sensation that my body and soul was capable of when I was used to nothing at all.

My gaze flickered from my computer screen that had taken all my willpower to focus on, not the wolf eyes that belonged to a man who owned me. Their pull was magnetic, every force in the air was yanking me to them. With the practice of years, I managed to resist any of my baser emotional urges to settle on the small man standing in front of me.

He was not small in stature, but that wasn't how I measured people. I knew enough about him to make him no taller than a thumbtack.

I raised my eyebrow, regarding him without greeting him or inviting him to sit, I didn't plan on him being here for long enough for that.

He stayed silent, glistening hands limply at his sides. Sweat like what was on his forehead. Despite his expensive suit, three-hundred-dollar haircut and Ivy League education—not even half of my employees had a college degree, I didn't agree that they denoted intelligence—he was afraid.

As he should've been.

His Ivy League education didn't teach him a lot, but self-preservation seemed to be in the curriculum.

"Do you know what I have a lot of?" I said after the silence that was long enough to make him uncomfortable.

He shook his head, sweat beaded in droplets trailing down his overly tanned forehead.

"Money," I answered for him, tapping my pen against the desk. "It's rather crass to say, I admit, but it's not exactly a secret is it?" I moved my eyes around the corner office boasting million-dollar views of Manhattan.

Another head shake.

More sweat.

"Money can buy a lot of things. Cars, jewelry, men...women." I quirked my brow as roses blossomed at the sides of his cheeks. "Contrary to popular belief, happiness is also on that list, if you know where to shop." I stopped tapping my pen. "Do you know what money can't buy, perhaps the only thing other than health and talent?" my voice was flat.

Another head shake. Was he mute? Or was he a very lifelike robot having a computer glitch? Or simply a bully, that had a lot to say in the playground, but nothing to squeak in the principal's office?

"Time," I said simply. "Time is a luxury to no one. Everyone has it. Loses it, steals it and wastes it. Which is precisely what you're doing now. Standing in my office, clutching your masculinity like it's your prom date's panties and dripping your perspiration over my favorite rug. I don't like wasting something I can't make, earn or control. So how about you listen to what you know I'm going to say without actually making me say it." I paused and let my words sink in. He can't have been dense enough not to know why he was here, everyone that worked for me was highly intelligent, and this was his third HR complaint, which was why it was being brought to me.

"You're a smart man, considering your parents paid for an education that would've been more useful as a house deposit," I continued. "You know why you're here. And you know the only reason you won't be leaving here with your potted plant and framed fraternity pictures of your glory days in a box, is that you just so happen to be good at your job. When you're actually doing it and not living up to every stereotype one could think of from an upper middle class, entitled, and misogynistic white male." I paused again, wishing I could fire him. No way did I tolerate sexual harassment in the workplace, or any other place, on either side of the gender divide.

"Do I need to say anything else?" I asked. "Or are you going to waste my time some more and make me forget you're good at your job?"

There was a pause, one that had me quirking my brow in warning.

He left the room quickly. I think he might have sprinted if he wasn't clutching the last shreds of his dignity.

I didn't hold an ounce of guilt for that.

He was only simpering and weak in front of powerful women who held his paycheck in their hands. Others, he thought were beneath him. I would have fired him for that alone, but it was very hard to fire someone these days. I could have, I had lawyers on retainer for these very scenarios, but I was tired. Too tired to deal with that. So he got three more strikes than I usually gave. A glimmer of a fourth and he was out. And I'd make sure that he never worked in this city again.

My gaze, of its own volition, flickered past the door to the corner of the room where he stood.

I swallowed roughly as the energy flickered, turned so charged even the letter opener to the left of my trembling hand couldn't cut it.

He no longer was the statuesque mute he'd been moments ago, and he traveled the distance of my office in long, unhurried steps.

I did nothing but sit and watch until he rounded my desk, yanked my chair around roughly and leaned his muscled arms on either side, boxing me in as he bent down.

"You missed one," he murmured.

I blinked at him, drowning in his gaze. "One what?" I managed to choke the two words, the powerful CEO from moments before was now a puddle on the floor.

175

His mouth was so close to mine it brushed it when he spoke. "Passion. You can't buy that shit." He moved so his rough stubble scratched my skin and his mouth landed on my neck.

I clutched the arms of my chair as his teeth grazed my collarbone.

"You can buy a lot, Boots," he continued, voice thick. "Fancy clothes." His rough hands caught on the delicate silk of my blouse. "Sparkly shit." They moved up the column of my neck to brush against the diamond studs in my ears before moving back to the arms of my chair. "But you can't buy an orgasm that makes you fly from this earth the moment I sink my cock inside you." Wolf eyes met mine. "You can't buy me," he growled. Then his mouth claimed mine with ferocity that had me spiraling in my own head, clutching for coherent thought and moaning in protest as his lips left mine. "You can't buy me, but you fuckin' own me already."

He straightened, the air cold and bitter where he used to be. I felt empty without his body touching mine, desire fizzled over my skin and beads of perspiration blossomed at my temples from my body's crazed reaction.

His face was a mask once more yet the wolf was in charge of his eyes.

My thighs pulsed.

"Take off your panties," he ordered, voice flat.

My nails raked at the sides of the chair. In a painful motion, I tore my eyes from his to glance at the oak door which had slammed shut moments before. It was unlocked. Since the first time in the office, I'd made sure it was locked for the other times —there had been many—Jacob fucked me on my desk, or the sofa, or against the window. I had multiple pairs of fresh panties in the bathroom directly off my office.

Which was essential, since Jacob and I didn't use protection. There was no need to. I had his medical records. He had nothing that I could catch. Nor did I, I'd been religious about protection, though it was impossible for me to get pregnant. I'd gotten my tubes tied at twenty-four.

"What if you change your mind?" the doctor asked, *with no small amount of judgment. I thought I paid her enough not only to not judge me but to not question my decision.*

I glanced to the framed photo with her and a young boy on her desk. I nodded at it. "What if you change yours? Your son is all you wanted when he was young and pure. But what if he grows up to commit some horrific crime? Assaults women? Or just turns into an ugly person whether it be by nature or nurture? You can't change your mind then, can you? Blood dictates the fact you can't. So my decision is no less permanent than yours. If you have a problem acting in the capacity in which your doctorate dictates you should, then I'll happily find another doctor."

She performed the service, though her bedside manner left a lot to be desired.

Not that I cared.

She did her job, there were no complications and I was satisfied.

Still, even though the chance of getting pregnant was eliminated from that surgery, I always practiced safe sex. Even though I got my sexual partners to show me their latest STD results.

I was nothing if not careful and businesslike in all corners of my life. The men I chose to have sex with were much the same so they didn't hesitate to provide the papers I requested and took the ones I offered.

Sex was polite and ordered. Just another business transaction.

Not with Jacob.

I didn't even *think* about protection. There was no protection with Jacob. The only thing he protected me from was death. Everything else he took himself.

And I didn't want anything between Jacob and me. I wanted it raw, I wanted as much of him as I could take.

"Do I have to ask a second time?" he warned.

I swallowed, my body responding with more hunger at his

harsh tone.

"Eyes," he growled. "You'll give me your eyes while you do it."

I immediately snapped my eyes to him and swallowed a little moan at the contact. I lifted my ass slightly so I could push up my skirt to gain purchase on my lace panties.

He hissed a breath between his teeth and his hands clenched at his sides as I pulled them downward, but that was his only outward reaction. His face was blank.

His eyes were feral with desire. Ice and fire.

I dropped my soaked panties to the ground, my eyes never leaving his.

"Jacob," I pleaded.

I leaned forward with my arm, intent on yanking his belt buckle to bring him toward me.

The pure energy exuded by his glare stopped me. "I tell you to move?" he hissed. "You don't move. You don't speak." He paused until I lowered my hand once more. "I want you to touch yourself."

I sucked in another breath at his controlled words and the erotic command. I should've bristled at his command. I didn't take them, I gave them. Both inside and outside the bedroom. But not with Jacob.

"I'm not patient," he warned.

My breath was shallow and frenzied as I trailed my hand up my thigh.

"Spread your legs."

I complied, my hand still moving.

My skirt was now hitched to almost my waist. I was exposed to him, at his mercy, things which shouldn't have turned me on yet the moment my finger touched my soaked flesh I cried out with the contact.

His jaw hardened and the veins in his arms pulsed as his eyes didn't leave mine. Didn't move down to my inner thighs, where I was bare and exposed.

No. He was watching me.

I regarded him through hooded eyes and decided this was the most erotic moment of my life. A moment filled with passion, violence and I wasn't even being touched by anyone but myself.

Then in a blur of movement, my chair was shoved back behind my desk, Jacob at my back. Before I could speak or even move my hand from its spot, the door burst open.

"Don't stop," he growled in my ear before straightening and stepping back slightly.

Vaughn entered the room, his kohl-rimmed eyes focused on his iPad.

"We've got three contracts that have just come in and I've got this new software for you to look over and approve. It's not cheap but—"

He cut off abruptly as his eyes left the screen and fastened on me. Then Jacob. Then back to me.

My hand was still on my sensitive, soaking bare flesh, every inch of my body was pulsating, yet I kept my gaze even and blank. I imagined Jacob did the same though I didn't dare look at him.

Vaughn obviously saw through our facades, or at least mine, because he grinned. "They can always wait," he said slyly, clutching the iPad to his chest.

I nodded. "Yes, I'll go over them later on this afternoon," I replied, my voice ice. Only because I needed it to disguise the fire in my lungs. My finger continued rubbing, the authority from Jacob pulsating through the room with an energy that didn't need words. This was quite possibly the craziest thing I'd ever done.

But I couldn't find the control to stop.

I didn't want to stop.

Put me in Times Square, I'd likely still lightly be brushing my sensitive flesh as long as Jacob was there. As long as Wolf Eyes fastened on mine.

"I want you to check over HR files and see if we can find a way to let go of Derek without a lawsuit, and if not, go and talk to his secretary and make sure she hasn't been keeping quiet about something," I added, changing my mind about trying to fire him immediately.

Vaughn kept grinning. "Consider it done." His eyes flicked to Jacob. "I'll let you get back to....work. I'll ensure no one disturbs you."

On that promise, he turned on his spiked heel and left.

I sucked in a breath.

Silence echoed through my ears, my body thrumming with hot desire. My body was frozen, though I ached to move.

"Did I tell you to stop?" Jacob's voice was a low rasp as he stepped forward, his callused palm running down my neck in warning before slipping under the lace of my bra.

"The contract," I breathed. "It's more than a standard employee agreement."

I didn't know why I brought it up at this moment.

No, I knew *exactly* why I brought it up.

Because having Jacob's hands on me, inside me, having him in ways I'd had no one and giving him things I didn't know I had to give, I wanted to make it clear, what I'd done.

His hand circled my nipple and I cried out. "I know."

My gaze snapped up. "You know?"

He circled my neck with his other hand, tilting my head backward. "Of course I fuckin' know. You control everything around you. And you were faced with the one thing you couldn't control, me. What I awoke in you." His hand moved from my nipple down, mouth on my neck, he threaded his fingers against mine and entered me.

I bit my lip as a new intense pleasure erupted over me instantly and violently.

"So you wanted to control me. Moreover, you wanted to control yourself." His finger moved and his eyes watched my reaction. "What did it say, Boots?"

"Tha-that," I stuttered as another finger entered me. "That you were mine. That you were to engage in no sexual relationships with any other females while you were in my employ."

"I was yours the second I entered that alley," he growled, accusing me of that, as if it were under my control. "Don't need a piece of paper to tell me that. And no fuckin' way could I touch anyone before you. And after you? Impossible."

Then he fucked me on the desk.

ONE WEEK LATER

"You can cook?" I asked, though the pleasing smell of garlic and tomato answered my question for me.

I had changed out of my suit and was barefoot, barefaced and in my kitchen. With Jacob. My mask was not off, though, because neither was his. He was closer to me than I'd let any other human being, but there was a distance I'd never had with any person. Because of the part of Jacob that wasn't a person. The part of me that wasn't one either.

Jacob refilled my wine—the pink stuff that I usually hid from company, it didn't make sense to hide anything from Jacob since he had ripped me apart and inspected all of my hidden depravity.

"Gotta eat," he replied. "In every other part of my life, been eatin' shit—metaphorically, of course. So when I'm feedin' my body, I may as well give it somethin' worth eating since my mind is force fed rancid shit."

I blinked at him rapidly. At the personal and philosophical and heartbreaking sentence. It seemed that Jacob was done hiding things from me too. Some things.

He didn't break my gaze.

"Though it seemed just as my mind was getting used to being fed with garbage I get something more. Something much more," he said, letting the words soak into me like the smell of his cooking, and then he turned to the stove.

I watched his back, muscled and large, covered by a plain tee. His ass was nothing short of magnificent in faded jeans.

My sleek, white and chic kitchen was designed for a lot of things. To make a statement, to be timeless, to make sure I lived up to the image I portrayed to the world, to distance me from the homely yet shabby kitchen of my youth. But it wasn't designed for *Jacob*.

My life, carefully structured, curated, controlled, hadn't been designed for Jacob, but somehow it felt made for him at the same time.

"I've never done this," I said.

Jacob waited a long time to speak, as was his way. I imagined he was still unaccustomed to having conversations such as these. Or conversations at all. The clank of cutlery against plates took the place of my words before he answered.

"What? Eaten dinner somewhere that wasn't your desk or some pretentious fucking restaurant where they serve two bites of food and call it dinner?"

I raised my brow. "Have you been talking to Molly?"

She hadn't returned from India, had decided to extend her trip, as I knew she would. She checked in now and then, her security checked in twice daily.

He sipped his water, not beer—he didn't drink. Nor did he answer. Jacob never answered rhetorical questions, nor actual questions, well, not with anyone else but me.

"No, I mean sat down at my dining table that cost twenty-five thousand dollars and eaten a meal on it," I replied, putting the food in my mouth, savoring the flavors. Savoring the feast that was Jacob sitting beside me.

He watched me, as he always did. "So what you're saying is we're eating a twenty-five thousand dollar dinner." He paused, regarding his half-eaten plate. "Not bad."

I stared at him, the corner of my mouth turned up to a smile. Not something anyone but Vaughn or Molly had made me do.

It was a pivotal moment with the man who I always thought would bring me pain—and I'd been content with that. He was giving me more than pain. He was giving me a reason to smile amongst the pain.

It was terrifying.

Because he was Jacob, he sensed the way the air changed with the moment, he didn't say a word, he continued to eat the food he'd made at a table that I'd never sat at, while I lived a version of my life I never could have imagined.

A life I never wanted.

I wasn't even sure if I still wanted it now.

But it wasn't about want with Jacob.

Or need.

It was just Jacob.

I continued to eat the food he made, while my soul digested the truth, his permanence. Molly was right. A man like this was never going to be temporary. I'd feel him here, at this cold table, in my cold apartment, inside my frigid heart, long after he was gone.

And he'd go.

Because I was getting close to finding a way to take Kershaw's company out from under him. And once I did that, I'd take his power. He'd no longer be a threat.

He might try and kill me again, but I doubted it.

So Jacob would leave.

And I'd have the cold table, colder heart and agonizing memories.

My plate was swiped from under me, I hadn't even realized I'd finished.

Jacob's fingers snatched my chin, forcing my gaze out of my own mind and into the present. Into his present.

"I can think of some other things we can do to get your money's worth of this table," he growled.

I was wet instantly.

He didn't waste time in lifting me up, splitting my legs, ripping yet another skirt and pair of panties and having an entirely different kind of meal at the table.

One that was worth quite a lot more than twenty-five thousand dollars.

I hadn't forgotten about the painting.

I could never.

But I also never let myself entertain the idea that Jacob would have a reason to be inside my bedroom and therefore have a reason to see it.

And when he walked into the bedroom for the first time, after he'd given me two orgasms at twelve thousand dollars each, my legs were wrapped around his hips and he was inside me, so I didn't expect him to be focusing on the décor.

But this was *Jacob*.

He was not a man to be distracted, even by the best sex of my life. I knew the second his eyes met the gaze of the wolf on my wall. Because he froze, his already painful grip intensified.

My head turned with his. "Molly painted it," I breathed, my voice fractured. "She made me hang it here." I paused. "But I would've put it here anyway. It's where you belong. Watching me."

He jerked. Then his eyes, the ones that had watched over my nightmares focused on me. He didn't say anything. He kissed me. And then he fucked me brutally, without holding back, without anything but the wolf inside him.

And that was saying it all.

14

My thoughts were soft around the edges, fuzzy. Like I'd drunk two bottles of pink wine. Fermented grapes or strong liquor was the only thing that could affect me like this. Even those didn't have me feeling so...content. My thoughts were usually hard, angular and ordered. Not subject to emotions. And certainly not subject to a man.

Until now.

Though nothing was fixed. Or sorted. He was still an enigma, still holding me at arm's length with words left unsaid that nearly burst the room apart, but it didn't matter.

Not in this moment.

It didn't even matter that Kershaw may or may not still be plotting to kill me. That my uncle might have a hand in it. That my company's stocks were suffering while I publicly seemed to be doing nothing since the pull out of the merger.

That was out *there*. Floors below. In the real world. The place I always lived.

I hadn't taken a vacation in six years. I was enjoying one now. Not an island, because Vaughn was right, no woman was an island, even if I lived on one. Jacob was an island, with rugged, dangerous cliffs, like the backdrop of Cathy and Heathcliff's story. I always knew I'd find a vacation in darkness and pain. In Jacob's darkness and pain.

I ached to know more about his captivity. How he got out. I wanted to claw at his demons, make my mark on them. But there was nothing more said. And I had yet to expose some of the ugliest parts of me.

The harsh ringing of a phone interrupted me, cutting through my mind. I frowned, it wasn't my phone, but out of instinct I hopped up and padded across my bedroom to Jacob's jacket.

My hand outstretched, I paused.

Jacob was private. He barely spoke to me. And while we spent all of our time together, he'd just done the most intimate things anyone had ever done to me and killed for me *twice*, answering his phone seemed like a personal gesture. One for boyfriends and girlfriends who enjoyed simplicity.

Simple would never be a word to describe Jacob. Or me. Or us.

Despite that, the logic of it all, my hand had a mind of its own and snaked into the jacket and had the cool metal at my ear before I could fully understand what was going on.

"Hello, Jacob's phone," I answered, putting on the professional voice I'd distanced myself from as late. Well, distanced myself from insofar as I didn't adopt it with Jacob.

I was met with a small intake of breath, then silence.

I waited a beat.

"Hello?" I repeated, my eyes on the door to my bathroom, were the sounds of a shower still pattered lightly in the background.

"Um, hi," a small female voice greeted, sounding uncertain. "This is Jacob's phone?" she clarified.

"Yes, it is," I replied.

I knew I shouldn't have done this. The way she said his name, the emotion drenched in that one word told me something.

Had I just addressed a woman he was sleeping with? An ex-girlfriend? His secret wife that lived on Long Island with two kids and a dog?

Inner me shook her head. No. Jacob didn't even wear suits because they caged him. A wedding ring? A promise of forever? No. He would never.

"I-is Jacob there?" she asked in a small voice.

I glanced at the door where the shower was still running, gritting my teeth. "Yeah, he's just in the shower for a moment, would you like me to take a message?" I asked politely.

It wasn't this soft-spoken woman's fault that Jacob had more than one woman on the go and I didn't want to be rude. Though my insinuation from the shower wasn't exactly kind if she was his estranged wife.

She sucked in a breath. "He's in the shower?" she asked, and instead of anger or jealous, she sounded strangely exuberant. "And you're..." She trailed off.

"Charlotte," I replied with hesitation. Was she waiting for my name and then going to try and stalk me and kill me? Because I already had one person trying to do that and it would be awkward for her to meet Jacob as my bodyguard when she came in to go all *Single White Female* on me.

"Charlotte," she breathed. "You're Charlotte and he's in the shower," she almost sang the words.

My eyes never moved from the door. "And he is taking an extremely long shower, too," I muttered. "He better not be using the last of my Jo Malone body wash."

She immediately burst out laughing and the sound was like bells. Literally feminine and light and nothing I could ever reproduce. It reminded me of Molly. It caught me off guard, mostly because I wasn't used to making anyone laugh, nor was I used to uttering thoughts out loud like I just had.

"I don't mean to be rude," I said when she finished laughing. "But who are you?"

She paused. "I'm Tina," she replied, waiting a beat, for me to say something. When I didn't, she continued. "Jacob's sister."

I pursed my lips. "Oh right, Jacob's sister," I said, trying not to betray my surprise.

I had assumed he was some kind of rogue orphan who was raised in the woods. He certainly didn't seem like he had a sister whose laugh sounded like bells.

"He usually doesn't answer my calls," she said, her voice not as cheerful as before. "I'm a little surprised to get one, and with a woman on the other end," she explained.

"Yes, well, I'm surprised to answer it. My hand had a mind of its own," I replied honestly. "Curiosity killed the cat, but I'm totally hoping it won't do the same to the Charlotte."

Another laugh. "Well, I'm glad you did. Answer that is." There was a pause. A loaded one. One that seemed to travel sadness even across the phone line. "He's...okay then?" she asked in a small voice.

I paused. Could anyone ever describe Jacob as okay? Unhinged? Yes. Homicidal? Definitely. Addictive and dangerous? Double yes.

But okay? Never.

"Yeah. He is," I replied simply. This woman was obviously concerned, yet she still laughed easily, and despite Jacob not returning her calls, she still called him. The shower turned off. "I can get him for you, if you want?" I offered, not liking the wrath I would get from Jacob.

But his sister sounded, concerned. Nice. And overall, haunted by whatever lurked behind his eyes.

The fact that he hadn't answered her calls in what I guessed was a long while had me willing to risk the wrath. I couldn't imagine not going a week without talking to Molly. Even if I was lying to her. Though I guessed I could rule out one lie, Jacob and I *were* dating. In the sense that he followed me around and tried to stop someone from killing me and fucked me within an inch of my life.

"No," she shot quickly. "No, no. He'll answer, when he's ready. It's just..." She paused. "I'm happy that *you* did. Answer. And I really hope I meet you one day." Her voice was small.

"I do too," I told her back, just as honestly even though I knew that was never going to happen.

Jacob was never going to be in the space to be okay enough to be around a sister who still laughed, whose voice was still light and whose heart was obviously still hopeful.

He'd told me that who he was before was dead. I believed him. He wouldn't show this woman the ghost of himself. Or the monster he'd turned into. I wondered if she knew that, deep down.

Probably not.

People that laughed with strangers normally hadn't abandoned hope.

"Bye, Charlotte," she said, more than a whisper. "And thank you."

Then she was gone.

Then the door opened, and I was presented with the male goodness of Jacob, dripping wet with droplets of water trailing down the ridges of his abs. He took me in too. Not hungrily. No, he focused on the phone at my ear.

Yeah, here came the wrath.

I waited. Held my breath in fear and anticipation.

But his face stayed empty, eyes flaring slightly over my naked body, covered in bruises from his beautiful assault.

"Your sister called," I said after a long silence.

His jaw twitched. The movement was tiny.

But it was movement.

It was reaction.

Maybe there was hope yet.

"And you answered," he replied.

I nodded. "Are you mad?"

He moved across the room instead of answering. He came to stand in front of me. His towel was slung low on his waist, revealing the scars that proved why Tina was calling her brother's ghost.

Well, it explained some of it.

The deadness in his eyes explained the rest.

"I thought I might be," he said by reply.

"But you're not?"

He shook his head once. "Not mad. But I think I might punish you anyway."

And I let him.

"Will you tell me about your sister?"

My words broke the long and easy silence that had followed the long, not at all easy and definitely not silent sex.

He tensed underneath me, his arms tightening.

I didn't think he was going to answer. Even now, with the entire dynamic between us in tatters, with us being more intimate than I guessed he had been with anyone, he still picked and chose which of my questions he answered. Especially the personal ones. I didn't press him, demand answers, demand respect like I would've with anyone else. Because he gave me his respect without having to demand it, and the answers were when he chose to do so. I got all the answers I really needed in a meaningful glance.

"She's younger than me," he said finally. "Three years. Looked up to me since she could hold her own head up. Don't know why, even before, I wasn't exactly the person anyone should be lookin' up to, but that was a responsibility I took on, like I did looking out for her. Tried to make myself into someone worth looking up to."

He paused. And I heard a lot in that pause. *Felt* a lot in that pause. A whole lifetime that might've been, had reality not been so cruel.

"I did a good enough job," he continued. "For a while. Then I took a road so well paved with good intentions. But I'm not makin' excuses, placing blame. Every choice I made was my own. Every life I ended, every trigger I pulled, that was done with purpose, for a start, then with a kind of sick satisfaction as I fed some kind of hunger that I'd created." His arms tightened around me, finger pads pressing into my hips creating fresh bruises to accompany the fading ones he'd already put there.

"Hunger turned into something altogether different being locked in that box, unable to feed it. So I started gnawing on my insides, killing parts of myself if only to feed the wolf. I wasn't human when I got out. What I did to the fuckers who put me in that box..."

He trailed off.

I waited.

"When I came home, I knew I wasn't gonna fit there," he continued. "Knew that I had buried whatever part of me that belonged there in that hole I'd been kept in. In the holes I'd put others in."

He gritted his teeth. "But I also knew that my sister would hurt if I didn't. My whole family went through hell thinkin' I was dead. So I tried to come back from hell and pretend it hadn't turned me into a demon. Didn't work."

I felt his words deep down, in the part of me I'd covered with ice in order to come back from my own hell.

"That was apparent the second they tried to hug me, touch me, fuckin' *look* at me," Jacob said. "They were scared of me. Knew that. They tried to hide it, of course, 'cause I come from a good family. Solid people. But people who hadn't seen shit that I had, hadn't seen monsters like I'd turned into. But they tried. I tried. Worked on the farm with my brother in law. He was mindful. Good man. So he kept his distance. Made sure I was never

ANNE MALCOM

alone with his wife, kids. Though I'd never hurt them. Consciously."

He pressed harder into my skin.

I bit my lip, drawing blood so I didn't cry out. I knew what pain he was going through to answer my question, so I wasn't going to complain about a shadow of it being projected onto me. I wanted it all projected onto me. I would cut my skin open just so I could have scars like his.

"Didn't sleep well. Nightmares," he continued, voice cold, detached. Clinical.

But it chilled me, because of what a nightmare must've been to a man like Jacob. He'd gone through most of what other people couldn't even comprehend, but the human mind could always conjure up a worse nightmare, depending on how hellish reality got.

"Lack of sleep got the best of me, rested my eyes for a few seconds while my sister's husband was out," Jacob said, his brow twitched slightly, as if he were trying to call up a memory, an answer. "Must've done somethin' to bring Tina into the room. She was worried. Kind, she is. And fearless in her own way. She tried to wake me up. I did wake up. In that hole in the ground thousands of miles away. Woke up as the man I was over there, and the man I was deep inside back home. Broke her arm before I could find my way back."

I was expecting something of the sort. It wasn't like I knew Jacob's story had a happy ending, considering his ending had him living in an abandoned warehouse, stalking the streets of New York finding someone to kill.

"Didn't blame me, not outwardly, of course," he said. "They were scared. Saw it. Plain as day. So I left. Did the thing I should've done in the first place, let them think I was dead. Since it's the closest version of the truth there is."

I waited. Because there was more. I was ravenous for it like

Jacob was for killing. It was pain that fed me, his pain. And he was a feast.

"The dead can still be haunted by the things they've done to the living," he said, eyes clear and cold on me. My breathing shallowed at the monster within them. "The day everything I've done stops haunting me, is the day there's nothing left of me but the monster I wore to do those things. That's the day you kill me. Or you run."

I didn't need to ask if he was serious. I knew it, some part of me knew from the beginning. He was there in the alley, not to save me from monsters, but to keep me for himself. There was a possibility one day, Jacob would stop being human. He was capable of hurting me. Killing me.

"I don't run," I said as response.

Something moved beyond his eyes. "Then you better prepare yourself for death."

I swallowed roughly at his words and let silence take us both captive.

"I don't like the thought of you there, in the middle of all that ruin, living in that," I admitted after the words left unsaid needed to be drowned out with yet another admission.

Why? Does bein' surrounded by something pretty somehow dress up ugly thoughts?" He glanced around the bedroom pointedly.

"No," I said, shocked at how close his words were to my witching hour thoughts. "But it's not worthy of you."

My admission wasn't planned. It betrayed more of my feelings toward him.

Jacob's eyes darkened the same time his hands tightened around me. "You don't know what's worthy of me," he growled.

"Or maybe *you* don't," I replied, not shying away from his brutal gaze.

"It's your tell," he said instead of responding.

I straightened my spine. "What is?"

ANNE MALCOM

"You blink," he said, fingers trailing my eyes. "When you're scared, hesitant or unsure, you blink. Rapidly. Outwardly every decision you make is made with confidence and surety a reigning monarch doesn't likely have." His hand ghosted the sides of my face. "Except for this. The blink. It shows you're scared."

I met his eyes, willing myself not to blink. "I'm not scared. I don't get scared."

"I am," he said. "Freely admit you fuckin' terrify me, more than any war in a desert has or ever would. Because you can destroy me so much more than they ever could." He paused while my heart was in my throat. "Wanna make it, at least with us, that you don't need it. To hesitate. Want you to have something in your life that just...because, without blinking, Boots."

I choked on his words. On the fact he watched me that close to pick up a motion that was as natural as breathing and connecting it to reality. He was watching me. Every inch of me. I knew that. It's what I'd hired him for. But I didn't think he actually *saw* me.

15

I didn't know how he got past the doorman.

I'd fired the original one who had let my would-be murderer in. Not that it had technically been his *fault,* the killer was a professional who excelled at getting his targets, the doorman wasn't exactly trained for such things. But it didn't matter about fault. It mattered that it happened. And though we had somehow been able to keep both incidents from the public, it wasn't something Charlotte Crofton did, let people get away with such things. So I fired him. Not before arranging another job for him with the same salary at a different building.

The new doorman had been vetted and was supposed to be among the best of the best.

Yet the man still got past him.

I wondered how.

A distraction.

A disguise.

Or maybe he'd killed him.

It didn't really matter.

Since he was here, in my apartment.

I had been cooking.

Off guard when the elevator dinged.

I'd assumed it was Molly, here for an impromptu visit now she was finally back from India, or more likely an interrogation about Jacob. Or Vaughn, feigning something about work but likely for the same reason.

It wouldn't be the man himself.

He never said when he was coming, just disappeared and appeared. I was not in control of when I saw him, or what things were like when we were together. But he'd spent every night so far in my apartment. We'd structure our days the same as before, run at five, then shower—together—and to the office. He'd leave before me so he was at the curb when Ralph pulled up.

He knew my schedule. Which meant he knew that this was a rare night I didn't have a meeting, on the books or otherwise. He and Ralph were the only ones who knew about the business meetings I took to acquire various companies and influence Kershaw's shareholders. Talk to lawyers. Not that I was technically staying within the law. But trying to kill me to put a business deal through wasn't within the law either. We were above the clouds in our offices, and above the law in our lives.

Jacob knew everything, he even helped with suggestions late at night, after my body was bruised, scratched, sated, and ruined. His voice was tighter than normal, huskier, because he knew about Ethan Kershaw. But he wasn't so dense as to try and stop me from taking care of it myself. He was not that kind of man, and I was not that kind of woman.

Nor was I the kind of woman to be drinking wine, cooking dinner and trying to pretend I wasn't expecting Jacob to walk through the elevator doors.

But I was doing all of that.

Which was why my guard was down, my half empty bottle of pink wine being replaced into the fridge when I heard the elevator.

Chicken was sizzling on the stove.

I wasn't hungry.

But it was time for food—dinnertime—and I hadn't consumed enough today. It would be foolish of me to neglect my health just because of him. He'd torn my emotional health to shreds, it only made sense to control what I could about my physical body until I gained enough strength to figure out the emotional part.

Turned out the physical part was going to be ruined too.

With just the ding of the elevator.

The heavy footfalls were what put me on alert.

Vaughn's heels would've been thwacking on the marble, sharp and echoing. Molly's chunky heels would've been slightly softer.

These weren't soft.

This was a man.

It wasn't Jacob.

Not his boots.

It took longer than it should've for me to register all this, be it the wine or the mess my mind was. But I still snatched my phone, not hesitating to dial Jacob's number. The ringing started the second the man rounded the corner.

The second to enter my apartment to mean me harm.

I scrambled for the knife I'd washed and put on my drying rack after I cut the chicken, the phone glued to my ear.

The man was faster than I expected.

Three things happened at once.

My hand fastened around the handle of the knife.

Jacob's voice sounded in my ear. "Boots?" His voice was urgent, concerned.

And the man crossed the distance between us, snatching my wrist holding the knife with such a brutal grip I cried out and dropped it.

I wasn't sure if the crack I heard was the metal against metal or my bone snapping in two under my attacker's grip.

"Boots!" I heard one last roar in my ear before my phone smashed to the ground and the beating began.

JACOB

He considered himself a man immune to most all human emotions. Made sense, since he didn't rightly consider himself a human. Hadn't for a long time.

There were only so many times you could take life, draw blood, cause pain before you were no longer worthy of the basic label as human being.

There was a certain number of graves you dug, then you became something else. Something a lot less. And a lot more.

Because unburdened by human emotions, killing came much easier.

Life came much harder.

Which was why he'd killed. To make it easier.

And then it led him to her.

Who made everything so much harder.

She who showed him he was not immune to human emotions, only immunized against everyone but her. She was a fucking plague to his soul.

He loved her.

With whatever ruined, rancid and rotten part of his organ he had left.

He hadn't admitted it to her. Not with words. He knew she knew, on some level. Because she was *her*. She cataloged every-thing around her like a fucking black ops agent. She read people in a second. Could destroy them in just a few more.

She'd done both to him.

Eventually, he'd have to make the hardest kill he'd ever made. Whatever it was between them.

Eventually.

When the threat was eliminated.

The thought of someone actually succeeding in hurting her filled his thoughts with acid. But on some other level, he *wanted* that

"Was it you?" I interrupted, my own tone smooth and cold.

He flinched. Physically flinched as if I'd hit him. Never in my life had I seen my uncle react outwardly to anything. It could've been an act. There was nothing to trust right now. Not even my instincts. Especially not my instincts. I was off-kilter, only half of me breathing, existing.

"Was what me?" he choked out.

I sipped vodka out of my water glass, tacky but it afforded more room for the liquid.

I didn't taste it.

"Were you behind Molly's death? It's obvious that her murder was to do with the merger, since she is not a human being who could physically make an enemy that would want to do..." my voice trailed off.

Blood and strawberries.

Torn skin.

Flesh on the outsides of her body.

Her tattoos obscured as someone had flayed them from her skin.

"*That*," I finished carefully. "No one would do that to someone like Molly unless it was for a purpose. A message." I took another sip. A bigger one.

Still nothing.

"And you made it clear how far you were willing to go in order to make sure this deal went through," I continued, eyeing my uncle evenly. "Made it clear blood didn't mean anything to you. So it stands to reason that if it didn't matter who you shared it with, you wouldn't mind spilling it."

My voice was flatter and colder than I'd ever heard it. It probably should've scared me. I had nothing to be afraid of anymore.

He was gaping at me. I knew Jacob was staring at me. He'd been doing that the entire time. Apart from his handful of words as Abe arrived. Before that, there had been nothing. No empty words to placate me. No empty comfort. He watched me pour the glass to the top, didn't say a word, and he wasn't saying a word now about me accusing my uncle—the only family I had left—of ordering the brutal murder of my sister.

He was used to people doing depraved things, likely.

I knew he was waiting, watching. For Abe's reaction. To catch a whiff of a lie in his inevitable protest. I also knew if he did, that he'd kill him right there in front of me.

I couldn't bring myself to care.

I only hoped if it came to that, he wouldn't get blood on the rug.

Abe was gaping at me. His face turned gray. So gray he looked like he might faint. It looked natural. But what was natural?

"C-charlotte, how could you even—no..." he trailed off, his words fractured. "I took you in," he said little more than a whisper. "I watched you both grow into two different and extraordinary human beings. I love Molly—" He choked out a painful sound that resembled a sob. "I *loved* Molly. I would never." He paused, long and hard, regarding me with his red-rimmed eyes, his gray face.

No doubt he was watching for some reaction, examining my own dry eyes, my placid expression. I'd graduated past him in my business endeavors, and it seemed I'd done the same in my emotional ones.

There was most likely something wrong with me. Even Abe, who I'd been so sure was some kind of sociopath, was having a violent emotional reaction.

I was having that same violent reaction. Inside I was screaming. Tearing at my flesh from the inside out. But that was a me I'd banished to the depths of my mind. She was screaming deep from within some well, never to surface.

"You really think I could do that?" he asked, voice a whisper.

"I think greed makes anyone capable of anything," I replied. "Greed and defeat. Dangerous combinations. And someone wanted to hurt me. They had to know me well enough to know the one and only way to do that was to get to Molly. Anyone who knew my surface would think to destroy the businesses I've built from the ground up, put my everything into. Most everyone who would want to destroy me would destroy my world. Only people who had intimate knowledge of me would know that to destroy me, you would have to destroy my universe."

He flinched again, but he didn't splutter or cry. His eyes evened. Cleared. Turned cold and calculating like that of the uncle who was more recognizable. I found comfort in that. "It wasn't me," he said, voice firm.

I regarded him. Tasted his words. Waited for him to say more, give excuses, explanations, protests, even to blow up on me for accusing him. It's what a guilty person would do. They wouldn't be comfortable in the silence where a lie could be found. Well, a true professional like Jacob could do so, but not many others.

Abe stayed silent.

I nodded once and stood, walking to the bar and pouring him a drink.

He took it when I handed it to him.

"We'll get them, Charlotte," he said. "Whoever did this to Molly."

I drained my drink. "Oh, I know."

I filled my water glass up once more.

Abe clutched his, eyes focusing on my hands. The blood on them. His own hands shook as he put the glass up to his mouth and took a long drink.

I did the same. My hands were not shaking.

"We should put a protection detail on your mother," Abe said after a long silence.

I glanced up from my inspection of the floor. "Why?"

He furrowed his brows. "Because Kershaw is targeting your family, trying to hurt you. She could be in danger."

I smiled. It unnerved him, I could tell. "If he was trying to hurt me, he would not touch my mother. If his intel on me is as good as

I suspect it is, then he'd know leaving my mother alive while killing Molly is the worst thing he could do. If he hurt my mother, he'd be doing me nothing but a favor."

Abe gaped. "She's your *mother*, Charlotte."

I tilted my head, surprised by his shock. "No, she's not. My mother died the same day as my father did. When her cracked psyche finally shattered as she stabbed him to death." I sipped my vodka.

It didn't burn going down.

I walked to the sofa, sitting because I wasn't sure how much longer my legs would hold me.

Jacob watched.

Said nothing.

I looked at Abe. "Maybe there's bits and pieces of her floating around that prickly and black pit of thorns that we can call her mind, but not enough. Shreds. Fragments that will never fit together to make her a person. He would be doing me a favor by killing her, and he doesn't want to do me any favors."

"Something went wrong with you," he said, taking a sip of his drink. No, a gulp was more accurate. His hand was shaking, but now his voice was not. He was slowly regaining control. I never lost it in the first place. "I don't know when it was, but it went wrong. Something was taken from you." He leaned against the bar. "Maybe it was all given to Molly. All that feeling, all human emotion. It was all taken from you at some point and now you're barely a human beyond winning, beyond collecting power, influence, revenge."

"See, if I was a man, these qualities wouldn't be listed as something that was wrong, they'd be something to make me *right*. Make me *better*. Or make me the same as all the rest." I drained my glass. "But I'm meant to be soft-hearted with a kind soul, otherwise I'm wrong, broken, empty? Maybe I'm all those things, but it doesn't matter right now. I'm focusing on the long game. And if you'll remember, you're in bed with the man who had my sister brutally murdered. I'll trust you to show yourself out."

Abe didn't heed my dismissal. "I wasn't in bed with him," he bit out. "I was angry at you for making what I thought was the wrong business decision." He gripped his glass. "And now I see that it was the right one. If only I'd seen it earlier, maybe..."

"There's no time for maybes in reality," I cut him off. "There is no maybe about what I found on your computer."

"No," Abe agreed. "But I've been around the world trying to gather what I can to help us acquire his companies under shell corporations, or at the very least stage a hostile takeover."

I raised my brow, quietly impressed and surprised. My uncle was a good businessman, so it stood to reason he'd have the same idea I did. "I don't think you understand what being fired means."

He gave me a long look. "I don't think you understand what family means."

He was right.

"My brother was a good man," he continued. "Different than me in a lot of ways. Better than me in every way." His eyes had a faraway look, not seeing me or the penthouse. "A good father. Husband." He blinked away the past. "He was to me what Molly was to you. And I know the pain of losing him. Now we've lost Molly in the same way. This world seems to think taking the better parts of our family is going to ruin us. And it will. It already has. But it will not beat us. Fired or not, I'm going to do every-thing I can to fight for my remaining family. I'm not going to ask you to trust me, because I know you well enough that under the best of circumstances you hesitate to trust anyone. This is far from the best of circumstances, therefore, you're going to trust no one."

His eyes flickered to Jacob.

There was a knowing in them that surprised me.

"Almost no one," he added. "But I don't need you to trust me in order to help you."

"I don't need help," I said immediately.

"I know. But I'm going to give it to you anyway. For my brother. For my niece. And for you."

His voice was resolute. Brokered no argument. Usually, there was never a time I would have let him take such a tone with me. But I was tired.

So I sighed and nodded once.

I filled my glass again.

And then I tried to get comfortable with an empty soul.

1 9

The next day was the same.

I woke up at five.

Jacob was in my bed. I didn't remember getting there. My entire body ached with the loss of her, my limbs screaming and nerves exposed to the root. An animal part of me ached to cower under the covers, cower from the world.

I threw them off me instead.

I went for my run.

Jacob was beside me.

I had my shower.

Jacob fucked me in that shower.

I dressed myself in my armor.

And I went to work.

Ralph hugged me. Murmured apologies. There were tears. I responded appropriately to everything he said.

If he registered surprise at the fact he was still driving me to the office, I didn't notice it.

There was a difference when Jacob entered the car.

He did not sit across from me.

He sat beside me.

His hand circled mine and he rested it on his thigh. He didn't say anything else. I didn't pull my hand away, though I should've.

I made it up the elevator, happy that it was only Jacob and I, and I didn't have to see anyone. Abe had emailed me everything he'd found, and it was a lot. Almost enough to prove he didn't have anything to do with Kershaw beyond those emails.

Not enough to make me trust him.

He was right last night. The only person I would trust without question was lying on a metal slab in a morgue somewhere.

And maybe one more stood beside me in the elevator, holding my hand. It wasn't by choice that I trusted him. Like everything with Jacob, it was by force.

He let go of my hand as we stepped out of the elevator and I felt the loss, only slightly, since most of me resembled the human-shaped slab of ice that all of my employees believed me to be.

As they always were at this hour, the offices were empty.

Well, almost empty.

It wasn't unheard of for Vaughn to be here at this time, but I didn't expect him. He'd only left my apartment after midnight, and he had drunk less vodka than me, but that wasn't saying much at all. I hadn't wanted him there in the first place, but he hadn't given me much choice, either, turning up with tear stained makeup and two bottles of Grey Goose.

To his credit, he'd only made me suffer through one long embrace before he'd sat in my living room with me, drinking and hardly speaking.

Vaughn stood up, blinking at me as I walked past him. "Char, I didn't expect you in today."

"Why? Because my sister was murdered yesterday?" I asked.

He flinched.

"She's going to be dead whether I'm here or at home," I said. "I've got work to do, this is an important day and it can't be rescheduled for a death in anyone's family. I think I even made that rule. It wouldn't be proper for me not to abide by the rules I made, would it?"

I didn't wait for his answer.

"Get the board members on the phone, confirm with each of them that the meeting is going ahead as planned, in case any of them has some kind of idea I wasn't going to be here."

Again, I didn't wait. I walked into the office, closed the door and got to work.

I once traveled to Serbia on a business trip. A security contract, I think it was. Such things weren't unusual. I had a company jet for this precise reason. I had been to a lot of different places in my work. War-torn, some of them. I'd been to Bosnia, seen the scars on the city, cut by a neighbor that on this visit seemed absent of any wounds.

I was walking somewhere when I saw it. Amidst the rest of the perfectly formed concrete structures, sat a ruined and half standing building. It couldn't have been large, especially when I was used to being swallowed by sky scarring buildings in New York, but it was big enough to tower over my head. Half of it was missing. A chunk ripped out from a bomb in the long-buried war.

It still stood, though. Even though it had been years since destruction tore through it, and most likely should have been torn down.

It was still there.

I remember it striking me, how the building looked perfectly intact everywhere else, could have been serviceable, inhabitable, if not for the huge chunk exposing its skeleton to the world. To the elements.

I didn't really understand how it could still be standing, with half of it ripped away.

The wind whistled through the graveyard and then whipped through the open and exposed part of me.

Now I knew why that building still stood. How it could still stand. Because I was that building. I had something ripped away from me. Torn brutally. The part that would make me whole. Inhabitable.

Now I just stood there, watching the casket, the priest in front of it speaking. The concrete stones, stark against the too green grass.

I was the building that would stand, maybe out of habit, maybe because no one wanted to tear it down. Maybe because the reminder needed to be there. Of horror.

Of the blood that might be able to be mopped up, bullet holes plastered over, but it would always be there. The one building that could neither be torn down or used again. That lived half in this world and half in the next.

In the worst sort of limbo because it was dead and it was alive and it was both or neither.

Or maybe that building was just *there*. Nothing else could explain why. It just *was*. And it wasn't.

Whatever the reason, I was that.

It was the cheese in the fridge that did it. It wasn't the funeral. It wasn't the photos her friends had put together for her. It wasn't any of the many moving speeches that various people said.

It wasn't even watching the coffin containing half of my sister's cremated remains being lowered into a grave.

No, I kept my composure through all of this.

I didn't shed one tear.

I did what was expected. I signed checks for funeral directors, for the grave plot. I greeted mourners. I answered emails.

Jacob was by my side the entire time. He didn't hold my hand, didn't placate me with empty words like everyone else did. He was silent. But he was there.

And he was there, in my elevator as we rode it up on the day that we buried my sister's coffin.

That's what today would always be.

And the next day would be the day after we buried her.

Every day after that would be the same.

I wouldn't be counting time in Mondays, months, years.

I would be calculating it to the proximity to this day. To how long my sister's ashes had been inside a grave.

"You don't have to come in," I said as the doors opened to my apartment.

There were flowers everywhere.

Deliveries likely accepted by my housekeeper.

Meaning well.

I'd have them picked up and donated in the morning.

He didn't answer.

I turned to face him, to look at him for the first time I had today. I'd done everything I could to avoid making eye contact.

Because I was afraid.

Even though I was so sure that I had nothing left to be afraid of. I was afraid of him. Meeting his eyes and having to face the truth in them.

I was proud of the fact I didn't react to the pain that speared through me with his gaze.

"I need tonight to be..." I trailed off.

Alone.

That's what I was. Whether he was present or not, whether I was in a crowded room, a city teeming with people, living on an overpopulated earth—I was alone.

"You don't need to stay," I said. "I don't want you to."

It was a lie.

I wanted him to more than anything.

Precisely why I didn't want him to.

Why I *couldn't* have him staying.

His jaw was granite as I spoke, his hands fisted at his sides, not taking his eyes from me.

"I'll see you tomorrow," I continued. "On our run."

He still didn't speak.

"Jacob," I said his name like a prayer. But my voice only cracked slightly. A hairline fracture.

A muscle in his jaw ticked and he nodded once, stepping back into the elevator.

I exhaled in relief or disappointment, preparing for the doors to close. They started to, then a large hand attached to a muscled arm shot out, stopping them.

In two rapid blinks, he crossed the distance between us, gripping the back of my neck and yanking me into a brutal kiss.

I didn't intend on responding. But with Jacob, I didn't have a choice. My mouth moved against his, matching his violence, never surrendering to him. It was all the words he hadn't said since it happened, all the words he wouldn't say, poured into that kiss. It speared at my soul, sparked all those nerve endings I was so sure had died with Molly.

I was in his arms, my clothes being torn from my body as he slammed me against a wall. A resounding crash echoed through the apartment as the wall in which Jacob had slammed me sent a mirror shattering on the marble.

I barely noticed.

My body reveled in the pain shooting up my back from the impact, from Jacob's fingers pressing too hard into my soft skin. I wanted more of it. Blood trickled over my hands as I raked my nails through his flesh.

He let out a hiss, releasing me from the kiss and yanking at my hair to expose my neck. His teeth grazed the skin.

"I know you're in too much pain for me to take it away, so I'll give you more, because I want to give you something," he rasped.

"Give me everything," I demanded, my voice a rasp.

And he did.

Enough pain to forget about the rest of the world.

For a while at least.

I forgot what I'd even been looking for in the fridge once my eyes touched that single packet of cheese.

My hand went out and touched the plastic hesitantly. It was shaking.

This was the last time I'd ever see a packet of cheese in my refrigerator again. One that Molly had bought. Touched. Soon the world would be absent of things that she had touched while alive.

Apart from her art. That was her.

But ordinary things. Her clothes would stop smelling like her eventually. Her apartment would be rented out by someone else.

I didn't know how many of those mundane things I'd run through my head. I must've blacked out, because I was on the floor. The same floor that I'd crumpled onto after a nameless thug left me beaten but not broken.

I was broken now.

I found myself wishing, clutching that packet of cheese, that he had killed me that night. That he had smashed my head against this cold marble, crushed my skull and left me to die. Because if he had, then my sister would buy more stupid cheese, she would wake up at noon in an apartment full of chaos and Chinese takeout boxes. She'd paint great art. She'd live.

If only he'd killed me.

I'd been so fascinated with my own death for a long time. I'd never really *wanted* to die. I didn't even want to die now. I wanted to die *then*. When my death would've made a difference. When my death would've saved her. I didn't yearn for my death anymore. I needed my life in order to devote it to revenge.

He found me on the floor.

Clutching cheese.

Wishing for death and planning revenge.

I didn't know if he said anything. If he did, I wasn't in a place to hear it.

All I knew was that I was in his arms, on the floor of my kitchen, he was holding me like the time I'd been beaten but not broken.

He was holding me now I wasn't beaten but broken. Shattered. Destroyed. Pulverized.

His lips touched my hair.

I clung to his jacket, letting the cheese fall to the ground.

And I cried.

I wept.

For the first time in years. Likely for the last time too.

He didn't let me go.

I stared at the array of colors linked together in a mosaic. It didn't make up an image. Not a conventional one at least.

"I don't want to paint what everyone else sees. I want to paint what I feel when I see what everyone else thinks they see."

She wanted to be half in the earth, half in the air. That's what she said. Why we'd buried a coffin with another urn, with half of her inside. There were no instructions on where to scatter the ashes.

"You'll know."

It was a joke.

I didn't *know*.

The person who was the other half of me, the person who I filled my heart with, who I thought I knew in life was a stranger in death. Maybe that's what death did to people. Turned them into strangers. Because it was easier to bury a stranger.

I didn't *want* easier.

I needed it to be hard every day.

I need to know her again.

The urn was open before I quite realized it. My hands scooping up the grit the color and consistency of grainy sand. The charcoaled remains of the other half of me. Someone so big, so vibrant and colorful was nothing but gray sand falling through my fingers.

I shoved them into my mouth, bitter and stony.

Swallowing her ashes, I found I didn't feel as empty. Greed overpowered me to devour all of it, her to fill me up, to give me more of her. To know her better. I was closer to her. I remembered her now. Snatches of conversation I didn't realize I'd forgotten.

"Don't you ever want to fall in love?" Molly asked, peeling strips off string cheese that wasn't cheese.

"No," I replied without hesitating, not glancing up from my laptop.

"Why?"

I sighed and glanced up to my sister, leaning on my kitchen island, beautiful and naïve. "Because if I fall in love, I lose everything I've worked my life for. Everything that means something to me. All my power."

She smiled. "Love isn't going to take that away from you. Not the right kind."

I didn't smile back. "Right or wrong, love always takes power away from everyone. It's one or the other, Mol, and I'm happy to be powerful without love than helpless and with it."

With shaking hands, I replaced the lid. I had to make her last. Keep her here.

And she had wishes.

Molly, of all people, who didn't balance a checkbook, who never did taxes or had health insurance, had wishes in the event of her death.

I glanced down at the pieces of paper that had been staring at me since the lawyer delivered them.

I picked them up.

Gray ash stained the white paper.

Paper that Molly had touched, and now I was staining it with her charred remains.

I bet this is a surprise to you, right, Char Bear? I wish I was alive just to see the unflappable Charlotte Crofton shocked by her decidedly flappy sister.

Well, I just wish I was alive.

I'm hoping this letter finds you when you're old. Not gray or wrinkled because you'll have six weekly salon appointments and six-monthly Botox injections. You'll be flawless and beautiful like always.

I'll be wrinkled, gray, with frizzy hair, with a collection of tattoos, memories and not flawless.

Well, in my head, I am.

I'm not sure you're reading this when you're old.

I know you balk at this kind of stuff, Char, but I've had this kind of...knowing I'd die young. We all die young, really, since I don't know what old is, but I had a feeling I'd go before you. Before my older sister, who is likely blaming herself for whatever has befallen me. It's not your fault. Unless you murdered me. Then it totally is your fault.

If you haven't murdered me, you'll be heartbroken and shocked at this letter. You likely have all sorts of plans in place for your death. I'll get everything I need, the company run by Abe and Vaughn and trusted advisors, appropriate charities donated to.

I don't have anything but this letter. Because I know you'll take care of the other stuff, I know that you'll need to take care of it. To keep you busy. Keep you on the run from those emotions you're so afraid of. The knowledge that you're human, and despite what you think, your heart isn't blackened or damaged.

I don't have many requests. I want my art to be displayed somewhere where people can see it for free. I want all the proceeds from my estate to go to free art classes in my name for talented youths.

I have another request. One you'd hate me for if I'd asked when I was alive. Or at least give me the ice queen glare and that would be that. But I'm dead now, so you have to listen to me. No one can say no to the dead.

I want you to go and see Mom. Because you need to. Whether you admit it or not. And because with me gone, she's the last piece of our memories, with pink wine and tiaras, that we have left.

Once.

That's all I ask.

My greatest wish, is that my sister, my soul, my better half, is not broken from this. I wish you to find love, happiness, a life that doesn't exist in a corner office. I am so proud of you, of everything you've built, the empire. You are a force. But without it all, you're still a force, you're still someone. You're still everything.

I promise you, when you take it all away, stop focusing on the next goal, the next rung in the ladder, the next brick in your ivory tower, I promise you that you're not going to fall apart.

Or maybe you will.

Humans tend to do that, Char. Falling apart doesn't mean you can't put yourself back together.

You're not her, Charlotte.

That's why I want you to visit her, to see that.

I hate to think of you in pain, I feel it, even now. But I guess I have to feel it now, because I won't feel it when I'm gone. I'm gone from this life, but not in another. I'm still here, with you, inside you.

I love you. I believe in you.

My tears mingled with the ashy stains on the letter.

Then I ripped up the paper and ate that too.

JACOB

She was falling apart. Jacob could see it. He was somewhat specialized in spotting the signs of a human detaching from themselves.

Mostly because he'd been responsible for that happening. Many times, half a world away in a dark interrogation room, rank with mold, blood, and sweat.

He'd watch the pieces fall from them like snow in January.

Reveled in it.

He did not revel in this. Seeing Charlotte go about the motions, her beautiful face nothing but ice and her soul nothing but gravel.

But she was also excelling. Never had he seen a person fall apart while bringing something together at the same time.

She was going to take Kershaw down. Something multiple governments hadn't been able to do. Something some of the most powerful men in the world had died trying to do.

But he watched her.

And it was nothing short of magnificent.

Charlotte had done it.

Almost single-handedly. First, out of her need to win, for power. Even after the attacks on her, it wasn't for revenge. She knew that those attacks were part of the game. She took the hits in order to gain the upper hand.

But Molly.

He shuddered thinking about it.

Fucking *shuddered.*

Him.

The scene in the loft, her body, he'd actually been forced to swallow bile, that's how close he'd been to losing his lunch. Never had he had a reaction to a body. Corpses were just empty flesh to him. There was nothing to fear from the dead.

But he'd met Molly. She was part of Charlotte. And she was able to pierce through whatever he had left in him to warm with her smile, jokes, her *light.*

"You love my sister. I know it. I've waited for you. You're not perfect. You're wrong in all the right ways. She's good for you. I don't think she'll heal you, and you won't heal her, but you'll create new and beautiful wounds on each other," she'd said the first night he'd met her.

The first fucking night.

He didn't say anything.

But she didn't wait for him. Just winked and sashayed away.

Seeing her body, it had fucked with him.

More than he cared to admit.

Seeing Charlotte in so much pain that she actually shut down all her emotions and operated robotically, it scared the shit out of him. Because he wasn't entirely sure she was going to come back. Be human anymore.

He was terrified she was going to turn into an even bigger monster than him.

CHARLOTTE

"I don't like this," Jacob bit out, hand tight on my hip.

"I don't care," I replied, not looking at him.

I couldn't.

It was imperative that I stayed even for this meeting. That I kept my mask on tightly and didn't give away an inch of the sorrow that was carefully covered with makeup, clothes and the trademark Charlotte Crofton glare.

"I don't like it, but I know you have to do it," he continued. There was a loaded pause as the numbers on the elevator climbed. "Proud of you, Boots."

The words hit me, because they were heavy, because they were from Jacob. But I didn't react. "There's nothing to be proud of," I responded in the cold tone that was necessary for my survival.

His hand clenched the back of my neck in a grip most would call an assault, but with Jacob, it was a caress. "I disagree."

The elevator doors opened, and I didn't have time to argue. Or react. I exhaled in relief.

I didn't hesitate to step out, and Jacob didn't stop me, though I knew he wanted to. He hadn't tried to get me to stop and talk about my feelings, to slow down, like Vaughn and Abe had. He'd silently watched me as I worked myself to the bone, helping where he could. He'd taken me brutally whenever he could, every time being more violent than the last, as if he could sense how numb I was and he was trying to make me feel the only way he knew how. With pain.

I liked it. I was becoming addicted to it.

To him.

And walking through these offices, to the conference room with the view above the clouds, I was making sure I'd have to go cold turkey.

Because after this, the threat would be gone. Jacob wasn't

conquering it for me, fighting my battle. I was in this conference room to fight it myself.

I knew I'd win.

In one sense of the word.

I'd lost in so many others.

Kershaw rose as I entered the room, eyes flickering over me, face warm as if he were greeting an old friend and not the women he had beaten, attempted to have killed and murdered her sister.

"Charlotte," he said. "You look well."

I didn't reply, just pulled out a chair and sat. Jacob stood behind me. I didn't look at him.

Ethan did, for a long moment before he sat.

"First, I would like to offer my condolences for your loss," he said. "Misfortune seems to follow you around."

I didn't react. Though he didn't likely expect me to. He was testing me. Prodding, softly at first, then he'd press harder until he drew blood. Little did he know, I'd already drained him dry without him knowing.

"Misfortune follows everyone around," I replied, voice flat. "Only the majority of people are too obtuse to notice it."

He nodded. "Everyone with a heartbeat, at least."

Another prod.

I didn't lower my gaze, or even flinch. Nor did I bleed. Whatever warm blood I had was spilled in a paint-spattered loft and was little more than a maroon stain behind police tape.

Because the police were still investigating. Detective Maloney still clinging to his naïve view of justice and its reach. It was nothing but a spec from the conference room we sat in.

"I'm not here to exchange more threats with you, idle or otherwise," I said. "I'm here as a professional courtesy, and to educate you on how battles are won. Not with assassination attempts, beatings, or blood." I glanced around. "But in boardrooms. I'll admit the decorating leaves a lot to be desired, but my designers should be here before the afternoon is out. They'll make sure to remove all of the toxic masculinity."

Something flickered in Kershaw's face. "What are you talking about?"

I leaned forward, reached for the water jug in front of me and slowly poured. It was a rather elementary power move, but I enjoyed it. I took a sip.

"I mean, this conference room is mine now," I said after I put the glass down. "Along with this building, and every single one of your companies, including RuberCorp." My expression didn't crack as I met Kershaw's eyes. "You really think because I didn't react to your violence that I've been idle? You underestimated me. Don't worry, most men do." I paused, thinking of the one man that didn't, the one standing behind me, taut and wired, waiting for a chance to kill.

I knew it's what he wanted.

To rip Kershaw apart. Feed his hunger for violence. Death. Feed his monster.

But I was doing that in my own way.

And I had my own monster to feed.

"While you were plotting murders like some second-rate gangster, I was actually achieving something," I continued. "I was acquiring controlling shares in your companies under various shell corporations, possible because you run your businesses poorly. Poorly compared to me, of course." I took another sip.

"You can't do this," he said, still smiling, thinking of the aces he didn't realize I'd snatched from his sleeve. "I have half of Congress in my pocket. You try and take my company from me, you'll be hauled in on the Patriot Act and never seen again."

The threat was real. I knew that he would've been capable of orchestrating such a thing. He had, with many of his adversaries, still rotting in prisons that didn't officially exist.

"You *did* have half of Congress in your pocket," I corrected. "I'll admit, seeing some of the things you were blackmailing with even shocked me, and I thought I was too jaded to be shocked. My hackers certainly were. But that's because they're not at all jaded by the outside world since they live in the virtual world." I paused. "Well, they actually rule it. Since they were able to get past all of your firewalls, discover every alias, locate and destroy every piece of blackmail you've been using to control the Hill and our government," I said. "I know that you're not stupid enough not to have physical copies. But I found them too." I glanced to my watch, the one with the scratch on the face I'd worn specifically for this day.

"My security team should be at each of your residences and have obtained all physical copies, right about now," I continued. I knew they were, since I'd gotten an alert on my phone as soon as I walked in. They were the top mercenaries in the world. Not conflicted by conscience or morals, the only people you could trust in such matters—the most trustworthy of them all.

Kershaw's grin froze on his face and his eyes flared with naked panic before he masked it.

"You're bluffing," he said with a certainty characteristic of men who considered themselves untouchable.

"You killed my sister," I said, my voice flat and cold. "You did it because I'm guessing you caught wind of *some* of the things I was doing. Or maybe you just had her killed in order to distract me, to target my emotions. You expected me to react like a woman to that. But I don't react like a woman. Or a man. I react like a winner. And I do not bluff."

He stared at me, gauging my words, my even tone and my likely empty expression. That's what the victory felt like, even as realization dawned on his face and his phone began to buzz—it was all empty. I'd beaten the man who had tried to kill me, had me beaten to a pulp, had my sister murdered. It all meant nothing.

I stood, mindful of Jacob's proximity as he likely expected Kershaw to lash out, to go for the gun I knew was taped under the left-hand side of the head of the table.

I knew better.

"I'm now the majority shareholder at RuberCorp," I informed him, glancing to his phone. "Your board, all of whom you've intimidated, paid or extorted into submission are happy about the change of leadership, to say the least. I've funneled every last cent in your personal accounts to the charities trying to help your victims. Your car, home and jet are being impounded as we speak." I paused, looking down at where he was still trying to process what had happened. "Everyone's a victim, at some point, Ethan," I repeated his last words from our first meeting. "Even the most powerful of men. Or women. There's a point where power doesn't save you."

And then I turned on my heel and walked out.

Empty, hollowed out, and victorious.

The ride back to my office was silent.

As was the trip up the elevator.

And the walk to Vaughn's desk. Then I gave him the news. The bare bones, at least. There was a weariness about me that had me unable to go through the specifics. But the specifics didn't matter anyway.

Vaughn gaped at me, something moving behind his eyes that was more than shock. Betrayal, perhaps. He was likely hurt I hadn't involved him in the process, as he considered us close, and me hiding such a pivotal move from him was almost unheard of.

I didn't explain myself. You didn't get to the top by explaining yourself.

Vaughn blinked rapidly and his eyes flickered back to normal. "Champagne," he declared. "We need champagne to celebrate this moment. You're now the top cybersecurity firm in the world, Char."

"Celebration follows a *happy* event," I said. "This wasn't an event, nor was it happy. It cost my sister her life. My acquisition of RuberCorp was nothing but necessary. *Celebrate* by getting me a press release drafted announcing that Charlotte Crofton is now the head of the top cybersecurity firm in the world. Up our rates by thirty percent and do background checks on all top-ranking employees with security clearance. If there's a hint of anything suspicious, fire them," I instructed.

Vaughn blinked rapidly. More foreign emotions that I couldn't quite pinpoint flickered behind his eyes.

I didn't have time for Vaughn and his emotions and I certainly didn't have the capacity to deal with him if he decided to do something like bring up Molly.

So I didn't wait for an answer. I turned to walk into my office.

I stared out the window as Jacob closed the door behind us.

"I used to think about what it would be like to jump," I said, regarding the skyline to avoid the truth of what this victory meant.

Jacob's heat kissed my back, but he didn't touch me.

"I would be fascinated with the feeling, the aftermath of such a fall," I continued. "On what it would be like to die. For it all to be over." I steeled myself and turned. "And it is. Over."

The words echoed through the office.

Jacob didn't react.

"The threat's been eliminated," he agreed, voice flat, empty, like always.

I wished there was something more behind it. Something more behind his cold eyes. Something to hold onto.

There wasn't.

Or maybe there was, and I was making sure I didn't see it.

I couldn't trust my own eyes when it came to Jacob. I couldn't trust my own mind. Which was why I had to walk away.

"Your job is done," I replied.

His jaw ticked. "With you, Boots, my job is never done."

The jaw tick. The words. They hit me in that space reserved for my heart. I sucked in an unsteady and agonizing breath. "It needs to be. We need to be. You know this much the same as I do. There's nothing left for you here. I have—" I cut myself off abruptly. I had nothing but an empty apartment and a fractured soul. I straightened my spine. "I have a job to do. Businesses to run."

He wouldn't stop staring. Stop picking apart the bits of me that he owned with his eyes. "There's more to life than business, Boots."

I shook my head. "No, life is always business. And that's the only way I can live mine. My uncle was right. Something with me is...*off*. I don't have the capacity for anything more. If I did, that's been buried, and the gravestone reads Molly Crofton. I don't want to have to pretend otherwise. I'm better as I was before."

"Empty?" he pushed.

I nodded once.

He didn't speak. Didn't try to change my mind. To fight for me. The strongest, most violent man I'd ever encountered was refusing to fight, for me. He was surrendering after a handful of my cold and empty lies.

Or truths that I wished were lies.

He nodded once. The movement was violent.

My heart fell at our feet. Bleeding. Rotten.

He turned around and left it where it fell.

He didn't look back.

After Jacob left, I decided it was time to keep a promise.

The promise had me traveling to a quiet street, walking inside a nondescript brownstone and inside one of the best high-security mental facilities in the city, if not the country.

My uncle had arranged it once he'd gotten a top tier law firm to cover her case when she was charged with my father's murder.

The plea of insanity was a foregone conclusion, and it took a judge merely one glimpse at the shell that consisted of my mother to legally announce her not guilty by way of insanity.

My uncle's power and influence had her put here.

When money didn't let you get away with murder, it put you in a pretty cage.

But, facing my mother after more than a decade, it became apparent that her cage was not a brownstone in Manhattan, and it was not pretty.

"She doesn't do much more than this these days, I'm afraid," the nurse with the soft eyes and kind smile informed me.

My hard eyes focused on the skeletal frame sitting upright in an armchair facing the window.

The nurse moved forward to fuss with the pillows and brush a frizzy strand away from my mother's face. "She seems to like sitting by the window," she said, smiling wider at my mother's unseeing eyes. She focused on me. "I'm glad you're visiting. I was so sorry to hear about your sister."

Her words seemed genuine and her eyes watery.

"You knew her? Molly?" I asked. Her name was broken glass against my throat.

The nurse—Judy—wiped her eye. "Of course. Everyone here knows and loves...I'm sorry, loved, your sister. She was—"

"Thank you," I interrupted, unable to take her kind sincerity for another second. "I'll let you know if I need anything."

Judy blinked rapidly, likely surprised that someone with Molly's eyes and bone structure didn't have an ounce of her soul.

But she was a professional, and she nodded once and left the room.

I moved toward the chair, more afraid of the frail woman sitting in it than I was of the mass murderer I'd faced off with less than two hours ago.

We look at those people, you know, those *insane* people. The ones staggering around the East Village, muttering to themselves, or at least, muttering to people that only they can see. The people begging for change, cowering in doorways, dressed in rags, sometimes resorting to violence to get fed, or to get their fix. We dismiss them, more often than not. I say *we*, because it was in my practice to actively dismiss them, largely because of my past.

The past sitting in this chair, looking out the window at a well-tended rose garden, likely not seeing a flower.

Those people were a flesh and blood personification of everything that I feared. Of everything I was trying to escape.

Almost everyone thought of those people only in that moment. Where they passed them shouting at the air, or digging through trash cans. They are *defined* by who they are at that moment. We alienate them, imagining that they are like that because we tell ourselves they were *always* like that. When in reality, they weren't. Once upon a time, they were whatever passes for normal. They had a family, a life, drank coffee in the mornings, read the paper, muttered to other people about mundane things, who took the trash out—that was before trash became their livelihood.

Maybe we ignored them because, on some level, we knew we were only one failed marriage, lost job, injury, death, away from becoming them. One triggering moment to turn us into...*them.*

We didn't imagine crazy people having families. We didn't imagine villains having families either. I wondered about the dead man in the alley. In my apartment. Who they left behind.

Whenever we watched action movies where the hero cut through armies of people and called it a victory, Molly would focus not on the triumph of good over evil, but those faceless villains.

"What about their families?" She'd point at the TV. *"That's a child that's lost a father, a woman that's lost a husband, a mother that's lost a son. Who knows if they were even really bad. Maybe it was a job to pay the bills, feed the children?"*

That was Molly, always looking further. To her, the man begging for change was more than just that person in that second. She wanted to know who he was *before*, see beneath the surface of what he was now. Which was why she had worked at a homeless shelter whenever she had the time. Why she was the most beloved employee, and, why, when having dinner with me, she'd call them by their first name, talk about their lives, their experiences, their idiosyncrasies. Treat them like they were humans. Her friends.

She always saw the human underneath.

Which was why she had the reaction she did to Jacob. Didn't shy away from him as was human instinct.

It kind of irked me in a way I couldn't exactly understand. I thought we shared something, a connection that couldn't be described as wholly natural, something *more*. Yet I failed to comprehend who he was beyond those wolf eyes, before the night in the alley. I failed to remember that once he used to be a boy that skinned his knees and had a mother that would kiss them better. That he was human before the wolf took over.

What was that saying? Even monsters had homes and mothers.

I felt some of it when I answered his phone, heard his sister, heard the resemblance of my own loving, albeit crazy twin. It began to click just then. I figured out that he didn't just credit his origins to clawing his way out of the dirt. That he came from people, *family*.

A family that still called. A sister that laughed with a stranger, had children. A husband.

Jacob had something left of his past, even if his future was a wasteland.

But me, my past was nothing but a foreign woman, whose illness stole her beauty, her soul and my father.

I didn't speak.

Because it was obvious she couldn't hear me. Her eyes were glassy, bloodshot, staring at nothing. Her mouth, thin and pale, was open and slack, a thin stream of saliva trailing down her chin.

She was nothing.

I stared at her a long time, tried to call up some affection for her.

None came.

So I turned around and walked out, avoiding Judy's kind eyes as I walked out.

Walking toward the car, I sent a message to a number that I'd acquired when it became apparent that morals were absent at the top.

The text said nothing, but me sending it instructed the right people to ensure that Judy would find my mother's body tomorrow morning, having died of natural causes in the early hours of the night.

It would never trace to me.

I felt nothing ordering the murder of my mother.

"Home, Ms. Crofton?" Ralph asked, holding the door open, his words more of a suggestion than a question.

"Home, yes," I agreed. "The office."

I didn't meet his eyes and got in the car.

I worked for eight more hours. Long after the twinkling lights of the city snatched away the sunshine, and long after everyone abandoned the offices.

Vaughn left too. I barely looked up to say goodbye.

Because I was a coward.

I was avoiding his gaze, the sympathy, the kindness, the truth.

I was avoiding my empty apartment and the silence that awaited me.

But there was only so long you could avoid something. I needed to force myself into the discomfort of what my life would be like. So that's what I did. Made sure the distance between Ralph and me was further than ever, even shutting the portion between us so I didn't have the company of his silence. The entire ride, I focused on the mountain of work that came with my recent acquisitions. I set up meetings, performance reviews, overlooked press releases, RSVP'd to the appropriate events. Charlotte Crofton would not have a spare second in the foreseeable future.

Apart from the long seconds on the elevator ride up, I'd never felt more alone in my life as I did hurtling up to my beautiful, multimillion-dollar apartment.

My beautiful cage.

I stepped out of the elevator silently. My heels echoed on my floor. Everything I did was on autopilot.

Putting my coat in the closet. Placing my purse on the side table. Walking to the kitchen taunted by the emptiness of the apartment.

When I made it there, it was clear the apartment was anything but empty.

I didn't even stutter my step when I caught Vaughn sitting at the kitchen island. Nor when I spotted the gun resting on the counter with his hand placed casually on it. The barrel was angled toward me.

His eyes met mine.

The truth hit me half a second later.

"You're much more ambitious than I thought," I said by greeting, opening the refrigerator to retrieve wine and two glasses.

A bottle of cheap pink fizz.

An apt last meal.

My hands were still as I poured the liquid. My heartbeat was even, though I suspected I was minutes from death.

Jacob wouldn't save me from this one, I knew that with brutal clarity. He was not one to come and fight for a damned relationship. Or a damned soul.

Vaughn took the glass from me in the hand that wasn't holding the gun.

"I'm much more everything than you thought," Vaughn replied, spite saturating his tone and his expression.

"Or much less," I murmured, taking a sip.

His eyes flared with a foreign fury that had always lurked behind the faux kindness I'd thought was genuine for so long.

I wanted to be surprised at the betrayal. But I was so jaded from the world it didn't shock or surprise me. It hurt me, though. After Molly, I had been so sure that my ability to feel pain—whatever was left of it—was laying in my office where I said goodbye to Jacob.

Even the strongest of us were shown new ways the world could hurt us. Pain was the only thing on this earth that was infinite.

"You could've just taken the deal," Vaughn hissed, clenching onto the gun. "Then I wouldn't have had to do any of it."

I raised my brow and sipped slowly. "You *had* to do it?" I asked, placing the glass on the counter but holding onto the stem. "Ah, we're both much too intelligent to believe that your hand was forced to have me attacked, have my sister murdered, and frame it all on the obvious villain. You did it because you're greedy."

That flare increased and his hand tightened on the gun. But he wasn't going to use it yet. No, Vaughn was a drama queen and he wanted the theatre of a violent ending, after he told me all about how he'd done it. How much smarter he was than me.

He may have worn heels and eyeliner, but he was showing me he was just another man looking to crush me.

It hurt this time because he was the one—or one of the two—people left in this world who I thought I could trust.

Trust and love were two things wholly fatal to everyone.

"Greedy?" he screamed, leaning forward, wine sloshing onto my counter. "*You're* calling *me* greedy, the woman with *billions* of dollars, *thousands* of employees, dozens of homes and who is never satisfied?"

I smiled. It was the first time I'd done so since Molly died. "That's all true. But it doesn't come from greed. It comes from a need for control. And everything I've acquired, I did it with my own blood, not by spilling the blood of innocents." I paused. "I can understand how you could do this to me, but to *Molly*?" My voice cracked at the end. Only slightly, a hairline fracture.

Something moved on his face. Something human.

Grief.

Pain.

Ah, so not all of it had been a farce. Did that make it better or worse?

"I didn't *want* to hurt her," he said. "But it was you who taught me that once you committed to something, you never stop until you reach your goal."

I took another sip. "So I only have myself to blame for all of this, I assume?" I asked dryly.

He clenched the gun tighter. "No. You know about my past. I know about yours. We're both broken. In ways that make it impossible for us to be human. Don't stand from across the room and try and make me feel bad for putting myself first."

"You should get some kind of award for your performance," I said, struggling to maintain the ice in my voice. In the face of my sister's death and throughout her funeral, I'd managed not even a *hitch* in my tone. I stared down the man I thought responsible. I'd just said goodbye to the first and last person I'd ever love. But in face of what Vaughn had done, I was becoming unraveled.

Maybe because death didn't have an affiliation, an affection, a loyalty to anyone. Death wasn't a betrayal, it wasn't a decisive action on the part of the person it happened to. Molly didn't die because she didn't love me, or because she wanted to hurt me.

But Vaughn had played this game, he had become someone to me, and he chose to do this. It hurt worse than losing someone.

"My award was meant to be my position at the head of one of the top security firms in the world," he snapped. "Not testing lipsticks and planning fucking eyeshadow launches."

I pursed my lips, the bitterness in his tone decades old. Rotten. I cursed myself for being blind to it. "Was it always the plan? From the start?"

His grimace turned into something softer, something more recognizable. Which hurt more, to see how easy he could transition between the two, changing faces. "No, Char," he said, voice more familiar. "I cared about you. You are one of the only people I have ever cared about." His eyes shimmered and the grip on the gun slackened for a second, his resolve wavering. In a split second, the monster inside of him took over and all softness, all humanity disappeared.

"But people like you and me don't let relationships get in the way of what we want," he continued. "We're not right, after what happened to us. We're missing something. You fed what you were missing with your power. I wanted to be more than your sidekick. I needed my own power."

"I'm *nothing* like you," I whispered. "If you wanted it so bad, I would've given it to you. All of it. None of it was worth what you took from me."

He sipped his wine, eyes shimmering, as if he could taste the memories of Molly inside it. "But it wouldn't work that way, if you gave it to me," he said. "You know that better than anyone. I had to work for it. Take it. Like you did."

"I didn't take anything," I hissed. "I *made* it. I didn't try to assassinate anyone. I didn't get anyone beaten up. I didn't kill—" I cut myself off abruptly, the words catching in my throat as the reality of it all sank in.

I knew the reality. I felt the wind whistling through the empty part of me every day, every moment she was gone I was a little less...everything.

It was one thing to lose a sister to an enemy. It was quite another to lose it to someone I considered a friend.

"You've been playing a long game," I sighed.

"I didn't plan it," he returned. "Not at the beginning." He lifted the gun, contemplating it. "I liked you. You were someone that believed in me, gave me opportunities. I wanted us to continue to take over the world together. But then you had to go and get *morals.* You. The ice queen. They say heavy is the head that wears the crown, but I don't think it's the crown that's heavy, it's the way you wear it. And you had honesty and ethics too high on your shoulders. Power is not gained honestly. Or without betrayal. You know that better than anyone. You also know about needing to get as far away from your past as possible. To build your ivory tower to get away from the skeletons of your past. I merely did that by creating some more skeletons of my own."

It was there that I lost it. In his cold and contemplative assessment of the actions that took my sister from me. Like power was something that was important enough to snatch away life.

All of the years I'd held onto my control, it all snapped, right there and then.

My now empty glass went flying against the wall without me quite realizing I'd thrown it until tiny pieces of crystal rained down on my floor.

"*You murdered my sister!*" I screamed. "You murdered her for a fucking crown that means *nothing*. For power that doesn't paint you paintings, that doesn't smile at you, that doesn't try to wake up earlier than you on your birthday. You are a sick piece of shit and I hope you burn in fucking hell. I cannot *wait* to watch you burn. Even if I have to go to the pit with you, I'll happily forgo heaven to make sure you're properly punished in hell."

He tilted his head. "Oh, Char, I thought you didn't believe in god."

I glared at him. "I don't. But you're giving me a reason to believe in the Devil and hope he's real. If not, I'll do my best to recreate his work."

He pointed the gun to me. "Assuming you'll live long enough to do so. You don't have the power anymore, Charlotte. It's my turn now."

I laughed. "Because you're holding a gun and tried to murder your way to the top? That's not power, that's cowardice. A weak man uses weapons, a strong woman uses wit. And despite your taste in shoes, you've just proven yourself to be just another asshole man." I rounded the counter, barely glancing at the gun that followed me. "And I'm sick of men taking things from me. So if it's my life you're trying to steal, then I'll take it myself before you have the chance."

Then I ran at him.

The gunshot echoed through the silence I'd been so afraid of.

It was a relief.

JACOB

He knew Charlotte didn't want Kershaw dead. And it wasn't out of nobility or goodness. She was remarkable, but there was no goodness in her. Whatever shreds she had was for her sister, and now she was gone, there was nothing.

Which was why he'd managed to stay with her for as long as he had. Why she was stuck in his rotten soul, never to be erased. She was crueler than him, in her want to keep the man she ruined alive.

Because she thought beyond the simple ways to inflict pain, she wanted agony, all the way down to the core. Jacob had first experience of that.

That's why she kept Kershaw alive.

But he wouldn't let that happen.

Because there was a high chance he'd scuttle back to a hole somewhere, rot away without everything that he defined himself with. Most likely would die by his own hand.

But there was also a small chance that he wouldn't.

That he'd use this absolute defeat, gather the scant scraps she'd torn off him, use them to clothe himself in desperation and try to hurt her.

Try.

He wasn't giving anyone even the smallest chance of hurting her. Killing was the better way. The surer way to protect her.

Once he was gone.

And he would go.

Because she might not be good, but Jacob wasn't purely bad. He was worse. And he'd corrupt whatever she had in her that was worth saving. He saved her life, but that was all he would do. He'd damn her in every way that mattered. And he cared about her too much to let that happen. Killing was always the better choice, and he'd kill what was left between them. He knew he'd already done it, walking away from her fucking empty eyes, those empty words.

She was not a woman that would accept defeat, but she had been praying for it when she dismissed him. Daring him to beat her. Fight for her.

Kershaw coughed, a thin spray of blood exited his mouth and hit the desk in front of him.

"I wasn't going to go after her," he spluttered, keeping Jacob's gaze. He hated the man, despised everything he was and everything he'd done, but he respected that he didn't lower his gaze, even in death.

"I know," he responded.

"Would've done the same thing, if I were you," Kershaw said, voice wet. "We're not that different. We're both monsters."

"We are," Jacob agreed. He was no better than the man in front of him, who'd done unspeakable acts, whose soul was up for sale. Who considered human life to have a dollar amount attached to it.

They were different in the fact that Jacob didn't kill for money. At the start, it was duty. Then it became something else.

But what was that difference, really? He still took something from death. It fed something. And maybe that was worse than killing for money.

He watched with silent satisfaction as Kershaw died in front of him. For once, the death was empty. Empty because he was. He'd thought he was hollow before, filled up only by his depravity. But then Charlotte.

Boots.

She showed him he was more than his depravity. Or maybe she showed him that it wasn't the death sentence he'd been so sure that it was.

He prided himself on his ability to walk away from people he'd once loved. His family. Because it was the old him that loved them. He held something for them in the emotional wasteland he'd adopted, enough to know he had to leave them for their own good. And sometimes, his empty spaces panged with a pain that might've been longing for his sister's jokes, his mother's cooking, the smell of his father's cigars and his niece's smile.

But it was manageable. And usually drowned out by the darkness.

He'd been away from them years.

It had been mere hours away from Charlotte and it wasn't a mere pang. It wasn't manageable. It was a need that he'd have to fulfil or he'd die.

He'd thought he was capable of the noble thing.

But he wasn't noble.

He didn't even wipe the blood from his hands, he went to get her.

Jacob knew something was wrong the second the doors opened. It was an instinct that once honed, never left. The ability to know death. To taste it in the way the air—usually sweet and bitter that was the mix of her smell—turned slightly rancid, colder.

It was different than when he'd come in here to see Charlotte crumpled and beaten on the floor. Bad. But better, because hurts healed. She was strong enough for that. It fucked with him to see her like that, but he was a man unsurprised by violence. It was the fact that it affected him at all that meant something. That it sickened the stomach that had stayed even during humanity's worst scenes.

He ran into the kitchen, and he found death there.

CHARLOTTE

"I get why you come here," I said, my voice flat, disembodied. It echoed through the space, bouncing off unseen demons.

Jacob's form entered my peripheral, he came to stand beside me, I could taste the electricity in the air, the way his energy told me he was strung out.

He likely found Vaughn.

He wouldn't be here if he didn't.

If he hadn't decided to come back for whatever was left of me.

There should have been some reaction to Jacob coming back for me. For us.

But there wasn't.

"It's empty. Ugly," I continued. "It's where you need to be. After..." I trailed off.

The echo of the gunshot was louder than I expected. The jolt up my arm was also surprising too. It had seemed so effortless in movies. But killing should not be effortless.

Taking another human's life should've jolted my soul like the gun jolted my arm bone.

It didn't.

It was barely a tremor, really.

Maybe if things were different, I might've felt more at ending the life of the one remaining person on this earth I'd cared about.

But things weren't different, and I didn't live in maybes.

I felt numb, vaguely satisfied that he was dead. Not much else.

"It was all him?" Jacob asked after a long silence.

"It would be easy, if it was, wouldn't it?" I asked. "Simpler. To blame it on one man, as if tragedy itself is dealt and decided by one person." I met ice blue wolf eyes. "It's unfortunately never that easy or never that simple. Or maybe it is. It wasn't *him* that took everything from me. It's what he wanted. Power. Absolute power corrupts absolutely and all that. But the lack of it corrupts, rots and decays the wrong kind of person." I paused. "I think I'm the wrong kind of person. In every way a person can be wrong."

That's when Jacob snatched me into his arms, brutal, painful. He clutched my neck.

"Yeah, Boots," he rasped. "You're the wrong kind of person. Which just so happens to be right for me. And corrupt or not, that power is yours. And no god will help anyone that tries to take it away from you again."

EPILOGUE

There was no ever after for Jacob and me.

Happy or otherwise.

Happiness was lost, buried beneath blood, bone, scar tissue that compiled together.

No marriage, because I didn't believe in it and I couldn't weather such a thing without my sister there to walk me down the aisle, fuss over my dress and just...be there.

Jacob wouldn't do it either. Because like a suit, marriage was just another chain to a life that would never be his, an identity that couldn't fit over top of the monster that he was now.

Marriage was too little for us.

Too hollow.

But we belonged to each other. As much as two people such as us could.

There were no children. There was no family.

Even if I was physically able, I wouldn't have let it happen.

We weren't cut out to be a family.

His sister was there. More than she might've been had it not been for me. But I wasn't the woman to bring Jacob back to the life he'd had before. If anything, I tore him further from that farmhouse, that family and the life that came with it.

There was just us.

The pain that we carried with us, the pain we brought each other.

He stood beside me, not as my king, but as something else entirely.

I'd learned a lot from my time so far with Jacob. Mostly about death. Pain. Pain was coiled up in losing Molly, love for her memory crippling, while my love for Jacob was paralyzing. Agonizing.

Love is an open wound. As long as I love, I never heal. I'll always hurt.

But when I stopped hurting, it'd be over.

So it wasn't the end.

ACKNOWLEDGMENTS

This is a book that has been hiding in a word document on my computer for a long time.

I had the idea years ago, and much like Birds of Paradise, I wrote a chapter and then moved on to other stories. I knew it wasn't ready yet. I knew it would call to me when the time was right. When I needed this story most.

And it did.

It came when I was ready to go dark again. When my mind was in a dark place. This story seeped into my bones and didn't let me go. It was hard to write.

Really fricking hard.

I count myself so very lucky to have people in my life that support me throughout the writing process. People who talk me off the ledge, who offer advice, love. I will tell you for certain I would not be here without these people.

Mum. You know the drill by this point. You are always here, right at the top. Because I would not be here, typing this, without you. You made me into the woman I am. You introduced me to books, you cheered me on and told me I could do anything. I love you.

Dad. You can't read this, but I know you're somewhere, having a beer, watching over me. I miss you always.

Taylor. Thank you for being my best friend. For supporting me. Making me laugh. Dealing with my meltdowns. Feeding me wine and treats when I'm freaking out about books. Thanks for going on this ride otherwise known as life with me. Forever and then some, babe.

Jessica Gadziala. You have been my constant support through so many meltdowns and dark periods of my life. You went above and beyond with this book, demanding to read it when I freaked out and thought it was total garbage. Thank you for being a true doyenne.

Amo Jones. Bitch. What can I say? You are my everything, ride or die. I would not make it through without you. And I'm never going to be without you. 'Cause you're stuck with me for life.

Michelle Clay. I don't even know what to say about you. You are one of the most special people in my life. You do so much for me and many other people without expecting anything in return. You support me, cheer for me and help me through so much. I am forever grateful that my words brought us together.

Annette Brignac. Another woman who is one of a kind. Thank you for being in my life. Thank you for reading my books. I am honoured to call you a friend. You are one of the best people I know. My life would not be the same without you. To the moon.

My girls, Polly & Emma. You're a whole world away from me and it breaks my heart. I miss you both every single day but I also know that no amount of time or distance will change our friendship. You two are my soulmates.

My betas, Sarah, Ginny, Amy and Caro. You ladies save me. Seriously. Thank you for reading my books when they are at their most raw. Thank you for helping turn them into what they end up being.

Ellie. Thank you for dealing with me. For editing this book. For not changing my voice. For being fucking amazing.

ABOUT THE AUTHOR

ANNE MALCOM has been an avid reader since before she can remember, her mother responsible for her love of reading. It started with magical journeys into the world of Hogwarts and Middle Earth, then as she grew up her reading tastes grew with her. Her love of reading doesn't discriminate, she reads across many genres, although classics like Little Women and Gone with the Wind will hold special places in her heart. She also can't get enough romance, especially when some possessive alpha males throw their weight around.

One day, in a reading slump, Cade and Gwen's story came to her and started taking up space in her head until she put their story into words. Now that she has started, it doesn't look like she's going to stop anytime soon, with many more characters demanding their story be told as well.

Raised in small town New Zealand, Anne had a truly special childhood, growing up in one of the most beautiful countries in the world. She has backpacked across Europe, ridden camels in the Sahara and eaten her way through Italy, loving every moment. She's currently living London, loving life and traveling as much as humanly possible.

Want to get in touch with Anne? She loves to hear from her readers.
You can email her: annemalcomauthor@hotmail.com
Or join her reader group on Facebook.

ALSO BY ANNE MALCOM

THE SONS OF TEMPLAR SERIES

Making the Cut

Firestorm

Outside the Lines

Out of the Ashes

Beyond the Horizon

Dauntless

Battles of the Broken

Hollow Hearts

THE UNQUIET MIND SERIES

Echoes of Silence

Skeletons of Us

Broken Shelves

GREENSTONE SECURITY

Still Waters

Shield

The Problem With Peace

THE VEIN CHRONICLES

Fatal Harmony

Deathless

Faults in Fate

Eternity's Awakening

A DARK STANDALONE

Birds of Paradise

Printed in Great Britain
by Amazon